FBI Agent Nicolas Hayes and his team are confronted with a murder series that started in Florida and continues in Virginia. When a wealthy company owner is poisoned to death at a party in Washington, DC, the agents investigate whether there is a connection between the victims. The killer is a master of disguise, and when the investigation stalls, Hayes needs the help of his lover and her friends to track down the culprit.

Umberto, a crime syndicate bruiser, shares his home with Michael, a dancing instructor. Their happy life is interrupted by the death of Umberto's boss, the mighty businessman Eduardo Vianone. Umberto has to move to DC to serve Eduardo's younger brother, Luigi, and his gang of thugs. His allegiance is put to the test when Luigi announces that he will expand his brother's enterprise along the East Coast and expects Umberto to clear the way. To his chagrin, Michael is also very curious about what his friend is up to and is not easily pleased.

The hunt is on when the FBI suspects Umberto of being involved in the murders. Will Agent Hayes find the true killer before he strikes again?

Clandestine Dealings
Copyright © 2022 Ann Raina
ISBN: 978-1-4874-3490-8
Cover art by Martine Jardin

Published by eXtasy Books Inc

Look for us online at:
www.eXtasybooks.com

Clandestine Dealings
Nick and Jacklyn 8

By

Ann Raina

Dedication

We celebrate twenty years of story development, creating main and side characters, and racking our brains about the best twists. Here's to you, muse! You are the best! And the cookies.

PROLOGUE

On the first of June—as on every warm summer morning—Eduardo Vianone sat at the pool of his residence close to Miami studying the newspaper, drinking his protein shake with strawberries and yogurt, and reminiscing about his family situation. He was thinking about how he could hand a part of his business to his younger brother, Luigi, without looking senile. After all, he was seventy-one and still had his wits together. If he retired from business without a plausible reason, competitors would smell weakness. He could not afford losing the empire he had built over forty years. The thought of losing face made him uneasy.

Without a solution at hand, he emptied the shake, folded the paper, and dropped his robe on the way to the pool. It was ten o'clock in the morning and already hot, and he longed to dive into the cool water to relax and, hopefully, gain new insight on how to proceed.

His younger brother, Luigi *Lou* Vianone, lived in the suburbs of Washington, DC, and ran his own business—racketeering and drug dealing, mostly. As far as Eduardo knew, Luigi was involved in the construction trade, too, and strove for expansion. Though it seemed wise to give up the leading role at his age, Eduardo hesitated. Luigi had never been the most successful executive. He had a temper that was hard to control, and since his business transactions lacked wisdom and foresight, he tried to compensate with rough retaliation. Eduardo doubted his brother would change his behavior once he shouldered a greater responsibility. He had been impetuous as a child, and unfortunately, that had not changed in adult life.

Eduardo decided to reach out to him for a conversation. After that, he would know better whether to hand him the honor of leadership or not. If he decided against giving his brother control over a part of the business, it would be wise to choose his successor from the most influential personalities in his large and complex company. It would have to be a man with enough stamina to stand up against Luigi, if need be. He had a loyal man in mind, a man of trust and resilience, a man with years of experience — tough but clever. He was the only serious rival to his brother, and he had known him for years. Eduardo knew he had to come to a decision, and the longer he pondered, the more he favored splitting his business and selecting two men instead of one. It could be considered a kind of sport — a competition of the fittest.

Slowly, for the water was cool, Eduardo entered the pool. His heart was beating fast, and his breathing accelerated as he pushed off the ground at the steps and swam toward the center. He turned on his back and squinted against the sunlight on yet another bright day with blue sky. Though the beach wasn't far away, he preferred the tranquility of his residence, where only a few employees were working and no one bothered him. They all knew that Eduardo cherished his solitude and wouldn't tolerate any disturbance. Later in the day, he would be happy to attend to the needs of his customers.

Eduardo swam to the rear end and back the same way. His mouth was dry and increasingly numb, and he licked his lips, pondering whether the shake had been off. While he continued his exercise, his face started itching, and the numbness spread from his head to his arms. His throat constricted, and when he opened his mouth to cry for help, he had no voice. Fearing that he was suffering a heart attack, for his heart was beating frantically, Eduardo tried to reach the steps and climb out of the pool. His arms didn't obey, breathing became difficult, and then his legs stopped working. Eyes wide with terror, he was unable to swim. Eduardo's head went under water. He made a last, feeble attempt at reaching the surface, hoping the butler would show up to clean the table, but it was too early. Eduardo had made it explicitly clear he didn't want to be bothered at the pool. His rules were law to the bitter end.

Eduardo looked up at the sun and the blue sky of southern Florida and thought that his life had been a good one and yet too short.

CHAPTER ONE

M ichael Grayden strutted across the parking lot toward the shopping center in central Miami, throwing in some dance steps here and there. It was mid-June and so warm that he carried his jeans jacket across his shoulder. He liked to show off his biceps and trained chest in a tight tank top. Aside from his dazzling smile, his body was his most valuable possession, and he tended to display it to its advantage. On his way to the dry cleaners he bought two doughnuts to share them — accompanied by fresh-brewed coffee — with his friend, Umberto, who would not be up yet. He loved to sleep in whenever he had a day off.

He smiled blissfully thinking of Umberto *Bert* Bianchi, his Italian friend, lover, and homeowner, who was kind enough to let him room in. These days, Michael tried to fathom what Umberto was to him — he was delighted every time Umberto announced he would like to move under the covers with his *friend with benefits*. Sometimes he called him lovingly his *sweet slave* without insisting that Michael had to do his bidding. Michael admitted that he tried to read Umberto's mind and do what pleased him, ever and again.

Since that dreadful night in Miami four months ago, when Michael had been robbed and beaten, Umberto had been his hero — his savior, his benefactor. He had shown courage — alone in a dark alley, armed with nothing but his fists. Michael had lain bleeding on the sidewalk, and Umberto interfered before the crook had the chance to kill him. That night, Umberto took him to the ER, waited until his wounds were treated, and took him to his home, claiming he could not let him stay alone after the narrow escape. Umberto spoke of psychological consequences, of a yet undetected trauma, and of the necessity to have someone around in case a nightmare shook him. Michael was utterly surprised by such chivalry, and he asked how he could repay him. Umberto had smiled and gently touched Michael's ear and neck. His look had indicated his thoughts, and Michael accepted the invitation.

Though it was partly flattery, Michael told Umberto repeatedly how much he adored his strength and appearance. Umberto had short black hair, thick eyebrows, and dark brown eyes. His face was chiseled like a classic sculpture, and he possessed a lean and yet impressively strong body. Not to mention, he was three inches taller, which added to Michael feeling safe in the older man's presence. Whenever they were out together, whether for a party or a night at the club, Michael stayed close to Umberto, behaving like a dog that was convinced its owner would keep away harm.

Umberto employed a woman to run the household, Margarita. She cooked if the guys wanted her to, but Michael enjoyed grocery shopping and the time in the kitchen, knowing that Umberto would smack his lips and laud him in rapid Italian, right before he cupped his cheeks with both hands to kiss him. Michael lived for those moments of pure joy, and his heart beat fast with love.

Looking back, there was nothing glorious about Michael's childhood. He hadn't known happiness in his youth, only drama and rejection, starting life without parents. Foster families tried to give him a home, but the relationships didn't last, and the families returned him to the orphanage. Two families claimed that Michael didn't get along with their own kids, another one said they couldn't name the reason, only that Michael tended to behave *out of line*. Michael was a good-looking boy, a heartthrob from the first day of his adolescence. The girls swooned over him when he was twelve, and they made him indecent offers when he was fourteen. However, he never got acquainted with any of them, partly because they mocked him behind his back for coming from an orphanage, and partly because he felt odd being with a girl, even if it was for doing homework together. Although he was a good athlete, the boys didn't want him in their teams. They treated him like an outsider, someone who would fail miserably and end up on the streets.

They were right. Michael finished school, didn't find employment, and was too arrogant to start as a busboy at a burger shop where former classmates would see him. After a month in a youth detention center at the age of fifteen, he swore that would never happen to him again. He left his hometown, met with all sorts of people while tramping across the country, and made quick money along the way, some of it illegally. One night, he encountered a much older man, who invited him for a drink. They sat at a bar together, and Vincent Decker, dressed in a formal business suit with vest and tie, chatted about his successful life and how much money he had made in the past ten years. Pleasantly drunk after a few gin and tonics, Michael accompanied Vincent to his motel room and could hardly believe when the older man said that Michael could make good cash if he stayed the night. Michael hesitated, and Vincent granted him time to think while he unpacked his bag and opened another bottle of gin. Vincent, gray-haired and wrinkled from too much time in the sun, complimented him on his good looks, his moves, and his manners. As the night grew late, Vincent recapped his youth and how he had struggled to accept his homosexuality. He claimed that the old days had been hard on men who admitted to love men, but now were better times, and Michael had the chance to live the way he wanted and make a fortune with his talents.

After three nights, Michael had learned more about himself and his abilities than in the previous twenty years, and Vincent was happy that they spent time on his journey together. The older man showed him around, introduced him to friends and executives, and taught him how to show interest without being blunt. Michael moved up from shady motels to expensive hotel suites and learned to dress and move and use the right cutlery at a dinner table. He took dancing lessons because Vincent stated he should be able to impress the ladies as well, and he learned so fast and easily that the studio wanted to hire him as a dancing instructor. Among developing various talents, Vincent also encouraged him to learn at least one form of martial arts. It was healthy, kept him lean and fit, and empowered him to defend himself.

For two and a half years, Michael's life was a bed of roses. He didn't think much about the way he made money. He saw the numbers on his bank account—an account Vincent had opened by claiming that Michael was his employee—and was exuberant about his success. Vincent spent a lot of time teaching him everything he needed to know, including how to disappear if things got rough.

Unexpectedly, Vincent died of a heart attack. Michael was in the adjacent room getting dressed for the night and heard a suppressed cry prior to the thud on the floor. When the ambulance arrived, it was already too late. Michael was devastated by the loss, even more so when he learned that Vincent had no family and had left all his possessions to Michael. For more than a month, he pondered what to do with his life, how to move on without forgetting Vincent and what he had done for him. He wanted to honor his trainer.

Finished shopping, Michael sat behind the wheel of Umberto's elegant black SUV and drove home. It was their last day in Miami. The next day, they would pack their belongings and move to Alexandria, Virginia, where Umberto was starting a new job at an insurance company. As he gazed at the beach, Michael couldn't decide whether he would miss Miami or not. He was open for a challenge, for meeting strangers, and for his new job as a dancing instructor at a small studio. He had filled out the application form, added a video from dancing lessons at his recent studio, and hoped his performance would convince the owner to give him a chance.

Michael put on his sunglasses as he steered the car off the highway into the residential streets. He looked forward to surprising Umberto with breakfast. His smile would make Michael's day.

"If you look at your phone one more time, I'll throw it out of the window," Nicolas groused in his deepest voice. "Jason, I mean it."

Jason Beckham, FBI agent and Nicolas's best friend, took back the hand that was going for the cell phone on his desk, but his look was murderous. "The baby will be early. That's what the doctor said. I want to be there for her when she goes into labor."

"You will be there for her." Nicolas stopped typing. He tried for a soothing tone. "No child's been born within a few minutes. Didn't you learn anything in the prenatal classes?"

"Didn't you hear of babies being born on the back seat of a taxi?"

"That's rare, and Elaine is a woman who knows exactly what to do. Calm down."

Jason emptied his mug and when he returned with fresh coffee, he found a new pile of files on his desk. "This is a joke, right?"

"It's certainly not." Nicolas sighed. "Four cases to work on, and two more just arrived. I don't think you can go on a vacation, Jason."

Jason bristled. "But I filled out and submitted the application weeks ago. Sullivan can't—" He stopped when Nicolas burst out laughing. "You're making fun of me. Thanks a lot." He took the first file from the large pile. "All right. I'll be so kind and work through the cases, but then—the moment this phone beeps—I'm gone. Poof. Just gone."

Nicolas's face sobered. "I hope Elaine gives birth to a wonderful healthy girl."

"How would you know it's a girl?"

"Because she told me."

"You talked to her? Recently?"

Nicolas looked at him until Jason understood the message.

"Oh. Well, certainly, you talked to her." Jason cleared his throat and turned the first page of the case file. "Interesting."

Nicolas shook his head. Since the day Elaine had announced her pregnancy, Jason wasn't the same man he had been before. It was a marvel that he was able to work at all, but Nicolas looked forward to Jason's vacation. It would be a quiet time, no matter the number of cases on his desk.

The truck of the moving company had already parked in front of Umberto's home, a stylish bungalow with a well-tended garden, pool, and a large, expensively furnished porch with side walls made of glass. Michael parked in front of the garage, carried the groceries to the kitchen, filled the fridge, and put the fruits into a bowl. He brewed coffee and decorated the doughnuts on a plate with a napkin. Content with the preparations, he took the tray to the porch, filled a cup with coffee, and smiled when Umberto appeared, his hair tousled and his eyes still puffy from sleep.

Michael handed him the cup and added a kiss on

Umberto's bare shoulder. "Good morning. I hope it's the way you like it."

Umberto chuckled, sipped coffee, and sighed with bliss.

"Yeah, I know," Michael said as he poured coffee for himself.

"Hmm." Umberto caressed Michael's bare arm, then let his hand travel upward.

It was a pleasant sensation when Umberto ran his fingers through Michael's long hair on top, but it was a thrill when his fingertips moved along the shaven areas above his ears. Michael shuddered with delight and spilled coffee across the small table.

"Oh, what a mess." Michael turned around, pretend annoyance in his voice. "You make a mess of me."

Once more, Umberto just smiled mischievously, sipped the excellent brew, and nodded toward the waiting truck.

"Are you okay with moving to DC?"

Michael tried to sound nonchalant. "I'm happy to go where you go."

"It's quite a change. You love your work at the studio."

"I'll find another job." Michael evaded Umberto's compassionate glance. It was true that he liked his job, but it was nothing compared to their blossoming relationship. Though it was a move of a thousand miles, he didn't regret his decision.

"If you don't find a new job soon, don't worry. I'll earn enough for both of us." Umberto kissed Michael's brow in a sweet, affectionate way. "Thank you for the great cup of coffee." He glanced across Michael's shoulder. "And the breakfast. You went shopping while I was asleep." He sat down, mumbling in Italian.

Michael didn't understand a word, but Umberto sounded affectionate, so he smiled and took the free chair. They ate the doughnuts, drank coffee, and chatted about packing boxes and taking care of emptying the rooms. There was still a lot to do.

However, when Michael got up to clean the table, Umberto pulled him down for a kiss and whispered, "We should give this house a suitable farewell, don't you think?"

Michael's eyes widened, and his heart jumped with joy. He was so happy he felt close to tears.

Chapter Two

Nicolas was astonished that Jason found his feet when Elaine told him on the phone that now, on this day, she was certain to go into labor. He put on his jacket, the phone wedged between ear and shoulder, and told her what to do while he sped home to fetch her. He waved goodbye to Nicolas and was out of the office so quickly that he almost ran over the mailman coming through the hallway. The elderly man shook his head, grumpy as always, and delivered a large box beside Nicolas's already full desk.

"What's this? From the bureau in Miami? Who told you to deliver it to my place?"

"Don't growl at me," the mailman replied scornfully. "I'm just delivering the stuff." He checked the paperwork. "FBI field office Miami sent it to Assistant Senior Agent-in-Charge Sullivan. He signed it and told me to hand it to you." He grinned, baring teeth worth of a predator. "Easy-peasy. Have fun." He walked on, pushing his cart.

"Fun, yeah, right."

Nicolas lifted the lid to find copies of five files. Each contained preliminary results of a murder investigation. The agents in charge had summed up that all murders had taken place in the larger Miami area and that the victims had been poisoned to death. Nicolas skipped through the documents, impressed against his will by the killer's skill. He or she had applied the poison so cleverly that the victim didn't notice it at once but collapsed well after the killer was gone. Despite FBI efforts, the killer—the profiler assumed it was more likely a woman — remained anonymous.

Nicolas leaned back with a cup of coffee and read the files one by one.

The first three victims were wealthy company managers with businesses in Miami, Fort Lauderdale, and Boca Raton. Their companies built streets, private houses, schools, as well as business skyscrapers. All of them were big in business and dedicated to restructuring parts of the cities and putting their nametags on the buildings. According to the police reports, it was possible but not verified that the companies had used illegal proceedings to obtain business contracts.

Nicolas assumed that competitors had wanted them out of the way.

The fourth murder victim was the Mayor of Orlando, Stuart Norton. He was found dead in his study, killed by a poisoned strawberry muffin, his favorite cake. The Miami Police homicide division had handled the cases up to this point, but now called for FBI assistance. The agents treated the four murders as the work of a serial killer, gave him the name *Rattler*, for the victims had died of very potent snake poison, and investigated the cases with their resources.

Though the pathologists had been thorough and found the real causes of death, the FBI didn't find tangible clues leading toward the killer. The poisons used were distributed by snake farms and laboratories, and also bought by clinics and other medical institutes researching ways to fight cancer. They could be ordered via darknet from snake farm owners, who made illegal money with them. Controls in that area were sparse, and many private farms existed without a veterinarian ever showing up. No matter where the killer had shopped for supplies, the FBI had been unable to detect the source so far. In one case, they assumed that the killer had intercepted a delivery to a clinic, but neither the laboratory nor the clinic confirmed the theft. The agent in charge summed up that the businesses wouldn't want bad publicity and that darknet users changed their profiles frequently to remain anonymous.

There were congruencies concerning the victims, though.

The three victims—Gerald Lubock, Hunter Boman, and Walt Matusky—had tried to expand their businesses to the north during the last five years. Lubock had acquired land in Orlando and announced he would erect three skyscrapers for companies and exclusive apartments. Boman wanted to create a huge complex with business buildings in Middleburg close to Jacksonville, partly financed by the government development program for that area. Finally, Matusky announced he would tear down an old quarter south of Orlando for a new resort with a golf course and a wellness area, designated to fulfill the wishes of retirees with money. Once finished, the compound would be worth a billion dollars.

All projects had come to a stop after the owners' premature deaths. The companies of Lubock and Matusky were struggling with loss of investment money, since the investors doubted the company's ability to finish the projects without the men at the top.

Nicolas went to fetch another cup of coffee and a bagel from the cafeteria. When he heard a loud conversation, he turned his head. Sullivan was browbeating Agent Montagna and ordered him harshly to leave his office. With the entire staff watching, Matthew Montagna stormed out of the office and directly toward the stairs. Nicolas knew the agent needed a cigarette to calm down before he could even think about working.

Nicolas returned to his desk and continued reading.

While the three deaths of company owners indicated a competitor's scheme to get rid of his adversaries, the fourth murder was a bold move against a sitting mayor. Nicolas studied the biography of Stuart Norton. Descended from a family of renowned politicians, Norton had started small as an assemblyman in his hometown of Lakeland and quickly made his mark by fighting illegal actions within the city government. He claimed that he would rid the city of corruption and put behind bars everyone who dared to accept bribes. Though party members considered him a lightweight in the beginning, he joined investigative police forces and helped convict two officials from the construction department who had favored builders in the granting of municipal contracts. The citizens then considered him a hero and elected him as Mayor of Orlando two years later. He was the youngest candidate to take over office. He was married and had three children.

"Yeah, the future looked bright for you," Nicolas mumbled as he looked at the photographs of the crime scene. Norton had slumped at his desk, his head resting on the polished wooden surface, eyes wide open and saliva dripping from his mouth. The crumbles of the poisoned muffin were still beside him on a plate. The pathologist wrote that the deadly dose had been in the strawberry — potent enough to kill him within five minutes. As with the other victims, the poison had been faster than he had been able to call for help, and the killer had chosen a time and place where the victim was alone.

Nicolas leaned back on his chair.

The killer knew the victims' schedules and habits, even their favorite treats. He studied his victims, and he got close to them or at least to an assistant or relatives to gather information beforehand. The agents in Miami had analyzed hundreds of hours of videotape recordings of the times prior to the murders in order to detect the man or the woman present near the victims and their beverages and snacks. They had questioned employees as well as postmen and workers seen prior to the murders at the scenes. They had also analyzed the companies to find connections with possible adversaries and angry competitors.

As a result, several employees as well as Norton's political opponents were under surveillance, and the agents had intensified their investigations into organized crime. The results were pending. The profiler believed the murderer to be female, in her early thirties, and remorseless. It was possible she killed for money, but her main motivation was revenge because of a wrongdoing she had suffered earlier in her life. She was clever, resourceful and so far, faceless.

Nicolas considered her a genius, for there was no video footage of a woman coming or leaving prior to the time of the victims' deaths, and the FBI had no woman on their watch list, even though all female employees had undergone thorough vetting. He wondered whether the profiler was wrong or if the woman was extremely adaptive and appeared as a man. In that case, observing the suspects wouldn't lead anywhere.

The fifth murder stuck out. The victim was a rich executive from Miami, seventy-one years old, a man who lived reclusively and led his huge company through intermediaries. Rumor had it that Eduardo Vianone had been the leader of a criminal organization for decades and would stop at nothing to execute his plans. Despite the persistent rumors, neither police nor FBI had been able to connect him to any specific crime. He was the gray eminence whose whereabouts were a secret. The FBI agent writing the report admitted that until the old man's death, no one had known of his residence.

In this case, the murderer had chosen a deadly dose of Tetrodotoxin, obtained from a pufferfish, and mixed it into the protein shake the victim drank every morning.

It was a discrepancy from the *modus operandi* or MO, and the colleagues in Miami shared doubt whether this murder fit the killer's scheme, considering both the murder weapon and the victim preference. Eduardo Vianone made speculative deals with companies, mostly successful. A small sector dealt with the building or remodeling of municipal structures, but he was no competitor to the big builders in the greater Miami area. Luigi Vianone, the victim's younger brother, was an aggressive company leader and had already promised a large reward for information leading to the killer. Since Luigi resided close to Washington, DC, he had placed ads in the Miami daily newspapers, much to the chagrin of the FBI agents, who considered their investigation corrupted.

The brother's belligerent actions were reason for the agents in Miami to inform their colleagues in DC about the pending investigation, concluding that it was possible the younger Vianone would go ballistic searching for the killer.

As a second reason, the report mentioned that the killings had suddenly stopped after Eduardo Vianone's death. Three of Eduardo's employees had moved to DC's suburbs and were currently taking up residence in Alexandria and Germantown. The agents advised their DC counterparts to have a close look at the men's doings. Names and pictures were included.

Matthew returned to the office and took Jason's chair, contaminating the air with stale smoke.

"Welcome to the show," Nicolas said quietly. "To what do I owe the honor of your presence?"

"Gimme someone to hurt or kill so Sullivan might live another day."

Nicolas pushed the files across the table. "Help yourself."

Five men had helped stowing the boxes and parts of the furniture in the moving van. They didn't talk much but were fast and reliable. There were six other men in Alexandria to help unload the van upon arrival. They carried the boxes to the designated places and would have unpacked them, but Michael interfered. So the helpers put the furnishings and paintings where they belonged, turning the house into a home.

Michael marveled at Umberto's talent for organizing the move. The helpers left with a sizeable tip, Umberto closed the door and turned around, smiling all over his handsome face.

"We're alone, finally." He went into the kitchen, and Michael followed, tired but happy. "I ordered the fridge filled and a bottle of champagne to celebrate the day."

He claimed the bottle while Michael rummaged through a box to find glasses, pondering who Umberto had ordered to go shopping.

"Take the first ones you find. My throat's dry, and I won't wait for you to unpack all the boxes, Mikey."

Heavy-heartedly — for it was exactly what Michael would have loved to do — he settled for simple water glasses.

"Oh, don't be glum! We did it. Look around. This is ours for as long as we want to live here."

Michael watched Umberto fill the glasses to the rim. The house was indeed a pearl amid a string of smaller pearls in the street. The kitchen was big enough to live in, the decor blue, and the oven, the stove, and the fridge shiny and new. The huge living room had the thickest carpet Michael had ever seen, and the classic dark wooden furniture was without doubt expensive. A part of the bookshelves was filled with hardcover editions of famous authors as if to signal that the owner read frequently — or could at least pretend to be bibliophilic. On the second floor were three bedrooms, a second large bathroom, and a studio overlooking the garden. Someone with a good and expensive taste had furnished all rooms. Michael felt at home instantly.

Every room in the house was bigger than those back in Miami, and Michael doubted Umberto's income was enough for such a high-end place to live. He didn't ask, though, anxious how Umberto would react to a question concerning the numbers of his bank account. Their relationship was so fresh that Michael always thought about what kind of questions he could ask on what topics without insulting Umberto. His caution saved him from precarious situations or even distrust. Michael wanted their relationship to last—he had longed for such a like-minded soul since Vincent's death twelve months ago. He didn't want to think about angering Umberto so much that—as an inevitable result—his lover would throw him out of this beautiful house. Michael had money to rent a place to live, but he would be alone again.

If anything, Michael feared he would work and return to an empty home every day.

He toasted Umberto on the new place, drank, and put down the glass while the champagne still tingled pleasantly on his tongue. "When do you have to start working?"

Umberto emptied his glass and set it on the table. "Not until the day after tomorrow. I told my new boss I needed time to unwrap all the stuff." He laughed, but briefly. "Don't worry, Mikey, I won't leave you alone so soon."

"I'm not worried. I do have a question."

"Yeah? What is it?"

"While I was packing, I came across a catalogue with . . . erotic stuff." Michael watched Umberto's expression carefully. "I wondered whether . . . I mean, I had a friend back in the day . . . he liked tying me up. And I liked that, too. Very much." He tried to smile but was too nervous to manage.

Umberto looked at him, frowning, not saying a word.

Michael's nervousness increased. If he had misjudged Umberto completely, and his friend rejected the mere idea of bondage in a relationship, he wouldn't unpack his personal belongings but carry them to a motel right away.

Umberto poured more champagne, glancing at Michael in a disturbing non-revealing way. He was as expressionless as a shark, his thoughts cloaked. He drank, cleared his throat, and turned the champagne in the glass, leaving Michael to guess whether he should prepare for a harsh reprimand.

"I didn't expect you to . . . enjoy being tethered." Umberto drank some more, then, all of a sudden, shook his head and laughed. "You know, I was looking for an opportunity, for an occasion to bring up the subject—that's why I got the catalogue in the first place—and here you stand, all sexy and desirable and ask me if I would like to tie you up." He set down the glass, bridged the distance and cupped Michael's cheeks. He sounded breathless. "Yes, Mikey, yes, I would love to tie you up and shower you with affection." He placed kisses on Michael's forehead, nose, and lips, hungry kisses that blew away Michael's anxiety and left him shivering with lust.

"I didn't know . . . I was . . ." Michael exhaled, smiling, lacking words to express his feelings.

"How should you? It's a somewhat delicate topic, isn't it?" Umberto put an arm around Michael's shoulders. "Do you know where you put the catalogue? We could have a look. We have a big bedroom we could equip with more than a bed and a wardrobe. What do you think?"

"I think it's a fucking amazing idea."

"Do you want to talk about your argument with Sullivan?" Nicolas asked as they left the office together.

As if he couldn't talk without smoking, Matthew lit a cigarette on the way to the employee parking garage. "Addleton and I were closing in on a bank robber group of five—ten banks robbed, several people wounded—and we might've needed two more days to gather the evidence for the DA. Two more days, okay? Then, all of a sudden, Sullivan decides that he wants me with your investigation." He shook his head. "I don't get it. He mumbles about organized crime and that the Vianone family has top priority. It's not even clear whether one of the Vianones committed a crime in the DC area. We have nothing to go on! What's so damn important? I read the files, and I don't see the relevance. We're searching for a woman—maybe—who killed five people—in Florida."

"If the last murder is on her list. Or on *his* list. I would like to keep it open whether we are dealing with a female killer."

"Fine. Whatever. I assume Sullivan has a promotion on his mind. Arresting the members of organized crime—no matter the color—would push his career. He's been drawing good vibes from the top brass for the cases we solved. He's able to twist the results of the investigations so that he looks great—in some cases without making a decision." Matthew snorted. "Remember the case of Timothy Egerton killing the women he considered responsible for his mother's suicide? I waited at Terry Winter's home that night because we suspected that Terry might become Egerton's next victim, but Sullivan didn't decide whether I could break into Terry's home. I made the decision myself, and in the end, we saved Terry from being murdered by his half-brother." Matthew stubbed out the cigarette. He blew out smoke through his nostrils. "I sent my report and mentioned that I had to break into the house to find the address where Terry and his lover were vacationing that weekend. Sullivan replaced the sentence and wrote that he had ordered the break-in to find clues to the possible whereabouts. Great, isn't it?"

"He really did that?"

"He made it look like he had granted permission when in reality I waited for thirty minutes until I decided that I couldn't wait any longer." Matthew pulled out the keys for his car. "Don't look at me that way. I could've reported him to his superior, but to what effect? He doesn't like me anyway, and I doubt that his superior would believe my words."

"You might be right."

Matthew stood beside the open car door. "So you have to work with me again." He shrugged. "Let's see if we can find the killer without Sullivan looking great."

Nicolas smiled. "Yeah, I bet we can do that."

Michael and Umberto lay prone on the thick carpet, next to each of them a pint of ice cream. They were leisurely browsing a thick catalogue with sex toys and making notes which ones they wanted to buy. Michael hadn't been so hyped up in his lifetime. It was a new world for him—a lover who asked him for his opinion and who was as excited as he to explore new frontiers—new ways of love making. He was close to pinching himself, disbelieving his luck.

While Umberto put in the order, Michael remembered Vincent's introduction to the sweet torment of bondage. In the beginning, Vincent used handcuffs that opened when Michael tore at them. Later on, the game had turned serious, including blindfolds and gags. Vincent taught him to relax and enjoy being helpless, telling him every time how much he adored him. Sex had been great, always, and Vincent had made him feel good. Giving up control had developed into a fantasy that aroused Michael quicker than any other kind of foreplay.

Michael loved to look back at the distance he had come—from the orphan who never knew his parents to the dancing instructor with a lover at his side who understood his needs.

"This is a game, Mick," Vincent used to say. *"It's over when you say it's over."*

Michael sat up to eat more ice cream and looked at Umberto's tanned neck and the crew cut. Exhaling with bliss, he looked forward to the games they would invent and how Umberto would use his power. "Did you do this before?"

Umberto turned around and rested his head on his propped up arm. "Yes. I was a handler before."

"And he was . . ." He let the question trail off, insecure whether Umberto was ready to talk about former bed partners.

"He was my puppy. A very . . . dedicated puppy." He looked hurt. "We . . . parted a while ago."

Boldly, Michael asked, "And since then? Any new lovers?"

"No. Not like this. Not like anything we have." Umberto turned back to the list, his tone indicating he considered the subject over.

"Did it have anything to do with your . . . colleagues and family? That they shouldn't learn of your kind of relationship?"

Umberto hung his head, sighing deeply. The silence stretched until he said, "I'm from Italy, Mikey. Italian men aren't gay." He glanced at Michael, and the pain in his eyes was raw. "Italian men are straight. All of them. Always. That's a rule. If you deviate from this behavior, you better keep it to yourself or you pay a price." Umberto looked him in the eyes as if his stare would hammer his words home. "Whenever we are with my colleagues, you are but a friend who pays a part of the rent, okay? Don't touch me. Don't make any moves that give you and me away. Do you get this?"

Michael nodded. He let the truth sink in that Umberto would never introduce him to his friends as a lover. He wouldn't become part of the family. Their relationship would bloom secretly, if at all. For the moment, he was numbed and disappointed. "I worked as a rent boy once," Michael said after a while.

"I thought so." Umberto finished the list and sent out the online order to the company. Inhaling, he sat up and spooned ice cream. "I don't mind."

"I like the work as a dancing instructor much more."

"Can you tap dance?"

Michael swung his hips around and lowered his butt on Umberto's thighs. Seductively and with a flash of a smile, he said, "I can do lap dancing much better."

"No, honestly."

"It's not that every dancer has to have it in his repertoire." Michael got up and looked around, but the only hard surface was in the kitchen. "I can do a few moves, but I'm not Gene Kelly."

Umberto cocked his head toward the TV set. "Let's watch a movie tonight, together. Any proposals?"

"What about *Singin' in the Rain?*"

Shaking with laughter, they changed places and got comfortable on the new leather couch. Michael settled in Umberto's embrace as he switched on the TV set.

CHAPTER THREE

U mberto stood with his hands clasped in front of the massive mahogany desk, facing the hand-tufted carpet. The room smelled of old leather, cigar smoke, and copious amounts of an expensive aftershave. Both doors toward the patio were open, and the soft warm breeze moved the curtains, grazing the room with fresh air.

Luigi Vianone, his new boss, had the sympathetic grin of a hyena and a devilishly friendly smile that chilled the marrow in the bones of his enemies. He was known to be ruthless, and yet he could be charming so that the women loved him for his flattery. The unholy discrepancy between showering his friends with gifts and stabbing his enemies in the back was terrifying for everyone who had the misfortune to come to know both sides of Luigi's personality.

The man with the Italian roots looked like a bad copy of Franco Nero, the famous actor. He had the high cheekbones, the impressive dark blue eyes, and the full curly hair but neither the charisma nor the moves. Dressed immaculately in a blue suit with matching tie, white shirt, and polished shoes, Luigi could waltz into any restaurant or meeting and fit in as if he had been invited. The perfect clothes concealed that he had a protruding belly due to a lot of food and even more booze. The clothes also concealed his weapons. Rumor had it that Luigi never left the house without at least two knives and a sidearm on his body.

He stressed repeatedly that his parents had arrived in New York with nothing but the clothes on their backs, and that his father had worked for the railroad all his life. Their sons Eduardo and Luigi learned that money was tight, and if you wanted something, you had to work for it, one way or the other. The brothers worked from their sixteenth birthday on and never depended on their parents' income. Both men were proud of what they had achieved, although Luigi never mentioned that his elder brother was more successful by far.

Umberto wished the meeting over. He knew from experience that Eduardo had been the more talented executive, in ways of moneymaking and dealing with employees as well as customers and competitors. He knew how to bribe a senator without making it look like he was bribing him. Now the elder brother was dead, and Luigi tried to get an overview of the company in Miami without looking dumb.

Luigi ranted about the building industry in Washington, DC, and that he would expand his business within the next five years — three years, if competitors understood that they'd better not mess with him. After three more equally loud and aggressive revelations, Umberto realized that Luigi was referring to the greater DC area as well as Miami and the bigger cities in Florida. He wondered whether Luigi was right in his mind — he needed skilled men to lead a company of that size. Not to mention the building industry was rough, no matter how many competitors Luigi could force to back down. As Umberto had learned previously, Luigi preferred cowing his so-called enemies rather than bribing them.

Umberto and the three men standing next to him waited for the end of the monologue and the tasks that would ensue. Until then, they were decoration, an audience Luigi needed to make him feel great. His secretaries stood at the opposite wall, taking down notes when Luigi mentioned one of the competitors by name. If needed, they provided information, statistics, and the family situation of the company owner. Then Luigi nodded as if he was already sharpening the knife to stab another competitor to death.

It would have been impolite to yawn, but the longer the meeting lasted, the more Umberto yearned for a walk outside, a drink, and a place in the shade. He was tired of standing on his feet. Tomorrow was the Fourth of July, and he had plans with Michael. After the boxes with the dungeon equipment had arrived, Umberto had sent Michael on a shopping tour so that he could assemble it in the meantime. However, they both had to work, and Michael's working hours were odd, to say the least. On some days, he came home close to midnight, claiming that private clients took their dancing lessons after the usual hours.

Umberto held his tongue. He was too happy with the arrangement of his lover rooming in to argue about Michael's time out of the house. Quite the opposite—when Umberto had to work late, Michael didn't complain or act grumpy with him. Umberto sensed that Michael needed to belong to an older and more experienced man. He was obviously satisfied when he could serve and fulfill the tasks given. Michael rarely mentioned what he wanted. Umberto didn't know whether this was good or bad. Though he had thorough knowledge of human nature, he was still trying to understand Michael's character and his motivation. It seemed unreal that a young man of only twenty-two years was completely happy with a man like Umberto, who considered himself boring.

"Hey, Umberto! Daydreaming again?"

Umberto snapped out of his reverie. "No, I'm right here."

"With your mind miles away." Luigi's brows twitched, a clear sign of annoyance. "You'll pay Trenton Polasky a visit. I haven't seen a cent this month."

Umberto strained to keep a blank face. Luigi switched from ominous threats against building competitors in two states to the petty task of racketeering. Instead of arguing that he should concentrate on one task—and that was a big one—to keep Eduardo's business running, Umberto headed for the door without a word.

It was a mistake.

"You think I'm not focused, right?" Luigi said to Umberto's back.

Dutifully, Umberto turned around. "Beg your pardon?"

"Don't play dumb, Bert. I know what you think. I know you adored my big brother. I know you don't approve of my methods — of me. But I'm in charge now. I need you to do your best. You understand that? You have to go where I send you, because I need the work done."

"Of course."

"Can I trust you?" Luigi asked pointedly when Umberto was about to turn away again. "Hey, can I trust you to do what's right?"

"Yes, Luigi." Umberto returned Luigi's stare without flinching. He had worked long years for Eduardo, tasked with more important decisions than collecting a few bucks from a dealer. He would never reveal his opinion.

"All right." Luigi nodded, chin protruding, the corners of his mouth dragging south. "Go ahead, make my day." He waved at him as if he was waving away an unwanted beggar.

Umberto quickened his steps and exhaled when he reached his car parked in the sunshine. It was hot inside until the air conditioning kicked in, but it was much better than spending another minute in Luigi's presence.

Relieved, Umberto started the engine and drove off.

If possible, Senior Agent Sullivan's mood hit rock bottom after the deputy director declared that observing the men presumed responsible for one or more murders in Florida tied up too many human resources and cost money. Sullivan's claims that the Vianone family in Washington, DC, must have something to do with the killings were dismissed because of a lack of evidence, and the agents of the surveillance teams, who had worked in Germantown and Alexandria, were assigned to new cases.

Grumpy as always, Sullivan declared that he wanted Luigi Vianone nailed for the crimes in Florida and, if possible, for more in the greater DC area. He would not allow organized crime to spread in the city.

After Sullivan had departed in a cloud of rage and frustration, Matthew dared to breathe again. He waited for the office door to close before he turned to Nicolas. "I heard that he lost a family member to the Vianone syndicate, but it was never proven. That explains a lot, but still doesn't justify tying us to this losing game."

"Do you have information I don't?"

Matthew went through a pile of papers on his desk. "The FBI bureau in Miami declared that they're looking for a woman, Leila Prescott, who pestered Mayor Norton two years ago, claiming that she blamed him for a lack of control at construction sites. Her husband had died in an accident at one of Lubock's skyscrapers in western Orlando. She demanded more controls and safety measures at the construction sites and higher insurances. Her demands were rejected." He looked up from the sheet of paper. "They're searching for her, but she left Florida — or so it seems."

"They finally found a woman," Nicolas mumbled, then added in a louder voice, "We'll split between the cases we got, anyway. By now, we're up to six, and none looks promising."

"What's your plan for tomorrow?"

Nicolas's expression was that of a man caught between a rock and a hard place. "We'll see."

"Dancing with the lady? Watching the fireworks? Escape trip to New York?" Matthew laughed, but Nicolas stared at his keyboard. "It's a holiday. Don't you like holidays anymore?"

"Let's say my ideas didn't meet with the ones Jacky had."

"Oh."

"And you?"

"My friend Bert's visiting from Chicago, and I volunteered to take a day shift. I plan to spend the evening with Bert and my dog, and take him inside when the fireworks start. Bingo is not so fond of the noise. Bert and I will then attend one of the fireworks close by."

"No date? I heard that Lisa from bookkeeping flirted with you."

"Then you didn't hear that she's allergic to dog hair." He laughed without humor. "At the moment, I don't want to choose between my dog that loves me and a woman who might or might not be interested in me. I'll stay with my dog." Matthew got up. "I have enough for the day. Go home, no matter Jacky's mood."

"It's not her mood that bothers me."

Michael packed his outfits and equipment, checked twice whether he had his dancing shoes, and looked in the mirror. He had washed and styled his hair, applied a little make-up, and shaved off his stubble. Vincent would have called it the *son-in-law look*. The elder man had taught him that the first impression was everything, no matter whether you wanted to impress a company executive or your lover. You had to wear the right clothes, polished shoes, and a few pieces of jewelry. A golden watch was acceptable, while rings and bracelets were not. Vincent had explained that no one liked show-offs. You impressed people by good manners, by politeness, and by intelligence. It was wise to have money, but it was unwise to mention it. His teacher knew how to flatter a woman and how to talk with a rich man to get into his inner circle of trustworthy persons. Vincent had possessed the natural skill of appearing full of integrity, and his reputation had been impeccable.

Smiling about the vivid memories, Michael took his full bag and headed from the dancing studio to the *Blue Mountain Hotel,* where the party would start in two hours. The day before, he had visited with his dancing partners for the last rehearsal, and he looked forward to their gig. If his perception was correct, the group didn't even look at him as a gay man dancing but as a classic performer, no matter his sexual orientation. One of the female dancers had asked him what he would do after their performance, and Michael had been so surprised he didn't say a word. She smiled and put a hand on his arm, mouthing he could decide later.

As he went through the hotel lobby, Michael noticed Umberto at the rear of the large reception hall in a conversation with two men in tuxedos. They drank champagne and looked much too serious for such a jolly night. Hiding his surprise and his presence, Michael mingled with the crowd and strutted through the main corridor toward the artists' locker rooms.

Umberto hadn't told him where he would spend the evening, and Michael pondered whether his lover had come to watch his performance or if he had been ordered to attend the party by his new boss in town. Michael didn't know whether his lover's new employer would attend the party. The last reason was acceptable while the first one bothered him — what if Michael's performance wasn't what Umberto expected? He wanted Umberto to be proud, not disappointed in his lover.

Taking deep breaths to calm down, Michael changed clothes and chatted with the dancers. Nervousness was their constant companion, but it should never interfere with the performance. When his colleagues asked about his career, Michael stated he had none. He was grateful for his talent that he had honed in uncounted hours at the studios, dancing every day, taking lessons, watching videos of famous dancers. He was able to glean from watching and could transform the moves into his own dancing skills. As if he had learned the steps during childhood, Michael moved gracefully like a ballet dancer. He was so flexible Vincent had described him as *snake-like*.

Maybe, so the others said, he could start a career that evening — performing in front of the upper-class executives of the DC metro, granting the rich people a glimpse of his talent. Michael joked that if there was a chance for another engagement, he counted on the other eleven dancers to be with him. He wasn't ready for a solo performance.

Their gig was the last one prior to the grand opening of the ball, when guests would dance. As the group entered the stage, the audience fell silent. Michael's heart beat in his throat. His usual calmness was blown away — he hadn't anticipated the hall to be so full of people. When the music set in and his partner strutted across the dancefloor into his arms, smiling all over her pretty face, Michael forgot about the crowd, about Umberto. The performance included rumba and samba, and the people cheered after each piece of music.

"This went great," his partner whispered as they thanked the audience for the applause.

The last dance was a jive. After the group took position to receive another warm round of applause, the music went on, and the dancers went to the tables to ask the guests to join them on the dancefloor. Michael charmed a lady way beyond sixty with his dazzling smile, escorted her to the dancefloor, and took position. When she confessed she hadn't danced in years, Michael's smile grew intense. "I'll show you — if you let me."

"Oh, my pleasure."

The lady was easy to lead and flushed quite nicely as

Michael enchanted her with his skills and his compliments. When the music faded, she beamed at him. "You're such a nice young man! If I had a daughter, I'd introduce you." She patted his arm affectionately as he led her to her table.

"Thank you." Michael didn't say that the introduction to her son, who sat at the same table, would be just as nice.

His mood lifting, Michael danced for another hour with various guests before he fetched his bag and retreated to the restroom, sweaty and tired. Now that his duties were done, the adrenalin level dropped, and his muscles felt heavy. He relieved himself, and when he left the cabin, saw an elderly man with a shock of gray hair stumbling right beside him. Quick-witted, Michael stretched out his arm and grabbed the man's wrist, stopping his fall.

The gray-haired man caught his breath. "Thank you, young man, that was . . . fast."

"Are you all right?" Michael asked as he helped him toward the closest sink. The guest looked shaken and stood, both hands gripping the rim, face pale and sweaty. He looked like he was about to collapse at any moment.

"I'm fine, yes, thank you. It must have been a slippery spot on the tiles." He took another deep breath before he corrected his black-framed glasses and looked up. "You're one of the dancers, huh? Small wonder you're so flexible."

"It comes with the job description." Michael smiled amiably while he washed his hands and reached for a paper towel. "I'm glad you are okay." He took his bag and when he turned around ran into Umberto, who entered the restroom. "Hello, sir."

Umberto didn't flinch and held the door for Michael to pass him by. Behind Michael, two men left the restroom and headed back to the party. Michael waited until the door snapped shut, and when Umberto didn't follow him for a chat, walked through the lobby toward the parking lot. For a second, he pondered whether to look for his dancing partner and spend some time with her in a bar, but then dismissed the idea and drove home.

Jacklyn could always tell Nicolas's mood when he entered their home. The way he dropped his badge and gun on the shelf, the way he took off his jacket and shoes, and the way he looked at her. This evening, he was tired but also grumpy.

She flashed a smile, smacked a kiss on his lips, and asked how his day had been.

"Tiresome." He went to the bedroom to take off his clothes. "Too many cases, no leads, nothing to go on. It feels like walking through molasses. Frustrating."

From behind, she put her hands on his shoulders. "We have a day off tomorrow. You can relax."

"Is that so? Just speaking of *frustrating* – this reaches a higher level." He turned around. "Do we have to leave at all?" He kissed her chastely. "Wouldn't it be nice to stay here and do nothing?"

She had heard the plea before. "We agreed on participating –"

"You told me we would spend the holiday with your parents at their home. You didn't ask for my agreement."

Jacklyn let go, shrugging. "My parents want to spend time with us. That's okay, I think. Not that unusual."

"Your mom doesn't want to meet with me. She wants to see her daughter, and you made it clear she can't have you without having me. That's different." He turned to the drawer for fresh underwear.

Jacklyn tried for a soothing tone, even though she was annoyed that they led the conversation in a loop every year. "It's not that she doesn't like you."

"She accepted her daughter's decision to live with a loser

instead of a rich banker."

"You forgot to mention he should be old and ugly." Her smile, meant to calm his mood, was wasted.

"She made it very clear she wanted a better match for her daughter, and I'm a walking disappointment she can't get rid of. There's more acceptance in a shark that he can't catch every prey." He went to the bathroom. "Every time I'm at your parent's home, she shows off with what they have and what you will inherit—always accompanied by a look that says that I shouldn't be the man to share that wealth with you." He dropped his underwear and switched on the shower. "She's probably happy we don't intend to get married."

Jacklyn took off her pants and shirt and joined him under the spray of water. She wouldn't follow the way the conversation was turning. "Don't be glum. Please, don't be angry about my mom. It's not worth it."

Nicolas turned to her, hanging his head. "Why can't we spend the Fourth of July here? Why the hassle? Isn't there any other time you can visit your parents? Without me?"

She cupped his cheeks and looked him deep in the eyes. "I'm proud of you, Nick. I'm proud that you are a successful agent, that you work hard and do a dangerous job. You risk your life every day."

"In your mom's eyes—"

"My mom's opinion means shit to me." She kissed him. "You should know that by now." When he still didn't look convinced, she added, "We'll make a deal. If my mom behaves badly again, we spend the next holiday here. Just the two of us."

"The next holidays I want you for myself and not to pay attention to your parents' interests, which are far away from the real world."

"That's not true. My father—"

Nicolas put a finger on her lips. "Deal." He pulled her under the warm water to kiss and embrace her.

Jacklyn melted in his arms, happy to have turned the mood around. The night was looking up.

Michael stepped out of the shower when Umberto appeared at the door, looking remorseful like a husband who had forgotten an anniversary. He was still wearing his formal suit and tie, dispersing the smell of stale smoke and vaguely of sweat and aftershave.

"I didn't know you would be there, at the party," Michael said, groping for a towel.

"It was a . . . short-notice invitation."

"By your new boss of the insurance company?"

"Yep." Umberto opened the jacket and took it off. "I watched your performance. You are really good." His smile needed work and faded quickly.

Michael pondered whether the praise was honest. He reached for his underwear. "Thank you."

"Stay like this," Umberto said.

Michael stopped in mid-motion, pulling the wet towel around his waist. Umberto closed the gap between them, kissed Michael's shoulder, neck, and, finally, his lips. Michael dropped the towel to open his lover's shirt and push it over his shoulders. The pants followed, and when he looked down, he gasped at the thick bulge in Umberto's boxer shorts.

"Will you be my servant tonight?" Umberto placed hungry kisses all over Michael's chest and abs. "Will you allow me to tie you up?"

"You want to christen the furniture?" Michael whispered as he lowered himself to kneel in front of Umberto and kissed his penis through the shorts.

"Yes, I've been dying to do this for a week." Umberto

tousled Michael's wet hair. "When I watched you dance, I wanted nothing more but to drag you away and fuck you blind."

Though Michael had hoped his lover would return in a mood to have sex, he was nevertheless astonished at Umberto's open longing. Umberto pulled him up, kissed him again, and then in one fluid move, turned him around and pressed him against the wall.

"I want you. I need you."

"Looks like we won't make it to the bedroom," Michael said, smiling.

"We have the whole night."

After the intermezzo at the restroom and his near-accident, Clifford Sorenson, son of Swedish builders and successful construction engineers, reached his limousine and slumped onto the back seat, breathing raggedly. He groped for a handkerchief and blotted his forehead, thinking about how well the evening had gone. Meeting so many important and influential people at one event was a rare and very lucrative opportunity to make acquaintances leading to deals in the future. When thinking about expanding his business in Maryland, he hadn't imagined how well you had to be *connected* to get a contract. The business executives present had—almost nonchalantly—discussed the bribes they paid to be in the mayor's favor. Sorenson knew he had to flow with the way business was done or he wouldn't win any contract for public constructions at all. Cautiously, he had explored the backgrounds and learned how to get close to the mayor without looking officious. He calculated the extra costs and decided that it was worth a try to get into the politician's favor.

Sorenson had swallowed a lump in his throat watching Luigi Vianone swagger through the ballroom like some arrogant stud out to impress and intimidate his competitors. Business here was different from Sweden—that much Sorenson had learned. But he wouldn't bow to a snotty-nosed little upstart who—if the rumors were right—stood in the shadow of his older brother. Eduardo Vianone had made a name with company take-overs, then turned into a profitable builder and a man able to restore buildings to sell them at a much higher value. The older Vianone was a legend, a man of integrity. Sorenson assumed that Eduardo had made his fortune partly illegally, but he didn't care. The branch had lived with such measures for centuries. He was much more worried about Luigi Vianone—he appeared to be a man who would walk over dead bodies to reach his goal and laugh doing it.

Breathing became more difficult with each passing minute of the ride. He poured a glass of scotch with trembling hands, but then left the glass untouched when his strength reeled and his dizziness increased. He pressed the button to tell the driver to stop. The limousine coasted to the sidewalk. Sorenson hoped that some fresh air would do him good, but the moment the driver opened the door, he turned to the side and heaved. He hadn't eaten much that night, so his vomiting bout was short. Still, he couldn't breathe normally, and he didn't hear what his driver said. He watched him dial nine-one-one and saw him speak.

His vision dimmed as he sank against the backrest. He felt his heart beat rapidly in his throat while he couldn't get enough air in his lungs. It felt terrible to suffocate. Then he lost consciousness.

When Michael walked toward the bedroom, he noticed that Umberto was staring at him. Staring in a way that told of hunger, lust—of feelings displayed much more openly than before. "What?"

"I'm admiring your perfect body. That's what it means to be a dancer, right? To train hard to look like this."

"Yes." Michael moved his hips left and right, smiling invitingly. He was pleased that Umberto noticed his well-developed muscles. He used to admire himself in the mirror every day.

Umberto gave Michael's butt a gentle squeeze. "You must dance for me some time."

"Pole dance, huh?"

"If you wish. But just for me."

Umberto's smile was back, and Michael was glad he could entertain his friend. He hoped for a wonderful time. The previous night, Umberto had left the house unexpectedly and hadn't revealed his destination the next morning at breakfast. He had mumbled about *obligations* without specifying what he had to do. He appeared grumpy about the question, so Michael had dropped the subject immediately.

Within their brief relationship, he had learned to accept barriers in their conversations. Should Umberto block a question or turn away, Michael didn't pry but waited for a better mood or didn't get to know at all what interested him. Umberto told him he worked for an insurance company and was obliged to travel from town to town to meet clients. However, if asked about details of his work, Umberto stated he had to keep company secrets or that his work was boring, then he changed the subject. Michael was curious but not careless. He wouldn't risk his relationship because of his thirst for knowledge. Every man had his secrets, and this included that Umberto forbade him to enter his study on the second floor. Michael accepted the order without discussion. If Umberto wanted to keep his privacy, Michael shrugged off the subject and moved on.

The construction in the bedroom looked like a cross between an examination chair and a St. Andrew's cross. It was comfortable, with dark red leather cushions and yet, when the victim was properly tethered, it was an inescapable piece of dungeon furniture, Umberto's latest acquisition. Michael exhaled while Umberto closed the cuffs around his ankles and caressed his feet, then his shins and thighs. Slowly, avoiding Michael's genitals, Umberto's warm hands explored Michael's abs and chest before he closed the leather cuffs around his wrists.

Umberto's eyes were shining with an inner light that was amazing. Michael couldn't recall Vincent's expression and whether he had felt the same happiness, but Umberto's devotion was one of a kind. The caressing went on, and Michael relaxed, feeling loved and taken care of. He closed his eyes to enjoy Umberto's hands on his face, shoulders, along his arms and torso. He was shivering with expectation and that was partly because he hadn't been tethered for a long time. Right after Vincent's death, Michael had thought he would never want that kind of lovemaking again, but here he was—so happy he could burst.

Umberto kissed Michael's growing member only to move upward again. When he stood beside his head once more, he whispered, "What's the safe word?"

"Picasso," Michael replied, thinking of Vincent again.

"And if you can't speak?"

Michael felt a shower of lust. "I'll snap my fingers."

"All right." Umberto tousled Michael's hair in a loving way and kissed his forehead.

Michael heard his loud breathing and knew he was touching himself to get hard. He hadn't expected the night to turn into a session. It was much more than he had hoped for. There was something about Umberto and his sudden appearance at the party that bothered him, but for now he was willing to put doubts aside and enjoy the night.

CHAPTER FOUR

Jacklyn handed Nicolas their two small bags. "Let's go."

As expected, Nicolas made a face and pretended to drop the bags. "I really—"

"We discussed the topic. It's settled." She took her purse and the keys. They left the house, and she locked the door. "Don't look so glum. You don't have any reason to complain. The night was—"

Nicolas grinned. "Pretty amazing."

"For standards—"

"And without a single shackle. You are awesome."

"I know how to tie a man to me."

Nicolas dropped the bags into the trunk and kissed her throat while his arms found their way around her waist. "Damn, you do."

She freed herself from his embrace. "We really have to go."

"I'll let you drive so I can nibble on your earlobe all the way."

"And ruin my concentration? You're with the FBI. You should arrest yourself for bad conduct."

"I like the way you say that. Maybe *you* should arrest me."

Jacklyn pointed at him. "I'm thinking about it." She slammed the trunk.

"Did you bring your equipment?"

"No. Why?" She slipped behind the wheel while he sat on the passenger seat.

"To keep me from running the moment your mother says the first words."

She slapped his arm. "Don't be ridiculous. Imagine her expression — bringing you in in handcuffs — gagged, on a leash." She pretended to envision the scene. "I don't think she'd understand."

He kissed her neck and cheek. "I do. I want that. Let's shock her a bit."

"And what shall I tell my parents? That I couldn't get you in the car any other way?"

He made a face as he buckled in. "Sounds realistic."

She started the engine and drove the car onto the street. "You're mean."

He leaned over and kissed her again. "I'm not mean. I love you and your mean streak. That's different."

She cast him a glance, half smiling, half serious. "I'm a mistress. Sometimes I'm mean."

"Then be mean with me. Right now. Pull over and show me how mean you are."

"Tempting, but no. I can't risk being stopped and checked by the police. How should I explain you being tethered in the backseat?"

Nicolas laughed aloud. "Yeah, great moment. We could call your mom and explain the situation — why we are late. Or not coming at all."

"It's getting better and better." She scolded him, but couldn't keep it up. "I'll have to make up for this trip. I get it."

"Big time, ma Belle. Do you want me to predict the first sentences she'll say to me?"

Jacklyn sighed. "Honestly, her bickering is enough. You don't have to imitate her on the way."

"Right." He reached out and caressed the curve of her ear and chin. "I'll spend my time distracting you from driving."

"Bad boy."

"That's what I am," he whispered in her ear. "FBI Agent *Bad Boy* Hayes."

No one wanted to work on the Fourth of July. Every year, employees were fighting over two or more free days to visit relatives and friends and spend the holiday together. Like any other public office, the FBI had to remain operational. One of the agents present was Matthew Montagna. Though his friend, Bert, had come to DC for a week, the festivities would start later in the evening, and Bert enjoyed Matthew's hospitality and playing with Matthew's dog, Bingo, during the day.

Getting off the phone with his friend, Matthew found a new email in his inbox.

"Now, look what we've got. Mr. Sorenson, owner of Sorenson & Gilmore Industries, died after a big party. Too many margaritas?" Matthew sat down and scrolled through the Washington, DC, homicide division report. "Another builder dead on a builders' festive event. Now that's interesting."

The lab had tested the victim's blood positive for fentanyl, but Sorenson's doctor stated his patient had no illness requiring a treatment with the drug. He had lived with a heart disease and a few other limitations that age brought forth, but nothing severe. The coroner concluded the dose had been high enough to be the likely cause of death. He couldn't tell, though, how the drug had been administered. The body didn't show any punctures, but it was possible that the drug had been swallowed or applied on the skin.

In a fact check on the internet, Matthew learned that either a highly-dosed pill or skin contact with an overdose of fentanyl—provided in a gel-form—was as lethal as the bite of a poisonous snake. Untreated, the victim died within thirty minutes of respiratory failure.

Sorensen had been rushed to a hospital, but was dead on arrival. He left behind a wife and a fifteen-year-old daughter, as well as a building corporation that was about to expand from New Jersey to Maryland. It was unlikely that the second partner, Gilmore, would lead the company with the same success. Sorenson had been the genius behind the deals—a well-known executive and a clever negotiator. Gilmore would lead on, but without the determination to expand the business.

Matthew also read that Senior Agent Sullivan had ordered the Washington PD and other police departments along the east coast to send file copies of murders marked with *death by poison, death of executives in the DC area,* and *murders of influential personalities* to the FBI. Obviously, the setback had not slowed down Sullivan's interest in bringing the Vianones to justice. Though Matthew still did not know with certainty the reason behind Sullivan's interest, he was glad his superior had placed the request. If the killer was the same woman or man as in Florida, the FBI could continue investigating within an already running serial murder case.

He called up the information about the cases in Florida and compared the details, thinking of Jason and his addiction to the whiteboard, plastered with the details of cases.

Jason had taken unpaid leave for two months—little wonder, with his father's money cushioning his family. Matthew wondered whether Jason would return to work at all, now that he had two people to care for. Maybe Elaine would convince him to accept an office job to stay away from danger. As Matthew remembered, Jason wasn't the type of agent who rushed into dangerous situations and welcomed the adrenalin kick in his blood. He was a cautious agent, a man who thought twice and found the best solution without risking his neck every time.

Matthew couldn't live without the rush of danger now and then, no matter the consequences. He had been shot while investigating. He had suffered injuries on a hunt, but no pain would keep him from doing the work he loved. His friend

Bert—always cautious bordering on being fearful—shook his head listening to Matthew's blood-chilling stories. He had three locks on his door at home, an alarm system, and a security company he could call in a case of emergency. He did not trust the police to react in time. When Matthew told him about closed cases, Bert shook his head and complained about a world gone mad with crime.

"Without it, I'd be without a job," Matthew mumbled as he listed the file details to get an overview. The FBI in Miami was still searching for Leila Prescott, the woman they considered responsible for killing the mayor, so far without success. Considering the circumstances, Matthew didn't believe she could be involved in the other victims' murders.

He doubted that Prescott had anything to do with the killings at all. Looking at the combined information, Matthew assumed he was looking for a highly intelligent murderer—male or female—who used disguises, slipped into different roles, and was able to blend into the surroundings. He or she had to be certain that only the chosen victim would eat the poisoned food. There were no known collateral deaths.

Matthew looked at the haphazardly attached post-it notes on the whiteboard. "Why did the killer change from snake poison to fentanyl?" Once more, he read the reports of his fellow agents in Miami. It took him an hour to find out that it was quite easy to illegally obtain snake poison in Florida, but harder the farther you came north. Statistics showed that the misuse of fentanyl and carfentanil caused sixty-thousand deaths per year along the east coast states, in most cases combined with heroin. It was easy to obtain and highly potent. "Small wonder you changed your poison," Matthew mumbled. "Now, all I need to know is who's your dealer. And what you look like would be nice to know, too."

He leaned back and folded his hands behind his head. It would be a long Fourth of July workday.

Upon arrival, Nicolas sighed deeply as he looked at the great old estate the Hollanders called their home. The buildings were located in a park-like property with high hedges and a fence around it, protected by security guards who looked as friendly as hungry grizzly bears. Though Jacklyn and Nicolas were expected, the two guards at the front gate examined their faces and checked the interior of the car and the trunk for potential weapons. Nicolas sighed again when they drove along the graveled path. He felt like he was slipping into another world, a world of mystery, crime, and suspense like that written by Agatha Christie. The few times Nicolas had visited Jacklyn's parents, he'd entered and left with a feeling of ineptitude, of being at the wrong place and misbehaving. Though the dark red stone building held the most expensive furniture and pieces of art, it lacked warmth.

Jacklyn killed the engine at the main entrance and looked at Nicolas with a sparkle in her eyes. "I know you can hardly hold back your excitement, but let me tell you this. No matter what happens, I'll drive home with you. All right?"

He kissed her with feeling. "Will two hours be enough?"

Jacklyn caressed his cheek with a finger. "I love you. You know that."

"Three hours?"

She laughed and got out. "Hello Herbert," she greeted the butler, who bowed to her. "How are you doing?"

"Great as always, Miss Jacklyn."

Nicolas knew he was stranded in a strange parallel realm and must stand tests of endurance to be allowed back into his own world.

The butler took the two bags faster than Nicolas could claim them.

Jacklyn linked arms with Nicolas and walked him toward

the door, seven stone steps up. "You look great, by the way."

"I feel like our roles are reversed," Nicolas whispered.

They reached the entrance, and another butler waited to lead them into the main living room. The Hollanders preferred the old English style—heavy furniture made of dark wood, highlighted by blue couches and chaise lounges with lots of small cushions. The walls were lined with cupboards with claw-feet, which contained porcelain and glasses. Many framed pictures were placed on top, showing Mr. Hollander meeting with dignitaries from different countries. Another board showed the family memories, and Nicolas was reminded once more that Jacklyn's beauty came from her mother.

Mrs. Beatrice Hollander appeared with measured steps, wearing a white knee-length summer dress with a sash and matching ballerinas. Her dark brown hair was styled in the latest fashion, and the make-up was elegant in an unobtrusive way. She was a woman that filled the description of being *sophisticated* to the T. She welcomed Jacklyn with an embrace and a light kiss on the cheek. "You look wonderful, my love, and I'm so happy you could make it." She turned to Nicolas. "Both of you. Certainly." Her smile withered around the edges. As usual, Beatrice was a beautiful gem and as warmhearted.

"Thank you for the invitation," Nicolas replied politely. He didn't expect an embrace.

"Oh, don't mention it." Beatrice waved her hand, and though she was much smaller than Nicolas, she looked down at him. "I ordered lunch to be served on the patio. I hope you don't mind."

Jacklyn smiled amiably. "Not at all. The weather is great."

Beatrice lifted a plucked eyebrow. "I will not lead a conversation about the weather," she decided and linked arms with Jacklyn to lead her through the room toward the open patio doors. "Tell me about your clinic. Are you expanding?"

Jacklyn looked left and right. "Where's Dad?"

"On the phone. He promised to come down for lunch." Beatrice pulled her daughter forward, and Nicolas knew his company was as desired as a herpes outbreak.

He pushed his hands in his pants pockets and lowered his chin while mother and daughter left the room, chatting rapidly in French. Nicolas strolled along the private exhibition of pictures, paintings, and collectibles. He stopped at Jacklyn's childhood photographs, smiling. Jacklyn had been a happy child. Her mother had obviously loved to dress her in skirts and blouses, in fancy dresses with lots of lace. No matter the outfit, Jacklyn had struck a pose and looked into the camera as if she had been born to strut along a catwalk. Nicolas thought about the career Jacklyn had made and was bound to smile. The jolly child had turned into a mistress who knew how to swing a whip.

Nicolas turned when he heard steps approach. "Oh, hello Frederic."

As at their previous meetings, Frederic Hollander appeared to come from a long lost decade. His clothes and bearing, even his haircut, belonged to the fifties, to a man like Cary Grant or Gregory Peck. Loafers and pants with creases were long out of fashion but looked completely right on him.

Frederic knocked his pipe on an ashtray and pulled a pack of tobacco out of his pants pocket. "Hello Nicolas. It's kind of you to escort our little princess home. Are you both doing well?"

They shook hands, and Nicolas felt better instantly. "Yes, we're doing fine. How about you?"

"The usual problems and small crises around the globe. If it was any different, I would be out of my job," he concluded with a wink and a smile as he continued stuffing his pipe. "Let's sit down. The ladies are already outside?"

"And chatting the day away." Nicolas sat down on the edge of the couch, keeping his thoughts to himself.

Frederic leaned back, found a lighter, and puffed on his pipe. "I heard about your latest case. My congratulations. Breaking up a ring of human traffickers is quite an accomplishment."

"Thank you."

"Though I didn't know him and as it may sound impersonal, my condolences for the loss of your friend Thomas."

"You know?"

"At my request, Jacklyn keeps me informed." The corners of Frederic's mouth twitched into a small smile. "She doesn't stop praising you for your outstanding work for society, so I asked her to be more specific. She points out the reports once they are released in the newspapers. I noticed that your name doesn't show. How come?"

Nicolas didn't intend to unveil the personal circumstances at the bureau. "It is common that the senior agent answers the questions of the press."

"Ah." Frederic's smile deepened, and his expression showed clearly that he understood Nicolas's attempt to downplay the situation. "Nevertheless, I admire you for your ability to stand in the line of fire almost every day."

Nicolas lowered his gaze toward his folded hands.

"How are you both getting along?"

Nicolas frowned at the change of subject. "Very well. Thank you for asking."

"I heard, though, that she would like you to take up a less dangerous job."

"And I won't. She's accepted that." Nicolas held Frederic's inquisitive stare. "We settled the subject."

"I heard that, too. Though she is worried sick for you every time you leave the house."

"My job's not as dangerous as it sounds."

"And how do you get along with her preferences in life?" Frederic blew out smoke, and the scent of dried rose leaves filled the room.

"You mean her being a physiotherapist?"

"I mean her being a very dominant woman who is used to command and get what she wants."

Nicolas held his breath, frowning and trying to understand Frederic's words as well as his cloaked expression. He was at a loss. "Be more specific, please, for I don't follow your train of thought." The words came out harsher than intended.

Frederic waved his pipe, obviously more amused than angry about Nicolas's tone. "Ah, the habit of diplomatic cautiousness." He put the pipe back between his teeth and took it out again after a brief pause. "I followed my daughter's career closely. I watched her every step—even the missteps, if you get my meaning." He made a gesture with his hand. "Her adventures in the dark rooms filled with instruments that belong to the Middle Ages."

"You are referring to her time as a mistress."

"Indeed. Do I assume correctly that your relationship contains elements of her desire?"

Nicolas lowered his chin, smiling. He put his hands together. "Frederic, if ever possible, leave out the diplomatic restrictions. Ask what you want to know."

With a sound of approval, Frederic bent forward. "All of the time, I wanted to know whether she continued her work at a club or if she restrained herself. Tell me, does she treat you like you are her . . . what is it called? Servant?"

"A submissive. She's the dominant and, yes, I'm the submissive."

Frederic's eyes widened. "Astonishing." He put the pipe in an ashtray on the table. "So you were . . . no, let me rephrase that. You tended to be a submissive man? She claimed she met you on the street."

"That's right. I helped her when her car broke down. To answer the question behind that—I was not a member of the club scene. Jacky told me and taught me all about the game."

Frederic sounded surprised. "All these years, you had no intention to be a woman's servant—pardon, *submissive* — until my daughter came along and convinced you? Or is this the wrong word?"

"Love appears in many different varieties. The bondage game is but one of them."

"That's a fascinating aspect I've never truly considered."

"How come you know and your wife does not?"

Frederic lifted and dropped a hand. His mischievous smile deepened. "She might know but denies the truth to keep up reputations—hers and Jacklyn's. Beatrice is a fine woman if you get to know her better, but she has sharply defined views of the world."

"Her daughter being a mistress would be a stain?"

Frederic laughed, a well-tempered sound that fit the English-style interior in its reserve. "Yes. Tell me one thing, Nicolas. Why do you play that game?"

Nicolas inhaled deeply as they locked gazes. "She helps me escape. You were right—sometimes my job's dangerous and stressful. Coming home and giving up control is a part of stress relief."

"Fascinating. Though I would like to listen to the stories you could tell, I'm afraid we are both expected to show up for lunch. Maybe later?"

Nicolas nodded, though he felt uncomfortable. He didn't know if it was possible that he had revealed details of his sex life to his lover's father.

The longer he thought about it, the less he wanted to be alone with him again.

Upon request, Matthew received hours of videotape feed of the Builders' Association Event on the third of July. When he unpacked the files on his computer, he moaned, learning how many different angles the cameras had caught and how many people attended the party. He checked the guest list. Everyone with a name in building and construction, as well as architects and sculptors of the greater Washington, DC, area, had been invited, plus several dignitaries such as the sitting mayor. He wiped his eyes and went to work with yet another cup of coffee on his desk.

Sorenson's driver had stated that his employer had been to the restrooms about twenty minutes before he entered the limousine. Matthew found out that neither the hallway nor the restrooms at the end of it were covered by cameras, which meant he had no means to determine exactly who was with Sorenson at the time prior to his departure from the party. According to the medical examiner's statement, Sorenson had been given the deadly drug about thirty minutes prior to showing symptoms, but the assumption depended on the way the drug had been administered. Matthew followed the man's actions backward and found him in a discussion with several other men and a woman. He was drinking from a short glass, probably filled with whiskey or another kind of brown alcohol, and chatting energetically, laughing in between. Matthew identified two men immediately — the Washington, DC, mayor, and the head of the Washington Architectural Association. He phoned the mayor's office to ask for help with identifying the other people present, but the office was closed for the holiday.

Cursing, Matthew went back to examining the recordings. He found nothing out of the ordinary until an angle of a camera in the ballroom showed Umberto Bianchi, one of the men working for the Vianones, who now lived in Alexandria. Frowning, Matthew emptied his coffee cup, put it down, and

spent another hour following Bianchi's movement throughout the party. At last, he found him leaving the camera angle
toward the hallway leading to the restrooms four minutes after Sorenson had gone that way.

"Now this is getting interesting."

Matthew counted seven more men heading for the restrooms in the time frame. He produced stills of all of them
for later identification, then leaned back, found the cup empty
and got up to pour another one, made of Jason's excellent coffee beans. He grinned as he put down the pot.

"Jason will kill me over that boldness."

But he wished Jason was back on deck.

Lunch was delicious, though Beatrice spiced it with remarks
about acceptable and inadmissible professions and the necessity of keeping a lady well supported.

Jacklyn countered her mother's remarks with ease, and
when Beatrice didn't stop, said, "You've had your share of
scolding Nick, now is the time to celebrate him. Without him,
a hundred men and women would still toil like slaves or fight
in illegal boxing competitions. More men would suffer as toys
for rich bastards who think they are above the law."

Beatrice put her elbows on the table and folded her hands.
Her face showed the tendency to smile but didn't accomplish
the task. "I did not intend to belittle his . . . achievements, but
still his *job* — "

"The Fourth of July is a holiday because in seventeen-sev-
enty-six, the colonies declared their independence from Great
Britain. The Declaration of Independence stated that they
would rule themselves and take care of their own fate. And I
don't accept being ruled by your opinion. I chose a tough,
very brave, competent FBI agent, and I'm in love with him.
That's my decision. I'm proud of him, and nothing you say

will change that. Consider the subject settled." She turned to Nicolas and found happiness but also astonishment in his look. Her kiss was chaste, meant as a demonstration, not as a challenge. She didn't want to pour oil on the fire of her mother's anger.

"Hear, hear," Frederic said, chuckling. He had a sparkle in his eyes that Jacklyn loved to see. "Now, that should truly settle the argument." He put a hand on Beatrice's arm, and his glance was enough to silence her.

Waving the argument away, Beatrice turned to tell the butler to serve dessert.

Jacklyn locked gazes with her father, then kissed Nicolas's cheek. "Love you, Nick, with all I am."

"Love you, too."

Late in the afternoon, Matthew had watched all the footage and taken notes about the persons in Sorenson's close proximity during the party, either by name or by looks. He hoped to identify the many men and women within two days to narrow down the circle of suspects.

His focus was on Bianchi, not only because Sullivan pushed for identifying the Vianone mob as the motor behind the murders, also in Florida, but also for the man's unexpected appearance at the party. But then Bianchi's presence wasn't so unusual, for Luigi Vianone also appeared on the tapes. Matthew was yet undecided about what job Bianchi was doing for Vianone.

Matthew dwelled on these findings, and then pulled the information the agents in Miami had collected.

After a lunch break consisting of a ham sandwich, more coffee, and a cigarette in the yard, Matthew went through the reports and the observation protocols of the agents in DC tasked with watching Vianone's men who had currently moved closer to the capital.

Only Bianchi had been at the Builders' Association Event. When Matthew checked the guest list again and compared it to Vianone's likely employees, he found out that Michael Grayden, who was living at the same address as Umberto Bianchi, had attended the party as part of the night's entertainment group. He was a dancing instructor, and the local dance club had been hired for a gig.

Leaning back, Matthew reviewed what he had learned. "Is it possible, Bianchi was at the party because Grayden danced?" He browsed the observation reports again. Grayden was said to be renting a part of the house where Bianchi lived. "A dancer and a bruiser? How does that fit?" Further reading revealed that Grayden, too, had recently moved from a small apartment in Miami to the north. "I'll be jiggered. Are they doing more than sharing the house?"

"Anything you would like to tell me about the ongoing investigation?" Senior Agent Sullivan asked, standing beside Matthew's desk.

"Yes ... yes, I think so." Matthew's heart caught in his throat. He hadn't expected his boss to show up on a holiday. He collected his wits and summed up what he had found out.

Sullivan huffed. "It's a start. Arrange a meeting with Grayden. Make it very clear that he's living with a criminal and might get accused of complicity should he not cooperate with us."

"Yes, sir."

"Very well. A happy Fourth of July." Sullivan left for the next desk where Agent Spring was chatting on the phone. His conversation stopped abruptly, and he stuttered an apology when Sullivan asked about his case.

Matthew sighed and started typing the summary for Nicolas to read the next day. He had as yet no idea of how to question Grayden without being blunt.

CHAPTER FIVE

Matthew gazed through the window to relax his eyes.
According to Vianone's company lawyer, a bald-headed man named Waldo Kurtz, Umberto Bianchi had been Eduardo Vianone's secretary. The FBI agents in Miami had no tangible clues that Umberto worked as a killer. A bruiser, maybe, but he had never been convicted. Bianchi operated in the shadow behind the old Vianone. There were rumors Bianchi had been treated like a son, a man prepared to do more than cow competitors or show up to demolish a store. However, after Eduardo Vianone's death, Bianchi had left Miami within fourteen days and was now associated with the younger brother.

The reports ended, and Matthew added two more headwords to his summary before he left the office.

"Now that we made it through lunch and dessert, you deserve something better," Jacklyn whispered as they left the patio toward the lush garden.

"You aren't saying—"

"Oh, no, I just wanted to show you the beauty of this property."

Nicolas didn't buy Jacklyn's pretended innocence. If he knew one thing about his lover—she was not innocent. "So we are going for a walk?"

"Indeed." More innocence as she blinked rapidly. "You were not suggesting that we—no, we won't do anything indecent on my family's premises. We might get caught — watched, I mean."

Nicolas stopped. "Jacky, where are you taking me?"

"Enjoy the view." She linked arms with him and led him toward the summer cabin close to the waterfront and the landing stage. "We didn't get here the last time because the house was under construction, and mother didn't want anyone here as long as it wasn't presentable." Jacklyn giggled. "Let's get inside. I haven't seen yet what they did with the old dump."

Nicolas stopped short as they crossed the last several yards between lush trees. He was breathless upon the sight. "An oceanfront home fit for royalty."

Jacklyn frowned. "Turning into a poet watching the sea? Oh, come on, not really."

"I'm not the one who lives in the Hamptons, ma Belle. That's your parents' lifestyle, not mine."

Jacklyn shook her head as she gently but firmly pulled him across the wooden path toward the cabin's entrance. "Come on, don't be grouchy because my father made a nice cut back in the day. Yes, the Hamptons haven't been that expensive all of the time."

"It's never been a cheap area to live in."

The inside of the cabin smelled of wood, polish, and the scent of unused fabric. The furniture was modern in a classic way, consisting of two couches and two armchairs, covered with white and blue striped cushions. In the center stood a coffee table, and shelves with books and seaside-themed knickknacks were placed along the walls. The cabin also featured a large bathroom with a shower stall and a bathtub, and a small kitchenette with a coffee maker, a microwave, and a small refrigerator.

"Whatever your parents do, they do it with style," Nicolas muttered. "Did he really make his money by working for the diplomatic service?"

Jacklyn made a face as she evaded his gaze. "Let's say, his family made some . . . decent money three generations ago. My dad is great at his job, but, yes, doesn't make the kind of money needed for this property."

Nicolas sat on the couch. "Now I understand your mom somewhat better. She expects you to increase the wealth you already have." He frowned. "You'll be one of the richest ladies on the east coast." He pulled her close so she sat on his lap. "I won't let you go. You're worth a lot to me." When she made a sound of doubt, he added hastily, "No matter the money, of course."

"Much better."

"And you stated your claim for me impressively, ma Belle."

She kissed his nose. "Ah, it was about time. We've been together for years now, and she's still thinking she could change my mind or push me in the direction she wants me to go." Jacklyn snuggled up to his chest. "I shouldn't have introduced my former lovers to her. She thought that I would end up with an ugly old man with a lot of cash in his pocket and only a year to live."

"Well, depends on the way you treat your lover."

"I know where your thoughts are traveling."

"Your parents won't come down here, will they?"

"And if they do? That's the salt in the soup of any adventure." She caressed the back of his head. "My brave, tough suitor. Is there something on your mind?"

"That's your turf. I'm trailing along."

She slipped off his lap, grinning like only a shark could. "Very well, Beast, you asked for it."

Michael woke at Umberto's side, still naked after the

nocturnal activities that had kept them awake until first light. The memory gave him goose bumps in the most positive way—a surge of lust that lasted longer than the act. Umberto had done him first in the bathroom, then while he was tied to the St. Andrew's cross, and once more on the bed. He was a taciturn lover, a man who acted instead of announcing what he was about to do, and Michael loved to play along, feeling perfectly safe.

This wasn't a small deed. Umberto was strong, could easily hurt him, and yet was circumspect to a degree he found amazing. Like he had done during their first meeting, Umberto was aware of Michael's constitution and didn't go too far. He couldn't say whether Umberto would ever want to add pain to the tethering, for Umberto kept quiet about this, too. However, it was indisputable that Umberto cherished him and loved him dearly.

Michael turned around so he could study Umberto's sleeping face. A smile crept into his features as he studied his lover's slack expression. Gently, without the intention of waking him, Michael finger-combed Umberto's short hair, relishing the feel of it. Right now, he wished nothing more than to stay with his lover until the end of days. He sighed. Nothing was ever easy in life and nothing lasted forever—he had learned that the hard way.

He ran his thumb across Umberto's eyebrow, compelled by affection. When Umberto stirred and his eyes opened to slits, Michael let his hand travel along his torso toward his midsection.

"Insatiable, huh?" Umberto asked, his voice still sleepy.

Michael hesitated. It nagged him that he couldn't instantly decipher Umberto's mood, even after they had been together for four months. Usually, he could judge people faster. "No. Just . . ." He let the sentence trail off, not knowing how to put his feelings into words.

"It's all right." Umberto cupped Michael's head and pulled him close for a kiss. "You were *a-fucking-mazing* last night. And this morning," he added with a wink.

"You, too." Michael's heart beat in his throat, hoping and not yet accepting the truth behind Umberto's words. Could he be so lucky to have found another man like Vincent, who accepted him, cherished him, and took care of him?

Michael slipped into Umberto's embrace, feeling safe. And horny.

"We're gonna play the obedience game," Jacklyn decided. "Undress."

Nicolas's gaze flipped toward the closed door. "Here? But what if—"

"No." She put a finger on his lips. "I play. You obey."

"All right." Grinning lopsidedly, Nicolas took off his polo shirt. He watched Jacklyn pull a soft blindfold out of her handbag. "You came prepared." He dropped his shirt to the side and took off his shoes and socks.

"Always." She blindfolded him. "Pants and underwear."

Nicolas obeyed, bewildered and also amused by her growing eagerness.

"There's a boathouse next to the cabin. We'll go there to play."

"Are you sure—"

"No talking. I didn't bring gags," she said when he smiled, "but believe me, I'll find a replacement."

She led him through the connecting door. The smell of salt-water was strong, and Nicolas heard the lapping of water against wood. He imagined small boats swinging on the water, oars placed within, waiting for their use.

"Wait here."

Nicolas felt the urge to cover himself or at least to glimpse from under the blindfold to be sure they were alone. Though he trusted Jacklyn that she wouldn't embarrass him in front of her parents on purpose, she had a streak of adventure exposing him in a compromising situation.

When he was about to put his worry into words, she was back in front of him. "Hands up front." She wound a rope around his right wrist. "Step on the bench to your right and lift your hands. You'll feel the crosspiece."

He followed her orders. She stood beside him and obviously unfolded a ladder because suddenly she was tall enough to flip the rope across the crosspiece and tie his left wrist. Nicolas exhaled, still uneasy with the prospect of uninvited visitors. He tested the rope, but Jacklyn knew knots he couldn't undo. He was caught.

"You haven't fidgeted this much since our first date," Jacklyn said and kissed his dry lips. "Relax. No one's gonna disturb us."

"And if your parents come looking for us? Say, to tell us about coffee time or whatever they intended to do in the afternoon? After all, you said we'd just go for a walk, not to stay away for an hour."

"You worry too much." She sounded cheerful as she stepped off the ladder and put it aside. "Do you want to know what else I brought?"

"I think—" Nicolas hissed through his teeth when Jacklyn pulled down on his testicles. "I can guess what."

Still in high spirits—Nicolas imagined her rosy cheeks and the sparkle in her eyes vividly—she tied a thin strip of leather around his testes and hung a light weight onto it. He liked the sensation, and yet the voice in the back of his head forbade an immediate reaction. "It's warm on my thigh. Is this thing open toward the water?"

Jacklyn giggled. "Of course, it's a boathouse. How should you get out with a boat without it being open?"

"But—"

"No one will see your gorgeousness but me." Jacklyn knelt in front of him and began kneading his member, careful strokes at first to get him into the mood, then harder when his arousal overrun his skepticism.

Nicolas moved into her warm hands and inhaled sharply when she placed her lips around his rod, taking him in. The change of sensation sent shivers up his spine, knocking out doubt and negative thoughts. The weights swung with every move he made, increasing his susceptibility to her warm lips and tongue. She was the mistress with the all-encompassing knowledge of the male physique. He moaned, louder now while Jacklyn was licking, sucking, and teasing him. He forgot about the rope biting into his wrists. His legs quivered, and he knew he couldn't stand her torment any longer. "Please . . ." It was the softest whisper, borne out of need, even though he knew she didn't tolerate begging.

Instead of granting his wish, Jacklyn raked her fingernails along the inside of his thighs and more gently along his cock and balls.

He lowered his head. "Fuck, fuck, fuck . . ."

"No such language, Beast. I'm not yet done."

Nicolas wanted to reply, but the words got stuck in his throat. After a pause for which he had no other explanation than Jacklyn keeping him on tenterhooks, her tongue made a frenzied dance across his glans, teasing so badly he would've squirmed if he had room. She took him in again, throwing Nicolas into the next onslaught of emotion. Her hands played with his balls and the weights connected to it. Her teeth scraped along the sensitive skin of his shaft, and then, as if the turmoil of arousal wasn't strong enough, Jacklyn put a hand around his pulsing member and stroked up and down hard enough to throw him into orgasm.

Nicolas cried out, for the pleasure bordered fiercely on

pain. He stood on quivering legs, panting. The sound of his frantic heartbeat outmatched that of the slapping of the slow wake against the boat. Gasping and shivering in the aftermath, he lowered his head, coping with the feelings his mistress had so vehemently evoked. He was dizzy as always after such an intense session, and when she stepped on the ladder to undo the rope, he imagined hearing a voice in the distance.

"Oh, for god's sake, this can't be," Jacklyn hissed.

"What?"

"My mom's here."

Somehow, after the fun and teasing had ended, Michael and Umberto made it out of the tangled sheets and into the bathroom, laughing themselves silly when Umberto staggered across the carpet, the end of the sheet wound around his right foot. They showered together, satisfied to be in each other's company.

"I want you to be my pet today," Umberto said when they stepped out of the shower stall. "What do you say?"

"Like we do at the club?"

"Yes. But because we're at home, you'll stay in the buff, and I'll prepare breakfast."

Michael was intrigued. Obediently, he put away the towel and dropped to his knees, looking up to Umberto, blinking rapidly. "Like that?"

"Oh, very much like that."

"And what's in it for me?"

"A day of no decisions."

Jacklyn untied him, and the moment he was free, Nicolas ripped off the blindfold. "Your mom's here?"

Jacklyn shouted, "In a minute! Go back, we are not decent."

"Are you crazy?" Nicolas hissed.

"Oh!" Beatrice exclaimed, and Nicolas imagined her touching her pearl necklace, grimacing with disdain. "Oh, I didn't think . . ."

"My stuff's in the cabin!" Nicolas didn't know whether he should laugh or be angry. "I can't get dressed. She knows!"

"Please, mom, go back," Jacklyn shouted. "We'll get there in a few minutes!"

"I—I just wanted to let you know we're having dinner a little early. It's quite a drive to see the fireworks tonight."

"Yes, all right." They heard her closing the door. Jacklyn turned to Nicolas, trying and failing to look contrite. The sparkle in her eyes remained. He knew she lived for moments of adventure, the thrill of the unexpected, the chance of getting caught while doing something naughty. "Sorry about that."

Nicolas shook his head, then looked to the right and to the open entrance toward the boat house. "This damn thing *is* actually open to the waterside!"

"Well, yes."

Nicolas turned back to her. "Are you out of your freaking mind? Someone could have passed by and seen us."

"So far, you liked it."

Nicolas shook his head, bereft of words. He stepped off the bench and untied the knot with the weights around his testicles. "Sometimes you're stone crazy, ma Belle."

"Yes, and you like me best that way." Jacklyn stroked along his arms and flinched seeing his chafed wrists. "I thought I was careful."

Nicolas handed her the weights, smiling knowingly. "No, you were not." He walked back into the cabin. "It's a beautiful place, by the way."

Jacklyn followed more slowly. "I liked being here when I was a kid. My father taught me how to swim so he didn't have to worry that I would drown if I came here alone."

Nicolas freshened up in the bathroom. "He had time for that?"

"Back in the day, he had more free days, not so many missions, and far less problems to deal with." Jacklyn shrugged. "When the Secretary of State learned of his diplomatic skills, he heaped on more and more tasks. That's why he's constantly traveling. It's astonishing that my dad's here today."

"No holiday around the world, huh?" Nicolas put on his clothes and shoes. "Do you think your mom—"

"I don't give a damn about what she says or thinks." She snuggled up close to him, looking into his eyes. "Anyway, aren't you starving after the exercise?"

He kissed her. "I wonder sometimes who's the beast in this relationship."

"Oh, I've seen you rage and rant." She patted his chest. "There's no doubt about the positions here."

"Very well." He kissed her hairline and linked arms to lead her outside. "Let's go and see whether your mom makes a scene out of what she . . . thinks we were doing."

Umberto's smile was worth the mild pain that resulted from crawling on hands and knees through the house. Michael accompanied his lover on all errands while the forenoon lasted, and he sat behind him on his haunches should Umberto resume working in the kitchen or the living room.

"Tell me," Michael asked after a while, "what shall I do should one of your friends or colleagues show up?"

Umberto's cheerfulness was replaced by guilt, and he stopped stroking Michael's head. "Go to your room and get dressed, please. And hope that no one sees you."

Michael couldn't suppress his disappointment quickly enough, and Umberto sighed as he squatted in front of him. "I'm sorry, Mikey, I know you deserve more, but . . . how can

I provide it? I can't risk ruining my reputation. If anyone learns that I'm gay, I'm ... susceptible to blackmail, you know?"

"In an insurance company? Why should —"

"You knew of the limitations when you moved in with me in the first place. The conditions haven't changed."

Michael hung his head, not only because of Umberto's harsh tone. The night and the last hours had been so fulfilling, he didn't want to hear the conditions of Umberto's business.

"Really, I'm sorry." Umberto continued caressing Michael's face, then lifted his chin. "Someday I won't be working anymore, and then we can do what we want."

"Are you sure this time will come?"

"Not this week, but maybe in a year or so." Umberto got up and put the used plates in the dishwasher, usually Michael's task. "If my plans unfold the way I want them to, I won't have to work for the insurance company anymore. I'll be my own boss."

"Sounds fabulous."

Umberto grinned. "Believe me, I know what I'm doing."

Michael dropped the issue to save the day. "I'll cross my fingers — okay, my paws."

Despite Beatrice's glaring, Jacklyn remained in such a fabulous mood that Nicolas didn't worry about being browbeaten. Quite the opposite. After dinner and while the ladies were changing into their festive dresses, Frederic used the time to approach Nicolas on the large porch. "If my eyes don't play tricks on me, your wrists weren't chafed when you arrived."

"That's right."

Frederic chuckled, stopped, and when Nicolas looked at him uncomprehendingly, his chuckling turned into laughter. "Oh, now I understand the incarnation of Pallas Athena that stormed through the house." He winked at Nicolas. "The Greek goddess of war. Beatrice had an expression . . . no, I don't think that I can come up with a better metaphor." He drew on his pipe. "Ah, how entertaining. So you were engaged in your mutual game during your visit to the summer cabin?"

"Yes." Nicolas stopped rubbing his wrists when he noticed what he was doing.

Frederic's brows twitched. "Was it worth it?"

Nicolas decided against going into detail, and the born diplomat discerned his hesitation in an instant.

"No, I take back the question," Frederick said. "It's impolite. My apologies. Let me rephrase it, though. Since being with my daughter, have you ever missed anything in your sex life? Do you want to go back to where you were before meeting her?"

"No. She has given me much and that isn't restricted to what we do in bed."

"If you do it in bed at all." He pointed with the pipe at Nicolas, frowning. "Don't call me ignorant, but you are a very strong man. Experienced in fights, trained in combat. Why does it appeal to you to give up control to a woman, who would be no match for you in a fight?"

Nicolas took his time to answer. "This isn't about my skills or that she's a woman without martial arts training. We enjoy the power exchange. It's a thrill. A really fantastic thrill for both of us."

Frederic nodded, pursing his lips. "I like men who know what they are worth. And I like that you are able to step down from the ladder of power to meet with my princess on eye level. She's a handful," he said quietly, turning and watching his daughter approaching in a wide-swinging summer dress with a wide-brimmed hat and sunglasses. She had chosen matching sneakers for the outfit and looked ten years younger. "And she's a goddess of her own making."

Nicolas couldn't agree more.

CHAPTER SIX

"Did you survive the day without damage?" Matthew asked Nicolas when they met at the office after the holiday. He scrutinized his partner. "Or do I have to pamper you today and keep you away from bad news?"

"And what would that be?" Nicolas put down his bag and switched on the computer.

"We ran out of coffee."

"Funny."

"Not so much. I'm addicted to the fancy stuff Jason buys." Matthew looked over his shoulder toward Senior Agent Sullivan's office. "The big boss wants us to lean on Michael Grayden so he'll help us with information about Umberto Bianchi's involvement in the *Rattler's* murders." He handed him the file about Sorenson. "Another builder is dead, and Bianchi as well as Luigi Vianone were at the party."

"You looked through the entire video footage?" Nicolas squinted at Matthew. "Didn't your eyes become square when you stared at the monitor for hours? I'm impressed. What's your suggestion?" he asked, putting down the file. He found another package of coffee in his drawer and threw it at Matthew.

"Ah, you came prepared. I appreciate that." Matthew went to brew coffee, content that he didn't have to go without. Until now, he had not known how deep his addiction ran. "I checked out Michael Grayden. There isn't much to know about him. I found out that he was employed at Vincent Decker's investment company for about two years without a clear function. Then Decker died, and Grayden started working at a dancing studio in Miami." He shrugged. "His occupation with Decker's company is unclear, but I didn't find illegal actions, not even tax fraud. Then he moved from Miami, Florida, to Alexandria in Virginia on a whim. But—and here it comes—it's the same address that Umberto Bianchi has. They moved in together."

"Are they more than two men sharing a household?"

"A man from Italy, who might be Vianone's bruiser, and a dancing instructor? I don't know what they might have in common."

"Any idea how we can meet him and not come across as FBI agents?"

Matthew switched on the coffee maker. "According to the surveillance protocols, Michael runs some errands during daytime, but they don't follow him closely. Maybe we can meet him on the way and . . . chat."

"Did the colleagues say anything about his preferences, and also about the possibility that he's gay?"

Matthew pointed a finger at Nicolas. "Ah, right to the point. Yes, they assume he's gay, though not in an obvious way." He put his hand on his hip and raised his voice as high as he could. "He's not swaggering up and down the street, honey-bunny. If you get my meaning."

Nicolas laughed out loud, and other agents turned their heads. "Yeah, right, I get it. How do we approach him?"

Matthew dropped the act. "Do you want to approach him?"

Nicolas shook his head. "I can pretend to be a broken guy without a job, but, for the life of me, I can't pretend I'm gay. So this is up to you."

Michael enjoyed spending time alone. Though he liked

Umberto's company a lot and strove to teach classes in classic dancing, he cherished hours without conversations, without the obligation to sense another man's wishes or needs. The relationship with Umberto worked so seamlessly because both men had time for themselves, either at work or while running errands. He would not have endured a partner who wanted to be around him twenty-four hours a day.

Being alone meant he had time to mull over things and to watch pedestrians, a hobby he had developed while living with Vincent. His old lover had told him it was always good to know who was around you.

As it had been his habit in Miami, Michael took Umberto's and his clothes to the dry cleaner. He was choosey when it came to cleaning and service, and he was disappointed when the shop owner announced he would have to wait twenty minutes for the last jacket to be ironed and ready for delivery.

Grumpy but reining in his temper, Michael took the second seat at the only table the establishment offered, across from a man in his forties with brown hair and a well-trimmed beard with some gray hairs mixing into the brown. He looked up with an inviting smile, and his expression and the quick lifting of his eyebrows signaled Michael that his looks were appreciated.

The stranger cleared his throat. "Do you come here often?"

"Occasionally." Michael returned the smile. "You're waiting, too?"

"Yeah, poured coffee over my jacket . . . and I need it for the next presentation. You know, I don't have extra clothes at the office."

"You should change that." Michael's smile brightened. "If you tend you spill your coffee on a regular basis."

"Thanks for reminding me." The stranger looked contrite. "I'm happy it wasn't my pants." He cleared his throat again when Michael laughed. "And you?"

"I had a gig and always take my stage clothes here."

"A gig? What's your profession?"

"I'm a dancer."

The stranger set up straight, obviously impressed. His brown eyes opened wide. "A dancer, huh? Classic dance or Latin?"

"Both. I'm also a dancing instructor at Myra's Dance Club." Michael liked the stranger's interest and the dialect he placed in the Chicago area.

"Interesting." And after a brief pause of checking Michael up and down, he added quietly, "As are you. You work out a lot, I see."

"Thanks." Michael couldn't help but cast down his gaze. Though admiration didn't come sparsely — from dancing partners and trainees — such a compliment from a total stranger was new to him. If he had been without obligations, the flirt would have been welcome. The stranger was handsome in a rugged way, was the right age, and had good manners. Judging by his clothes, shoes, and the manicured hands, he earned good money without digging in the dirt. Michael glanced over his shoulder to where the shop owner was putting jackets on hangers. "But I . . ." He turned back with a tentative smile. "I'm not interested."

"Darn," the stranger said, then got up trying and failing to hide his disappointment. He wiped his mouth. "Do you smoke? I need a cig. I've been waiting here for twenty minutes already."

Michael had nothing better to do, so he followed him outside and accepted the cigarette the stranger offered. He was intrigued by the older man's approach. There was a kind of restlessness about him Michael instantly liked. He was reminded of Umberto — the underlying urge to move, to do something instead of relaxing was the same.

"You live with someone?"

Michael pondered what to say. "Not really. We share a house." When the stranger didn't comment, Michael drew on his cigarette, the first one in weeks. "It's new. The house, I mean. We just moved in."

"Good for you. Where did you come from?"

"Georgia."

"That's quite a change." He pointed with his cigarette. "But explains the excellent tan you've got."

"Yes. Yes, it does." Michael didn't know where to look. The stranger appeared to devour him with his hungry looks, sighing deeply. He could not have been more blunt if asking him for sex around the corner.

"I moved here four months ago and still don't know a soul. Except for the few guys at the office, but they're . . . you know."

Michael understood the stranger's problems, so he pulled out a matchbook. "Here. Maybe you'll get more luck there. It's a nice place . . . quite exclusive. You should make reservations. Fridays are mostly . . . jam-packed."

"Thank you." The stranger's eyes lit up. "You go there, too?"

Michael flashed his dazzling smile, proud that he triggered another loud intake of breath from the stranger. "Like I said — it's a nice place."

The shop owner opened the door and told Michael that his clothes were ready.

Michael put out the stub and dropped it in an ashtray. "Well, it was nice meeting you." He was about to add a word about the stranger's good looks, but then dismissed the idea and turned away.

However, when he stood at the counter and the shop owner printed the bill, he glanced back at the sidewalk where the stranger was lighting another cigarette. Michael told himself he was in a blossoming relationship, but, hell, the stranger was worth taking the bait.

"What do you make of him?" Nicolas asked after Matthew had recapped his meeting with Michael Grayden.

Matthew replied in a high voice, "You want to know whether he found me attractive?" He pushed back his hair over his head, then blinked rapidly as he lifted his chin. "Yes, my love, yes, he did. If I had insisted a *touch* more, he'd have gone for me and then some." He sat down. His voice returned to normal. "Yeah, laugh it off, fuzzball." He drank the rest of his cold coffee and sat the cup down. "I'd say he's a nice and friendly gay man, soft-spoken, flattered by praise. He does look good, right?"

"You don't think he's in league with Bianchi?"

"If anything, Grayden is his toy. Look, he fetched Bianchi's clothes, obviously. The wardrobe wasn't his. Maybe they have a thing going, but clearly Bianchi will be the leading part."

Nicolas sat on the edge of the desk. "On the way back, I stopped at the dance school he works for and had a chat with the owner. She told me that Grayden is a good, a dedicated teacher. He doesn't meet with strange people, doesn't do anything out of the ordinary. He works odd hours sometimes, but she thinks that's perfectly normal because customers come in late after work, and the dancing instructors have to work overtime, too." He shrugged, found his coffee cup empty, and got up again to brew another pot. "The way she described him, he's the nicest employee she's ever had."

"And he probably doesn't know what Bianchi does for a living." Matthew snorted. "It'll be a hard wake-up when we arrest Bianchi."

"Then we'd better find some evidence."

Nicolas unlocked the door, and the conversation between Jacklyn and her girlfriend Lesley stopped abruptly. He swore he heard a notebook being shut, but when he entered the living room, both women were sitting on couches, drinking red wine, and smiling at him like goddesses who would never in the world — even if there was a reason — keep something from him. The notebook was on the small table. Nicolas resisted the urge to touch it to see whether it was warm from recent use.

He frowned. "Hello ladies. Everything fine here? Or do you need help to unlock your tongues?"

"The wine's doing the business already," Lesley replied, lifting her glass. Nicolas swore she sounded breathless. "And how are you tonight?"

She looked fabulous in a dark red leather outfit that stressed her feminine physique. She was thirty-eight, looked ten years younger, and behaved as if getting older was never happening to her. She operated two erotic stores and an exclusive bondage club in Washington, DC, and was the most severe mistress Nicolas knew. He suspected that the long-lasting friendship between Jacklyn and Lesley influenced his lover's behavior, but so far, to his advantage. The ladies met once a month at least, and tonight he was fortunate to come home while they were both still sober.

Nicolas took off his jacket and sat down on the remaining armchair. "I have a request."

Lesley lifted her perfectly plucked eyebrows. "Oh, and what would that be?"

He handed Lesley the matchbook. "We need to pay a visit to this establishment and find out what a man named Michael Grayden is doing there."

"The *Freaky Like Me Club*?" She made a sound of interest. "It's a new hotspot. Cosplayers, puppy handlers, hard bondage men. The entire menagerie." She looked up. "I've heard of it. Good place. Expensive, but the management is great.

They provide whatever the guests want without doing anything illegal. What's the occasion?"

"Find out more about a suspect. His background and whatever we can learn about him. I don't know what he'll be doing there, but I would like to know. In disguise."

Jacklyn's eyes widened with sudden interest. She set down her wine glass. "You are saying we should dress up and blend in? A night at the club?"

"I'm game," Lesley said, lifting a hand. "When?"

Nicolas grinned. He had known in advance he wouldn't have to beg for support. "This Friday. According to recent reports, he might be there."

"With company?"

"I don't know. Would you bring Raiden?"

"You want my beast at your side?" Lesley laughed, showing little white teeth. "Oh, yes, I'll bring my beast, all dressed up like a naughty puppy. What about you? Ready for a new experience?" She turned her attention to Jacklyn. "Did you ever dress him up like a puppy? With a muzzle and a tight collar?"

Jacklyn locked gazes with Nicolas. "We have to talk about the details, as I see it, but to answer your question—no, no puppy play so far." She winked at him. "This will be an interesting night."

Nicolas felt the items already lock around his face and neck. The idea came to him that his proposal might turn out differently than he expected. He inhaled and didn't know what to say. When both women stared at him inquisitively, he batted his eyelashes.

It was Lesley's term to laugh out loud. "Hey, suddenly squeamish? Don't say. It was your idea."

Jacklyn's voice was down to business. "What do you want to gain from that night? Is this man dangerous?"

"I don't think so. He might be accompanied by a criminal

or meet people of dubious backgrounds. We don't know that yet. So we have to get as close as possible without being obtrusive."

"Because you wouldn't learn anything coming as agents," Lesley concluded. "Good for you that you know two mistresses and another beast." She beamed at him. "Oh, I wouldn't have bet on the day that you'd need our professional help to nail a criminal. It'll be fun."

"Do you think Raiden would agree?" Nicolas stood to take off his tie. "He hasn't been so fond of the games after his kidnapping."

"Yes and no." Lesley emptied her glass. "He hasn't entered my dungeon anymore, but after months of, let's call it *celibacy*, he told me he misses the thrill. That's when we started playing at home." She turned the glass in her hands, then set it on the table. "We are not back to all the varieties of bondage he used to love, but getting there. He couldn't stay away from this forever. I was sure of that from the beginning."

"So he will be okay with a night of fun? If he considers it fun."

"I'll tell him you need his support. He won't let you down." Lesley looked at Nicolas with a sparkle in her eyes. She lowered her voice to give her words the power of a promise. "And we won't let you down. You won't forget that night."

Nicolas was convinced that the mistresses would keep this promise.

Umberto braced himself for yet another hour of both self-adulation and relentless bashing of competitors in the various enterprises Luigi Vianone presided over. Dressed in a dark blue three-piece suit with slim silver stripes, Luigi swaggered through his large office, setting his eyes on his secretary — a not-so-secret smacking of lips in appreciation of her short skirt — and his men — glare and distrust to keep them in line.

Umberto's family roots reached deep into Sicily, but he was estranged enough from the Italian mentality to speak louder the longer the monologue lasted. For the life of him, he didn't need to shout to be heard. Luigi appeared to fear his listeners would only believe his words if he spoke loud enough to wake the neighbors half a mile away. Umberto mused that this might be the case. He didn't believe the new boss's entitlement, anyway.

"It's fortunate this Sorenson-bastard is dead," Luigi concluded after a long rant. "He died like he deserved — like a rat on the street." He set his gaze on Umberto. "Almost too late, but, hey, we can't have everything, can we?"

Umberto didn't flinch and didn't reply, while his companions nodded and smiled in appreciation. He considered them idiots who would jump out of the window of the tenth floor if Luigi ordered them to, but of course he wouldn't say that out loud.

"I'm glad he didn't die quickly," Luigi went on, waving the hand with the cigar. "He got what he deserved. Anything about his partner, this . . . what was his name?" He swiveled to his secretary, snapping his fingers. "Now? Name?"

The secretary, a fake blonde by the name of Rosy, hastened to find the name in a file on her tablet. "Gilmore. Walter Gilmore."

"Yes. What about him? Is he trying to get public contracts in Maryland?"

She cleared her throat, but still her voice was high with nervousness. "News reports say he's still mourning the loss of his major partner. No word about his current plans."

"Ah, damn it." Luigi whiffed his cigar, contaminating the air with thick smoke. "I need to know if he's out to cause trouble." He turned to the man standing next to Umberto. "Guido, pay the man a visit. Be . . . subtle, okay? Let him know that Sorenson was only the first one to leave Mother Earth, okay? Make it clear, though, that he can join him underground, if he wants to. Six feet under, if you get my meaning." Luigi patted Guido's shoulder, grinning. "You'll find the right words. Go."

Umberto kept an unreadable face. Guido was a bruiser, an old-school basher with brass knuckles and a short club beneath his long leather jacket. He was as qualified to negotiate with a possible competitor as was Wile E. Coyote to finally kill the roadrunner. He imagined the two-hundred-pound goon entering Mr. Gilmore's house and stuttering about Mother Earth and how Sorenson fed the worms. It was such a hilarious idea, Umberto had trouble keeping the mirth out of his eyes.

"And you," Luigi said sharply, turning to Umberto, "take your fists to — ah, fuck! Rosy! What's the sucker's name?"

Umberto admired quiet efficiency under pressure. Rosy appeared to be smarter than her powdered cheeks, deep décolleté, and the checkered mini skirt suggested. She consulted the notebook again and looked up with an amicable smile. "Benjamin Cooper, owner of Cooper Industries. He builds concrete pumps, specialized in — "

"Yeah, yadda-yadda," Luigi interrupted her, impatiently waving a hand. He poked his feisty finger at Umberto's chest, getting closer with the next sentence. "You pay that man a visit and break a few bones. You know how it works. I wanted his year's production of pumps, and he dared to tell my proxy that they are already contracted." For the last time, he drew on his cigar and put it in the ashtray on his desk, thus granting Umberto room to breathe again. "Make it clear that I need the pumps, okay? My men tell me five of the old pumps are broken and can't be repaired. Without them, no concrete, and without concrete the building can't be built. Right? And Cooper has a patent on exactly the pumps I need. You get it?

I think you do. Take Drago with you. In case the fool has some bodyguards with him."

"All right." Umberto turned away, determined to leave the job to Drago, anyway. He signaled to him across the room.

"No comment, Bert? No *I can do this alone* shit? What's wrong with you?"

"I'll go and do my work." Umberto almost kept the annoyance out of his words, but Luigi was a better listener than a trained musician when it came to nuances.

"Yes, you'll do your work, but usually, you comment on my decisions, make proposals, try to . . . well, add your personal note to the job."

"Not today." Umberto didn't try to smooth his reply with a smile. It would've been false, anyway. "If you don't mind . . ." He pointed toward the door.

"Yeah, yeah, go. Report to Rosy later. I'll be off to Miami tonight."

Umberto saved that information for later use, nodded, and left the room with Drago in tow.

"You're in luck, the club owners know Lesley Gilbert," Jacklyn said as she chose her outfit for the night. She turned around, fumbling with the laces of the tight corset. "It was no lie that the *Freaky Like Me Club* is trending these weeks. Without her connections, we would have to wait until August." She looked up. "Stop staring at me and lose your clothes. This will be a major change, my Beast."

Nicolas rolled his eyes. "It would be much easier to walk in and show my badge."

She pulled his lapels, smiling. "But this wouldn't be fun, right?" She let go so he could take off his jacket and dress shirt. "Besides, you would get zip information out of anyone." As on many previous occasions, Jacklyn loved watching

Nicolas undress and revealing his muscular body. There wasn't an inch she didn't like, and nature had created him perfectly proportionate. Every hour of workout seemed to go directly to his arms, abs, and legs. She let out her breath. "Moving on. I've got some items that you need to wear tonight."

"All of them?" he asked as he stared at the display on the bed.

She chuckled at his worried tone. "If you can't stand a collar, all right, don't wear it. But the other devices are imperative to pass for the role you want to play."

"I feel like I'm being thrown into another fantasy world — right after mastering the Fourth of July in the realm of the Phenomenal Goddess of Cold Riches."

"You're exaggerating."

"No can do. Not concerning the unrivaled display of . . . qualities — what are you doing?"

Jacklyn knelt in front of him and pulled down his pants and boxer shorts. "Putting little Nick in a chastity device. Like I said before, there are some items you can't go without tonight."

"Ouch! I'm sure it's a size too small."

"Believe me, it fits. I've seen more penises in my life than you in yours." She went on trying until he stepped back.

"That's disturbing news."

"Nevertheless true. If you stopped fidgeting, this would be much easier."

He answered in his deepest voice. "I didn't want to wear this thing in the first place."

"If you want to go under cover, you'd better choose your costumes wisely."

"Stop chuckling, that's not fair. Ouch! It's not *your* junk that's pressed into a vice."

"Crybaby." She managed to adjust the device. "That looks

nice."

"A lock? Seriously? What if —"

"It's always locked." Jacklyn cocked her head, examining her work. The small golden lock was a stylish accessory, but so was her boyfriend. "Don't forget to use a stall in the restroom. It's impossible to use a urinal. You'd soil yourself."

"Fantastic! I'm womanized!"

Jacklyn kissed the skin above the device. "You're the manliest man I know. You really sex me up. I'm wet beyond decency, and if you don't lay me tonight, I'll force you to do so." As expected, her confession rendered him speechless. When she looked up, she knew he was torn between scolding her and fantasizing about how the night would evolve once the stakeout was done. "Collar?"

Nicolas heaved a heavy sigh and nodded.

Not for the first time, Michael was disappointed that Umberto insisted on driving to the club with two cars, claiming he had something to do before they would meet at the parking lot one block away from the establishment. Umberto argued it was better this way and that they didn't want anyone to know about their relationship, but Michael read anxiety behind his decisions. Vincent had been proud of Michael and had taken him everywhere. He had introduced him as his partner and that customers could trust him as they trusted Vincent. Back in the day, Michael had been proud how he was cherished for his character and appearance. On the way to the club, he mused whether Umberto was afraid of anyone at his company unveiling his secret and if it could be used against him in any way. Would Umberto be fired? Would the company owners give him an ultimatum to lose either his lover or his job?

The thoughts disturbed Michael's pleasant anticipation.

He had been to the club with Umberto once and was instantly thrilled by the interior, the music, the variety of guests, and the guests' easy-going attitude. You could be what you wanted to be, and no one looked at you condescendingly. The guests dressed up, played their games, and some had sex in various corners, in spite of the audience. The owner advertised on his website that anything was permissible as long as the participants agreed on the terms and no laws were violated. Never before had Michael enjoyed a night so much. Once surrounded by the semi-darkness of the club's enchanting main room, Umberto had relaxed and started playing with Michael. That night, Michael had learned much about his lover's preferences and a tad more about his character.

He parked the car and closed the collar around his neck. The leash dangled across his chest. His heart beat faster when he watched Umberto strut across the parking lot, dressed in black leather from top to toe. His hair—styled with gel—reflected the light of the parking lot's large street lamps. He looked like the villain of an old superhero comic book story sans cloak. The stern expression didn't change when he ordered Michael to get out of the car. It was time to slip into a role and play it until dawn.

Michael lifted his head to look into Umberto's eyes. His voice was quiet and obedient. "I will do your bidding, master."

"I bet you will," Umberto snarled and tugged the leash so hard Michael made a stumbling step forward. He slammed the car door and locked it. "You're mine. I'll do with you what I want. And you will follow every order given."

Shivers ran down Michael's spine. The night was looking up. "Yes, master."

Nicolas flinched when he got out of the car. The chastity

device pinched his sensitive flesh and pressed against the scrotum in the most unwelcome way. The tight leather pants added to the discomfort, as did the harness under the leather jacket. Despite Jacklyn's adoration and compliments — though welcome — he was uneasy.

"Don't fidget with the collar," Jacklyn warned. "You should look as if you do this frequently. Newbies stand out, and that's — "

"That's not what you want. I get it." Nicolas made a face as he watched his reflection in the car window. "My hair looks like I have spikes. What did you do?"

Jacklyn came around the hood and ran a hand over his head and along his clean-shaven cheek. "You look splendid. You'll be the night's greatest attraction. I'll probably chase a long row of envious guests out of the room. If anyone tries touching you, point him out to me. I'll do the rest."

"You? I think I should — "

"You're my pet. I protect you. No one gets close to you." She kissed him on the lips. "Believe me, it's better this way."

"There you are," Lesley said from behind. "I thought you wouldn't show up." She smiled at Nicolas, making big eyes. "Wow. That's what I call an outfit. You fill that piece of leather quite nicely. If I had no beast to show, I'd steal you right away."

"This is the oddest compliment ever." Nicolas straightened, flinching once again. He refrained from adjusting his junk. It didn't help.

"Tight? The chastity, I mean."

"You bet."

Lesley winked at Jacklyn. "First time, huh? How was it?"

"Don't ask." Jacklyn hooked the leash into Nicolas's collar. "And you?"

Lesley turned to where Raiden was patiently waiting for his introduction. He wore dark brown leather clothes but no shoes. Beneath the jacket, a thick studded harness showed on his olive skin. Despite the cuffs around his wrists and the collar complete with muzzle, Raiden looked perfectly at ease. Nicolas envied the younger man's equanimity.

"Are you going to keep him like this?" he asked, referring to Raiden's inability to speak.

"I can talk," Raiden replied faster than Lesley. "It's just a trick that makes it look tight."

Nicolas refused to ponder the unknown number of possibilities for restraining a submissive. He was happy Jacklyn hadn't insisted on him wearing a head harness or a muzzle shaped like a dog snout. He was overwhelmed already.

"What's the plan?" Lesley strutted toward the club entrance, Raiden trailing at her side like a tame lion.

"We choose a table and have a look around to see whether the suspect shows up and with whom." Nicolas turned to Raiden. "He doesn't know our faces, so we'll have a fair chance to watch him unobtrusively. We won't do anything else unless he's up to a criminal act. In that case, I'll step in."

Lesley purred loud enough for them to hear. "Oh, it'll be a show."

CHAPTER SEVEN

Thick gloves and kneepads allowed several pets in the room to walk on their hands and knees without hurting themselves. They looked up to Michael, telling him without words that they had handlers who knew about the real world of pet play and challenging him to copy their behavior. Michael would've loved to show such devotion, but Umberto had chosen not to dress him up in that fashion. When they reached their table, Umberto made Michael kneel beside the bench, which was at least a chance to demonstrate the handler's sway over his pet. Obediently, Michael lowered himself on his haunches and looked up, begging for Umberto's affection with wide eyes and his tongue between his lips. He was rewarded with a quick pat on the head.

"Don't you dare push me, Mikey," Umberto warned, squeezing Michael's chin between finger and thumb. "You get what I want you to get."

Michael lifted his chin. His voice was breathless. "I can't wait for that."

Despite his effort to remain a stern handler, Umberto was bound to smile. "You're doing it again. Now, shut up." He ordered drinks from the scantily dressed waitress. When she walked away, he put his thumb into Michael's mouth and his fingers under his chin. "Suck on it. Show me you what you'd do with my dick."

Michael let his tongue fool around Umberto's thick thumb, wondering why the man's skin was calloused. He hadn't seen Umberto work as a handyman, and as an insurance salesman, he held a pen or hit the keyboard of his computer but wouldn't move furniture. Michael was astonished he hadn't noticed the oddity before.

Umberto closed his eyes and squeezed his junk with his left hand.

Michael watched him, still sucking on the man's thumb. His penis was trapped in a chastity device of the latest fashion and left him with mixed feelings. He wouldn't participate in the sex game without his handler's permission, and yet he didn't want to, even if he could open the device. The thrill was one of a kind.

"Enough!" Umberto pulled back, leaving Michael confused whether he had done something wrong. He checked his watch. "Later."

The drinks were served, and Umberto held Michael's glass with a straw for him to drink. For a while, Michael was content with being patted and caressed and sipping his drink. He sensed Umberto's growing restlessness and was about to ask if he could do something when Umberto leaned forward.

"I need you to roam the club for, say, half an hour."

"You're sending me away?" Michael thought he had misheard. "We just arrived. What you're gonna do?"

"Stop whining, okay? I'm asking you to get lost for a while. There's nothing to it. Don't come back too soon."

Michael was about to object, to tell Umberto he hadn't imagined the night would take such an ugly turn, but the older man's eyes were hard as nails, urging him without another word to clear out. Michael got up, biting his lips and clenching his fists, and decided to take a stroll to the bar.

Nicolas pointed with this chin toward Bianchi and Grayden in the booth one table away from them across the aisle. He was still digesting the shock that both inhabitants of the house visited the club as a handler and his pet. Bianchi looked the part of the rough dominant partner in all details, while Grayden portrayed the shy and obedient pet hesitantly. He appeared insecure about whether his devotion was appreciated.

"It's not their first night at the club, but also not the fiftieth," Lesley stated after a few minutes of observation. "They're familiar with each other, but not here, not like this. The older man has this aura of constant alertness. He looks like you when you're on patrol, I guess." She flashed her white teeth at Nicolas. "I bet you're a wolf when it comes to hunting down goons."

"Anything . . . wait, what's happening?" From his position on the floor beside his mistress, Nicolas saw Grayden get up from his position and walk away with clenched fists. Bianchi ran a hand through his hair, looking contrite, but then hardened his gaze. When the next round of drinks was served, he emptied half his glass and ordered another one with a snap of his fingers. The waitress understood and returned to the bar.

"Not what I expected," Raiden mumbled behind his muzzle.

It was still strange to see this lion of a man tied up and collared. The handcuffs with the chain between them gave him the creeps, and yet Raiden assured him that he felt perfectly fine. Nicolas rubbed his chin along Jacklyn's knee and calf to stick with the image they maintained. "He's up to something." He turned his head to where the crowd of arriving guests thickened. It was after ten on a Friday night, and the fans of bondage and role play gathered for hours of entertainment.

"Much better than I thought it would be," Jacklyn said beside Nicolas's ear. "It has class . . . and still you have room to play. Did you see the three women over there making out? They aren't what I'd call subtle."

Nicolas preferred not to watch the couples and their

intimate actions too closely. Instead, he surveyed the badly lit room, taking in the details of the black and red upholstery, the oblong lights along the booths that gave just enough visibility to find the drink in front of you, and the separate corners where sex was not only permitted but encouraged. The room smelled of different fragrances but also the underlying scent of sex and its accompanying odors. Once more, Nicolas made eye contact with Jacklyn, this time to gain her attention. "Let me know if anyone joins Bianchi at his table."

"And you?"

"He's looking in our direction. Let's give him something to look at." He smiled lopsidedly, lifted his head, and fetched a kiss. Jacklyn rose to the occasion, and the kiss went deeper and lasted much longer than he had intended. "You taste like summer . . . strawberries."

"It's the drink."

"I want more."

She took a sip and shared the taste with him. Nicolas had decided to stay sober. When Jacklyn had mused about him lapping water from a bowl on the floor, he had grudgingly declined. The idea of being a pet seemed strange, even unsavory, but then when he thought about the possibility of discarding the daily grind, the suit and tie, the obligations and rules, the picture wasn't abnormal anymore. Jacklyn had taught him there was no sex game between two or more people that should be forbidden as long as all participants agreed and no one was harmed. As a mistress, she had seen the widest spectrum of sexual practices and was far from calling any of the fantasies abhorrent.

"He's getting company," Jacklyn whispered.

Lesley was a step ahead and used her cell phone to take pictures from behind Raiden's broad back. "It's not an ideal angle. Ideas?"

"The old *drink-poured-in-the-lap* trick?" Jacklyn suggested.

"Might get you into trouble," Nicolas warned. "Take Raiden down the aisle and pretend to make pictures of him."

"Here. You do this." Lesley handed Jacklyn her phone and got up. Raiden pretended to disagree with the arrangement, making a growly noise in his throat.

"Oh, come on," Jacklyn said, following the couple into the aisle. "Show a little backbone, pretty one." She moved graciously on her high heels, took some pictures from the left, then circled the couple to have one of the corners in the background and took some more.

Nicolas watched the new arrival. He was in his early fifties, gray-haired and slightly overweight. Though he wore a black leather cap and matching jacket with silver chains dangling on one side of his chest, he lacked the aura of a man accustomed to entering such clubs. He looked left and right when he settled in the booth, and stared at the lip-pierced waitress as if she had sprouted a second head. Umberto ordered the drinks, and the waitress left. The man squinted at Bianchi, then at the ceiling with the large loudspeakers. He appeared offended by the harsh beats of techno music.

Raiden pretended he didn't want the photos and moved left and right of the aisle, dodging Jacklyn's attempts to get a good shot of him.

"Man, you're a pain in the neck!" Jacklyn scolded. "Hey, do you want Jessie to tie you on the floor so that you can't move anymore? She can do that, believe me! Or you hold still beside her, I'll take a picture, and everything's peachy."

Raiden shook his mane, but after another harsh reprimand, sat on his heels close to Umberto's booth and the stranger until the photos were taken. Then, as if having enough of the scheme, he got up, pulled the leash out of Lesley's hand, and strutted toward the bar.

"Well, I was about to say you're a good pet, but now . . ." Smiling prettily while watching Raiden disappear, Jacklyn handed Lesley the cell phone. "May I return to my drink now?" She sat down and patted Nicolas's head. "You got what you wanted," she whispered. "And now?"

Nicolas grinned at her. "Now, I get more of what I want."

Umberto looked around, pondering whether he should have allowed Michael to stay. But when Ennio Marchesi entered the club, walking like a man pressed into a pipe and trying to wriggle free, he knew his decision was right. Eduardo's book keeper and long-time confidant looked ready to escape, more so when he encountered two women in the scantiest clothes imaginable making out in a booth, sucking and kissing noisily. Ennio would have no tolerance for a pet at Umberto's heel.

"Welcome, my friend," Umberto greeted him when Ennio settled across the table from him.

Ennio wiped sweat off his forehead, then adjusted his cap, only to put it down on the table a moment later. "No other place to meet? By god, this club is . . ." He shrugged, but his expression said *awful*.

"A perfect place to meet without being watched or overheard," Umberto finished the sentence. He signaled the waitress, ordered drinks for both, and when she left, bent so he could look Ennio in the eyes. "What's happening in Miami?"

Ennio stared at the drink already on the table, and when Umberto pushed the glass in his direction, emptied it in one long swallow. "Too much and nothing good," Ennio said, setting down the glass. "You know, when a builder was in financial trouble, Eduardo made arrangements, paid what was owed to the creditors with a threat in an envelope. The builder was out of the race, Eduardo had the building finished and sold it for a good price. Not always fair, but manageable."

The drinks were served, and Ennio waited until they were alone again.

"Luigi sends down his henchmen. They come, smash half a floor, topple over ladders and concrete mixers, and scream at the builder to either sell or lose everything." Ennio shook his head, took another swallow of his drink, and looked at Umberto for understanding. "This isn't business, Bert, this is warfare with lots of losses."

"Did you tell him there are other ways?"

"Mentioning Eduardo's name and way of doing business gets everyone into trouble. Luigi dispatched two of his proxies to run the business, and the boss has shown up from time to time, spouting off like one of the mob bosses back in the thirties. He's exchanging more and more of Eduardo's trusted men with stupid bootlickers." Ennio shook his head again. "I bet dollars to doughnuts, Luigi will ruin the business until the end of the year and find someone to blame."

Umberto wasn't shocked by the news, only by what a short time it took for Luigi to run Eduardo's lifetime achievement into the ground. "What about Arcuri and Farrini? Are they still in the loop?"

"They're still holding up, but for how long? No one can tell. Luigi is determined to get rid of the old guard. Not right away, but with excuses and explanations. He sent Opizzi to New York for a dubious deal and told him to stay there until another competitor is out of the race. That might never happen, but Opizzi's trapped and can't return if he doesn't want to anger the boss." Ennio emptied his glass and looked around. "People are having sex in public. That's so strange, I don't have words for it. We used to close the doors and the drapes when we wanted intimacy."

"Times are changing," Umberto said commiseratively. "I need to meet with Arcuri. How can I do that? He doesn't answer my calls."

"He doesn't dare." Ennio smacked his lips, then frowned as he watched a man that looked like a lion with a long brown mane get up from the floor and walk briskly toward the bar. "I'll let him know to contact you on a secure line. Give me your phone number." Ennio sighed when Umberto scribbled the number on a small piece of paper he carried in his jacket. "What do you want, Bert? I know you were one of Eduardo's favorites, but the old man is dead, and you can't just come along and claim your share. Luigi might tell you that you have guts, but he'll have you gutted the next day."

Umberto liked the play with words. "So far, Luigi thinks I'm doing his bidding. He sends me on errands, has me bash a builder here and a company owner there. I do what he tells me to lull him into safety, but that's not what I wanna do the rest of my life. Eduardo knew I had potential. He told me he wanted to hand a part of the company to me. Now look at me! I'm thirty years old, still running around with brass knuckles, a club, and a nine-millimeter to threaten business executives with my appearance."

Ennio frowned. "I'll tell you as a friend, you're playing with fire. Luigi is a killer, but a clever one. He doesn't shoot at first sight. He explores what you know and whether you're useful. If you are not—he'll have you killed and maybe create a cover story of a mugger in your street. You can't oust him easily. And think about everything you do,"—Ennio cut Umberto's attempted reply short—"because you're not only up against Luigi but his fellow goons. If Luigi smells so much as opposition, he'll come after you and probably after all of your friends. That would include me." Ennio played with his cap on the table. "And I'm not ready to die for your ambition." He put the cap back on. "Thanks for the drink, Bert. Be careful." He stood and left for the exit, casting his eyes down.

Umberto pursed his lips as he turned his glass between his big hands, digesting his friend's revelations and the conclusions he must draw.

Nicolas's heart pounded. The excitement of being trapped, dominated, forced to do Jacky's bidding if he wanted to lose the chastity device, turned him into the horniest man in the room. He couldn't wait for the device to come off and at the same time relished being his lover's prisoner. The clash of two equal desires left him breathless, sweaty, his mouth dry. He wanted to screw his beautiful mistress but also surrender his body to her to tie him up so that he couldn't wriggle anymore. The image got stronger with each passing minute, especially with Jacklyn sitting next to him in tight leather shorts and that wonderful corselet displaying a most inviting décolleté.

"You have that expression on your face," Raiden said quietly.

"What expression?"

"You want sex so badly I can smell it."

"No, you can't." Nick looked back toward Bianchi's booth to find him nursing his drink, starting at the empty bench across the table. The stranger had left without as much of a greeting and a smile. The conversation had been intense and important, and Nick wished he had been given a chance to eavesdrop.

Grayden returned to the table, sullen as a spoiled child. Bianchi pulled him down for a kiss and made him kneel in front of him. In a minute, Grayden had his head between Bianchi's legs. Nick didn't want to watch the men make out in public and turned away. Observing the men getting into the mood increased his desire. "I want to leave," he said urgently, only for Jacklyn to hear.

"Shouldn't we wait to see what happens next?"

Nicolas knew she was teasing him, yet he insisted. "Aside from them tearing off their clothes? No. If I stay another hour, I'll kiss your feet and beg you to make me come. Right here."

Jacklyn chuckled.

"No shit, ma Belle. This isn't what I expected. I don't know for how long I can stand this tension."

She frowned. "Your self-control is reeling."

"My self-control depends on the job I came to do. Now it's over, and if I stay I feel like I'll break down." He swallowed hard. "All of this is getting to me. I'm . . . I can't deal with it."

Jacklyn signaled Lesley that they would leave.

Lesley lifted her right eyebrow, a mocking smile playing around her lips. "Oh, hell, all sexed up." She kissed Raiden's brow. "Are you close to jumping your skin, too?"

Raiden winked at Nicolas, then grinned at Lesley. "I will jump on you anytime you want me to."

Lesley grinned. "We'll stay and watch what the men do. I'll report to you later tonight."

Jacklyn smiled and patted Nicolas's head. "We'll leave before he hyperventilates."

In the car, Nicolas slumped on the passenger seat, leaned back, and ran both hands through his spiky hair. The chastity device seemed to tighten by the minute, a painful threat and a welcome addition to his growing arousal. He was at odds with his emotions.

"It's the atmosphere," Jacklyn explained while she started the engine. "You've got a healthy sex drive, and that's why such a club entices you to make out. It's like living in a fantasy world."

"I feel like I'm regressing to an animal."

Jacklyn's frown was back, deeper than before. She steered the car onto the street. "If you mean that, I'll tie you up and let you rage and romp." She glanced at him. "If that's what you want."

Nicolas would have never thought there'd come a time he didn't trust himself to remain rational enough to control himself. He nodded.

Jacklyn floored the gas pedal and took them home.

Without an announcement or the slightest hint at what would happen, Nicolas had given Jacklyn more power than had ever been exercised in the years they had been together. She watched him carefully and yet unobtrusively. She didn't want him to think she was afraid or would dodge the game that was ahead of them. They had enjoyed different role plays during exciting weekends, sometimes spontaneously, sometimes planned ahead. Jacklyn had never before seen her lover hyped up like this.

"It itches, and it's damn tight," Nicolas complained as they entered their home. "I need to get this off." He took off his shoes and turned around. "And at the same time, I don't want you to free me."

Jacklyn knew she had to assess him instantly to steer his turmoil of feelings into the right direction. "I will play with you until you use the safe word. Do you hear me?" she insisted when he shook his head. "I want you as much as you want me, but I won't risk you getting hurt or feeling uneasy. No matter what happens, use the safe word. Is that understood?"

"Yes."

"Fine." Her eyes narrowed as she lowered her voice to order, "Drop your clothes, now."

Nicolas hurried to shed it all. The body harness and collar remained.

"On all fours." She saw the flicker of resistance. He wanted satisfaction, not prolonged torment that kept him from what he desired. "I said—"

Nicolas lowered himself onto hands and knees, never breaking eye contact.

She could see his puzzlement, and the spark of resistance

fired her arousal. She had told the truth that seeing him with a harness and a chastity device got her into the mood for sex before they had left for the club. Watching Nicolas hyperventilate surrounded by men and women eager to make out with each other had surprised her in the most wonderful way. If Nicolas hadn't asked to leave, she would have made the same decision within fifteen minutes. Her body longed for a touch from his big hands, and when shivers ran down her spine, Jacklyn bent to kiss Nicolas, telling him this way that his longing was her own.

"Stay here. Don't move." She left him in the living room to sashay on high heels into the bedroom. While choosing items from her cupboard, she heard him breathing right behind her. "I told you to stay away." They locked gazes. He could not have been clearer had he yelled at her that he couldn't wait to be taken. "Go back. Nothing happens until you do what I tell you."

Nicolas stood belligerently for a long moment, but then he abruptly retreated to the living room.

Jacklyn took her time — on purpose — and followed ten minutes later.

He attempted a growl as she entered.

Excitement ran through her like waves as she reached for a crop. "Oh, yes, my Beast, I will teach you manners."

The flicker in his eyes again — the silent challenge to dominate him. Jacklyn's heart skipped a beat. During the three years they had spent together, she had never before experienced her lover's hunger for sex like this. He wanted to rebel, to fight, to deny her orders and yet had the presence of mind not to hurt her. Once more, the power exchange went to her head. She wanted to subdue him and let him feel her dominance in the most blatant way. "Ass up and your head to the floor. Spread your legs."

Nicolas grunted as he lowered his gaze and then his head.

Jacklyn stepped between his legs to carefully insert a small, vibrating prostate massager. He breathed loudly and clenched his hands to fists so hard the knuckles were white. Jacklyn imagined how hard these fists could hit an enemy's chin. She thought of the fights he had toughed out and how easily he could bruise her. She wouldn't stand a chance. That image, too, aroused her. She shackled his feet and ordered him to kneel in front of her.

"Hands." Jacklyn handcuffed him with heavy irons. His chances for a successful attack diminished. "Open your mouth." She made him bite a small rubber ball. The attached chain ended in clamps she used on his nipples. "If you drop the ball, it'll hurt." Satisfied with her preparations, she used a crop on his butt, longer than usual but with less force. She felt superior, even when she crouched behind him to pull and tickle his balls. Again, his breathing accelerated, and he made sounds of restlessness in his throat. She hit him hard. Once. Nicolas fell silent. "Much better."

She saw his penis strain against the metal rings of the chastity device. The stimulation in his ass added to his discomfort. Once freed, he would try and bed her in two minutes flat. It was an intriguing prospect, so challenging that her resistance was fading. Her voice was breathless. "On the bed. Move!"

Dutifully, almost too eagerly, he crawled on hands and knees into the bedroom and clambered onto the bondage bed.

"On your back." Jacklyn pulled his arms up and tied the chain of the handcuffs to the headboard. The moment she had his feet secured, Nicolas tore at the shackles, startling her. He spat out the ball, obviously ignoring the ensuing pain on his nipples. Or maybe he wanted, needed the pain. He wasted his strength on the iron tethers, displaying his bicep muscles and tensing his abs. His fury had no words, only guttural sounds beyond the English language. Briefly, he stopped to watch her step out of her panties. Panting like a man on the run, Nicolas stared at her and strained at the chains again when she moved close.

"Take off that fucking chastity device! It fucking hurts!"

"Then you're gonna wear it a little longer," she said sweetly and kissed his chest. He hissed when she took off the nipple clamps and discarded the ball and chain. "You're under my heel, Beast, and nothing changes until I want to change it. No," she stopped his comment. "If you shout at me, I'll find another gag to stifle you."

He jerked the shackles again, but this time she had expected the move. Leisurely, she licked his now sensitive nipples and extended her licking toward his abs and his caged flesh.

"Ma Belle, don't prolong it!"

The sentence gave Jacklyn pause to look into her lover's eyes. With a curt nod, he gave her permission to go on. Grinning like a fool, Jacklyn continued licking the cock cage, his scrotum, and his inner thighs. He squirmed most pathetically, cursing and begging her to set him free. She took off her lace corselet and straddled his waist. Slowly, to let him know she wouldn't bow to his wishes, she lowered one of her breasts to his lips. "Lick me. Suck me. Do it right."

"I will bite you if you don't free me on the spot!"

"You will satisfy your mistress." She stared him down. "If you hurt me, I'll hurt you right back."

She read in his eyes that any delay was torment. He sucked her nipples, breathless, restless, but with the expected devotion. His bicep muscles strained over and over again while his lips and tongue satisfied Jacklyn's needs. Graciously, she moved lower so he could kiss her lips, but he was clearly not in the mood.

"You are a demanding bottom, my Beast." Slowly, letting him know she could prolong his ordeal, Jacklyn opened the chastity device. Nicolas pressed his lips tight, enduring the delay until it was off, and then sighed with relief. Jacklyn put the device aside and licked Nicolas's flesh, triggering low groans that resulted from both discomfort and arousal. She removed the prostate massager and bent to kiss Nicolas's rod with utter devotion. He was erect within a minute.

He looked at her, his eyes hazy with lust. "Fuck me, ma Belle, or I'll tear loose and grab you."

"Ow, you don't wanna be a loose cannon, do you?" she cooed, inching upward. She straddled him again, low enough to hover across his member. Nicolas panted loudly when she met with him. She was so wet he could've slipped in and hit her cervix instantly, so caution was the best advice. Nicolas lifted his hips, and she escaped the penetration.

"Fuck! Stop playing with me!"

Jacklyn put her hands on his heaving chest, deaf to his complaints. "You're wonderful to touch." Once more, he tore at the chains with all strength he could muster. She groaned as she made contact again, this time prolonging the penetration and getting into the rhythm. "Don't you dare rush it!"

"I . . . I can't hold this any longer."

She looked him in the eyes and gave permission with a smile, showing her anticipation clearly. The first thrust was the hardest, a force of lust finally set free. He arched his back and rocked up again.

She knew her weight meant nothing to him, did not even slow him while his mind shut off and his emotion ruled. Jacklyn was thrilled by his vigor, swept away by her feelings. This was the wildest ride she'd ever had and totally unexpected. Maybe in her dreams, she had wished for him to let loose all of his strength and not hold back for her sake. With every thrust he let her know that he was not holding back now. She would have to scream at him to make him stop, but she didn't want to. Finally, Nicolas revealed that he kept a beast inside that was only allowed to leave the cage of civilization after a night at a club with more temptation than the conscious mind could handle.

Hissing, then shouting, Nicolas pushed himself to orgasm, hands clenched to fists, and with his eyes closed. His body glistened with sweat—he was more adorable than any man she had ever met. Jacklyn felt his fast-beating heart, over-whelmed by his sheer force. Satisfied, she rested her cheek on his chest, relishing her lover's happiness.

Michael made a vain effort to conceal his disappointment when he returned to Umberto. The stranger had left, a man Michael had not seen before and who didn't appear to be looking for a sex partner. If he had to guess, the stranger had come for a chat, but certainly not about sexual behavior in a club. It nagged him that he had been sent away like a rent boy, a position he would never take up again. He didn't like the resurgence of a feeling of ineptitude, of not being wanted.

"Don't sulk," Umberto warned, then ordered him to kneel in front of him. "Get me in the mood, and I'll tie you up to-night."

Michael locked gazes, trying to judge Umberto's inten-tion—whether he was consoling him, making promises, or trying to distract from his unknown guest. As usual, Um-berto's expression revealed nothing, no hint at his mood or whether he had received bad news. Umberto put a hand on the back of Michael's head and pushed him toward his crotch.

Michael obliged. It was a way to avert his face and to oc-cupy his mouth with Umberto's sex instead of asking ques-tions that would not be answered.

Umberto kept his word. He paid for the drinks and ordered Michael to drive home. When he parked his small car behind Umberto's SUV at their house, Michael pondered whether he could live with a lover who concealed so much. Could he enjoy the partnership without looking into the other man's soul? Could he live side by side and never understand Umberto's deepest wishes because the man never uttered any?

Inside, Umberto told him to lock the door, undress, and follow him into the bedroom.

Michael obeyed when ordered to climb onto the St. Andrew's cross. Umberto closed the cuffs with sweaty hands, breathing heavily. Michael would have loved to know the reason for Umberto's sudden agitation, but didn't ask. His gaze fell on the shaving equipment. He had learned that the simple and yet delicate act of shaving calmed Umberto's mind. That had also occurred after Umberto had accomplished a stressful job. Sometimes, shaving led to sex, and Michael dared to hope that the night would be more entertaining than the hours at the club. He pushed aside the lingering question of why the stranger at the club had upset Umberto in any way.

Umberto looked him in the eyes. "Say the word whenever you want."

"Okay."

Umberto's face lit up to a smile, right before he kissed Michael's lips. "You're gonna love this." He showed him a short whip. "When I hit your body."

Michael swallowed, hyped by anticipation. "Oh, fuck, yes."

Every strike with the whip, every flash of pain was arousing, and Michael wished his penis wasn't trapped. The chastity device was tight—too tight—for this kind of reaction. He groaned, more out of frustration than out of pain.

Umberto noticed it, too, and chuckled about Michael's flesh straining against the cage. "You want to be freed, don't you?" Umberto whispered in his ear.

Michael didn't make the mistake that his opinion had been

requested. He was the submissive in this game, and he took what he was given. If Umberto wanted him freed and played with, he would do so — with or without Michael's comment.

When the chastity device came off, Michael knew that tonight, sex would be involved. Maybe he would be satisfied or would be allowed to masturbate, if his handler was in the right mood. For now, he closed his eyes and enjoyed the freedom he was granted. It was a marvel how deprivation enhanced your experience — the sensation of being touched.

Umberto laughed as Michael twitched in the tethers. "Oh, I love this sight." He ran his hands lovingly from Michael's shoulders to his thighs. "You are great to touch." He slapped Michael's butt. "You need a shave, and that's what I'm gonna do now."

Michael turned his wrists in the leather cuffs. This game wasn't for the squeamish, but his anxiety — that Umberto would be rough or ruthless as a consequence to whatever the stranger had told him at the club — proved groundless. Umberto's domination was subtle and took place outside the bedroom. Right now, Michael mused, Umberto showed his gratitude by shaving Michael's butt and genitals with the dedication of a man striving for perfection. If the look in his master's eyes told him anything, Umberto was absorbed in his task and happy with it. Dry shaving was done, and Umberto returned from the bathroom carrying a bowl with warm water, shaving cream, and a razor. Michael held his breath during the first minute as he always did, but after the initial fear of harm he relaxed. The lathering was pleasant and the moves of the razor arousing. Michael pressed his lips tight to hold back the words of begging that wanted out. He couldn't wait to get satisfaction, no matter how.

Done shaving, Umberto rinsed him with warm water, towel-dried him, and ran his hands across the smooth skin. Michael was close to jumping with desire. He writhed on the chair, whispering sweet nothings, hoping Umberto was doing this as a prelude and that they would have intercourse soon. The straps across his chest prohibited that he lifted his head far enough to check the bulk in Umberto's pants. He heard his labored breathing, though.

Michael wet his lips, kept on tenterhooks like any submissive guy who needed a vent after a long night of chastity. He lifted his head, looking into Umberto's eyes, trying to anticipate what would be happening next. But Umberto smiled that mischievous smile as he always did — unless he was angry — and didn't reveal his intentions.

Only when Umberto dropped his pants and stepped out of them was Michael free to smile. "Gag me. Please."

Umberto made a smacking sound. "Ah, since when does the bottom dictate the game?"

Michael's eyes widened with anxiety. Had he ruined his chances? "I'm sorry."

"Be quiet, not sorry." Umberto started rubbing his penis until he was erect, then lowered the upper part of the cross so that Michael's head was lower than his legs — the ideal position for Umberto to sink his member into Michael's mouth. Aside from the fact that Michael's blood went to his head, he felt great sucking on Umberto's cock. The man wasn't gifted with a remarkable size, but Michael would never let a word slip about it. He was grateful he wouldn't suffocate with that piece in his mouth.

It was a prelude, a delightful introduction, and Michael loved to be a marionette while Umberto was the puppeteer, controlling every move.

Slowly, her eyes still half closed, Jacklyn rose to a kneeling position to open the handcuffs.

"I don't know if I want to be set free," Nicolas said hoarsely as he watched her doings.

"Yes, you do." She kissed his sweaty face.

Nicolas embraced her, held her tight, and prolonged the kiss until they had to stop for lack of air. He laughed. "Tough mistress melts like butter once her lover hugs her." He tousled her hair. "That's a great headline. Looks like you had a lot of fun."

"And you should be exhausted. At least, you smell like a man after very strenuous work."

"If that was work, I'm in for a fifty-hour week." Pushed up on his elbows, he watched her opening the leg irons. "That was one hell of a ride."

"Are you okay?"

"Sore, probably, but . . . yes. Why do you ask?"

Jacklyn didn't put her concern in words, but was determined to take the question to Lesley about how the evening had evolved. "You seemed . . . driven."

"Is that a careful way of saying I was out of control? Raving like a madman?" He got up, groaning. "If so, I admit I haven't felt that way before, ever."

"Me, neither." After relieving him of the collar and the body harness, she ran her hands down his back, along the display of firm muscles rippling under his skin. *So much power, so much strength.* She was still intoxicated by his actions in bed. Once again, she wished he would agree to filming their sessions. So far, her memories were all she had.

Nicolas frowned. "Did I hurt you?"

Her gaze traveled toward the welts around his wrists. They were of a deep red and would stay for days, proof how hard he had fought the restraints. "No, of course not. You bet that I would have stopped you."

He turned around, still skeptical. "I hope you would. I would never —"

She put a finger across his lips. "I'm a grown-up woman,

your mistress. You only go as far as I tell you to go."

He sucked her finger. "Yes, ma Belle, at your service."

Then he devoured her with his kiss.

CHAPTER EIGHT

There had been a time when Benjamin Cooper ran five miles every morning without breaking into a sweat. He claimed that running cleared his mind and let problems look less nasty. Often, he returned to his company in Annandale with new ideas to improve the concrete pumps he was manufacturing.

Those days were over, for he found no solution to his current problem. It felt like arguing with a hungry tiger over which part of the man's meal he was allowed to feed when the tiger wanted to swallow the man as an appetizer. Not to mention that Cooper wouldn't be able to run for at least two weeks after a beating delivered by a henchman his competitor had sent to his home. Looking back, Cooper realized his enemy had been moderate—his wife and young son remained unharmed. However, Cooper wasn't in a grateful mood. While driving to fetch his son for their weekly meal at the diner in Falls Church, he pondered whether his immediate reaction of calling the police would backfire. He wanted, needed help, and yet the goon had told him should he involve the police, he would be dead. He had reported the attack to the sergeant in charge and later to a concerned-looking detective. He had assured Cooper that such information would be handled with utmost discretion. Cooper was guaranteed to receive personal protection, not in uniform but with police officers in plain clothes.

Cooper turned at the corner to the daycare where his son was being treated for autism. He was still reflecting on the threat to either sell the year's production of concrete pumps to an enterprise called Harvest Investment Group or face another unwelcome visit by thugs, maybe to cause more damage than two badly bruised ribs and a lot of superficial injuries. That day, he had defied the criminal's claim and felt bold and strong-willed. Right now, he couldn't stop thinking that the criminal might still resort to completely different measures. "Rely on the police," he said to himself.

Cooper's son Lionel welcomed him with the cool distance others would interpret as rejection, but his father knew better. Lionel was in a good mood, even exuberant, and followed him toward the waiting SUV without hesitation. He clambered up on the seat, used the seatbelt, and waited patiently until the ride began. He didn't answer questions immediately. Cooper had learned to grant him time to find the right answer and not repeat the question, as if Lionel was hearing impaired.

"It was a good day," Lionel said finally and nodded with conviction.

Cooper smiled, asked the next question and got an answer two blocks later. Considering that Lionel had refused to speak for about a year, this was a long conversation, and they arrived at the diner, each happy in their own way. Cooper had placed a reservation to get the same table every week, and the waitress knew their orders by heart. She smiled amicably as father and son sat down at the booth across from each other. Lionel rearranged the salt and pepper shaker and the bottles with ketchup so they were out of the way, for he didn't need them.

Cooper was glad they had established a suitable routine so that Lionel felt looked after and still explored his surroundings. For a time, Cooper remembered vividly, Lionel had not left the house, had even reacted violently when urged to play in the garden. Cooper and his wife had needed time to realize their son was autistic. Therapy and the love only parents could give had slowly but continuously improved their son's condition. There was hope that Lionel would be able to sustain himself when he reached adulthood.

The lanky teenager pushed a strand of his long brown hair out of his face, scrutinizing the diner's interior. Cooper bet he could tell every detail that was different from their last week's visit. When asked, Lionel listed the smallest items and even that the waitress wore a blue ribbon in her hair instead of a pale yellow one.

"You are a great observer," Cooper said, hoping against hope that his son would lift his gaze and look at him. "I didn't notice half of the things you mentioned."

"Capability," Lionel said, pointing a finger to his temple and offering his father a hint of a smile that made Cooper's heart burst with love. "There's room for more."

"Yes, there is." Cooper was flabbergasted at his son's wording. He was aware that Lionel was incapable of such reactions as irony or sarcasm and that his comment was meant exactly the way he had said it. And yet, every tiny action that enlarged his son's horizon was worth remembering.

Cooper thanked the waitress for the meal, said a quick prayer, and ate. His appetite was low, the pain in his torso too intense to enjoy the burger and fries like he was used to. He didn't want to upset his son, though, and told him he had enjoyed a late breakfast so he couldn't eat as heartily as he usually did. The lie went down well, and Lionel slurped his milkshake, munched on fries and two cheeseburgers, and pushed his empty plate to the side.

When the waitress came to ask for their wishes, Lionel said without looking up, "The dessert with cherries, please." The waitress was delighted.

Cooper was already stuffed and wanted to take back the order, but seeing Lionel's expression — the pride of having ordered the dessert by himself—made him close his mouth again and nod. *It is important to keep a routine.* Sighing, he stared at the vanilla pudding with cherries in heavy dressing, thick and sweet, which had been Cooper's favorite for years. He didn't know how the diner's cook made it, but he loved the taste and the texture of the dressing. Despite him being sated, Cooper dug his spoon into the cherries and pudding.

"Do you want some?" he asked Lionel.

"No, that's your dish. I don't eat sweet stuff. It's bad for my teeth."

Sometimes Cooper forgot that Lionel stowed information like a fast-running computer and could recall every conversation precisely. The dentist had shown him how teeth could be damaged by sugar and other sweetened food, and though it was meant to teach him how to brush his teeth effectively, Lionel had concluded that he would not eat sugar. It was wise not to tell him that even a hamburger bun and the meat contained sugar.

"You're right." Cooper took another spoonful of cherries and stopped eating when his stomach told him that it was by far enough. He left some of the pudding and apologized to the waitress.

He paid and added a tip—watched and counted by Lionel—and they left for the car. Cooper felt nauseous and put the blame on the amount of food. He swore he wouldn't eat anything else that day, even skip dinner if he could find a way to explain it to Lionel.

When his son was seated, Cooper rounded the car and slipped behind the wheel. His face was hot, and he felt his pulse racing. He put the key in the ignition, taking deep breaths, wishing he had emptied his coffee cup, for his mouth was dry suddenly. With utmost care, he drove the SUV back onto the street. Though he was wide awake, his reaction was slow, and he avoided colliding with a small transporter only at the last moment. The driver honked, and Lionel commented that the driver had the right of way, coming from the right. Cooper didn't care. Entering the highway four blocks later, his heart still beating frantically, he suffered from visual disturbances. He drove more slowly, tried to stay in the right lane and prayed he wouldn't drive into anyone's way. His heart beat in his throat, and he continued taking deep breaths.

There was a large truck in front of him, getting larger by the minute. Cooper braked to gain a safe distance, but still the truck seemed insanely big, hampering his view on the lane. He shook his head, but the picture remained. There was a large bull painted on the rear end of the truck, and it moved. A moment later, it started talking to Cooper in a most unpleasant way, and Cooper heard himself answer.

"Stop talking!" Lionel shouted from the back seat. "Stop it! This is nonsense!"

"It's not," Cooper replied, convinced of what he saw. "There, don't you see? The bull's talking. It's telling me to swerve to the right and overtake."

"No!" Lionel's scream brought Cooper back to his senses.

He steered the SUV back from the shoulder into the lane, sweating and panting. He couldn't explain his actions. "I'm fine," he assured Lionel.

"The driver has to know how to drive. Otherwise, it's not safe."

"I'll stay in this lane. Okay?"

"The car must change lanes in three miles to exit the highway from the left lane."

Cooper looked into the rear mirror, then into the side mirror. They were traveling in light traffic — it was early afternoon — but still there were other cars, and he had to judge correctly when to change lanes without accident. It was a horrendous undertaking. He managed to cross one lane, but in the next one, seven cars were driving closely behind one another.

He didn't see a gap, only cars and more cars, all of them blurring into schemes of different colors.

"One point five miles," Lionel said impatiently. "To leave the highway, the driver must change lanes."

His heartbeat still increasing, Cooper squinted at the mirrors and saw nothing but gigantic trucks hovering on the highway, closing in, threatening him. He pressed his foot on the gas pedal, and the heavy SUV jumped forward.

"Daddy!"

Cooper heard his son's panic-fueled scream and swung the car round to the right in an attempt to escape the highway's dangers. "I'm handling this, son, don't worry." He saw the garbage truck right behind him, but assumed he could avoid the impact. He accelerated the heavy SUV toward the non-existing exit of the highway, knowing and concentrating on the image that he must either exit the highway right now or be squashed by trucks. "We're doing just fine."

The garbage truck running at sixty miles an hour hit the SUV's right side of the fender and pushed it toward the shoulder and the guardrail. Cooper saw the railing getting closer, wondering where the exit had gone right before the SUV was hit by a second car and, since it was tipping over already, rolled and crashed against another car in front of it and then hit the guardrail.

Cooper's last thought was with Lionel and that he had not saved him from the gigantic trucks.

Nicolas entered the office at seven in the morning, eager to edit the pictures Jacklyn had taken with Lesley's phone. He saved all of them on his computer and started deleting Raiden and enlarging the image of the unknown visitor. Two pictures were of great quality, worth a try with the facial identification program the FBI possessed.

While the images ran through the system, he brewed coffee and checked his emails and snail mail. He couldn't concentrate. In his mind, he was back in the bedroom, back in Jacklyn's thrall.

Being released from the shackles had left Nicolas in a state of confusion, as if he was missing being shackled more than he enjoyed moving around again. He was about to ask Jacklyn to leave the handcuffs in place so that he could connect with the emotion he had enjoyed. He'd glanced at his electronic watch on the nightstand. One hour. He had spent an hour in chains since coming home.

Sixty minutes that felt like ten.

Nicolas had looked into Jacklyn's lovely, flushed face. He couldn't tell whether she knew of his inner turmoil, and he didn't want to ask. Could he get addicted to being tethered? Could he wish for the thrill of metal handcuffs more often and finally be unhappy without them? The idea of any kind of addiction frightened him. He was a rational guy. He was an agent because his mind worked with logic, with facts, and with common sense. He had never used drugs of any kind. He didn't smoke, and his mood wasn't dimmed should he go without coffee for a day. Addiction to being shackled sounded weird, to say the least. He wouldn't surrender to such a need, no matter the attraction.

"You're damn early," Matthew said as he put down his backpack on the second chair. "Everything okay at home? How was your night at the club? Did Grayden show up?"

"I made coffee. Maybe you should take a cup and slow down."

"No. I'm curious like a fox. How did it go? Is he up to something? Is he a crook? Did you talk with him?"

Nicolas pointed at the machine. "Coffee."

"You're no fun." Matthew fetched a mug, sniffed, and sighed with bliss. "Ah, that aroma." He sat down, holding the cup with both hands under his nose. "I have the coffee, you have my attention."

Nicolas summed up the evening's events without going into detail about his company or what they had done after the stakeout.

Matthew cocked his head and pointed. "You paid a heavy price for obtaining those photos."

"What do you mean?"

"The abrasions speak a blatant truth. Honestly, I admire your dedication to this investigation."

Nicolas pulled his sleeves down, knowing it was too late. "We're dealing with a couple, and I doubt that Grayden will testify against Bianchi, even if he knows about his illegal activities."

"Why did Bianchi meet with a stranger at a place so unlikely to meet? Because he doesn't want anyone to know about it. Perfect place, don't you think? You can't go in there in a suit and tie."

"Yes, he doesn't want Vianone to know, but why?" Nicolas checked the computer's progress and sent the pictures to the FBI agents in Miami, adding the request to identify the man.

"Maybe he's at odds with the new man in charge." Matthew sipped coffee, frowning. "Did you choose a clever disguise?"

"You're fishing for information I won't provide," Nicolas replied as he deleted the original photos from his computer. For the life of him, he wouldn't allow anyone to see Raiden in his *disguise*. "It worked. That's enough."

Matthew laughed. "If you don't tell me, I'll just imagine what you did to not stand out as an agent." He bent across the desk as far as possible and lowered his voice. "I read a lot about that club and what people do there. You either had a cloak that made you invisible or your dressed up much better than Mr. Unknown in your pictures." He sipped coffee, still grinning. "Lots of leather? Make-up? Handcuffs and such?"

Nicolas lowered his gaze toward the keyboard, hoping another piece of information might show up or that the telephone would ring. He couldn't stand the inquiry. "It doesn't concern you, so stop asking," he said gruffly.

"Hmm." Matthew leaned back. "It must have been an important meeting for both Bianchi and the stranger. Maybe they're planning an insurrection."

"I agree. It won't be enough, though, to get the surveillance teams back on track."

"That's something Sullivan won't like to hear." Matthew grinned broadly. "You tell him."

Two days later, Nicolas received a call from Detective James Bennett of the Falls Church Police. He told him about the death of Benjamin Cooper, a company owner from Annandale, who had died in a brutal car crash on July seventh. His son Lionel had survived the accident badly wounded and was still in intensive care. Bennett reported that Cooper had called the police three days prior to the accident to ask for help concerning a violent threat he had received from a bruiser, most probably working for Luigi Vianone.

"At first," Bennett said with regret in his voice. "I was unable to establish a connection between the attack on Cooper and the deadly car crash, since the circumstances didn't indicate that the victim's car was pushed off the highway and into the guardrail. It was more likely he had lost control over his heavy SUV. Witnesses stated that the SUV had swerved lanes, so it looked like he wanted to pass and speed up, but—" Bennett took a deep breath. "The widow claimed convincingly that her husband was a careful driver, especially with their autistic son riding with him. He would not have sped or driven irresponsibly, because any deviation from the routine would have upset their son." Bennett cleared his throat. "So I ordered the man's autopsy. The ME found an amount of atropa in Cooper's stomach that was enough to kill the man, even without the accident."

"You're telling me the man was murdered. Poisoned?" Nicolas sat up straight in his chair and took down notes. "If he had not caused or wasn't involved in the car accident, he would have died anyway?"

"That's correct. According to a doctor's statement, the toxin from the atropa causes hallucinations and vision disorders. I don't know what exactly happened, but according to the doctor's opinion Cooper was unable to drive the car."

"And you're calling me because the man was poisoned?"

"The FBI has flagged crimes committed by poison connected with victims within the building sector. Cooper's company produces concrete pumps for superstructures. He holds two patents for pumps and was a successful dealer in three states already. That's close enough for me."

"I understand. Who threatened him?"

"He didn't know the man's name, but I assume — and it's not something I can prove at the moment — it was one of Luigi Vianone's companies that placed the offer for buying concrete pumps only a week ago. If that's true, he's the man behind the attack and probably behind the poisoning." Bennett huffed. "You can bet I tried to link the bruiser to Vianone, but I failed. Cooper gave a description, but it wasn't good enough for an immediate identification. Now that the man's dead, I have nothing to go on."

"His widow didn't see anything?"

"She was at home with their son when Cooper was beaten up, but she stayed upstairs, trying to calm down their son. He's autistic and very sensitive."

"What did Cooper tell you about the attack?"

"He said a man came to his home and told him if he didn't sell to the Harvest Investment Group, he would *see Mother Earth and eat worms.*"

"Did Cooper describe the man?"

"Yes, I already sent you a copy of the artist's impression of the crook."

"Thank you." Nicolas opened the email attachment. The picture showed a heavy-boned face with narrow eyes and a broad nose, definitely not Umberto Bianchi. "What else happened?"

"The bruiser hit Cooper, hurt him pretty badly without breaking bones, and left. That's the thing. The bruiser was bold enough to show up in the daytime, but didn't touch the wife and son."

"An old-school bully," Nicolas murmured, his gaze still focused on the artist's impression.

"Yes, that's what we thought, too. By the way, the atropa was in the dessert Cooper ate at the diner. The cook and owner were questioned, but neither had a motive to kill Cooper, so it's up to you to find the killer. The file's on the way."

"Thank you, detective."

"You're welcome. We're protecting the widow in case the goons show up a second time to get what they want from her."

Nicolas frowned. "She isn't in charge now, right? Who's managing the company?"

Nicolas heard paper rustle in the background, then Bennett was back on the line. "He's got a representative, Anton Wicker. He runs the business when Cooper is absent."

"You should protect him, too. Vianone has a bunch of people working for him, and now that his intentions are foiled, he'll try to push his claim."

"Will do."

Nicolas hung up, stared at the image, and saved the file on his computer before he forwarded it to Matthew. "We have another murder case, probably the same killer, just a different poison."

Matthew quick-checked the facts. "Atropa?" He looked up. "Is the *Rattler* a master of every kind of poison? That's rare. Usually, a murderer sticks with what works best, his or her brand name, so to speak. He doesn't change his MO every day."

"He's adaptive, yes." Nicolas leaned back. "All the murders lead to the conclusion that Luigi Vianone is crusading against the building industry one way or another." He frowned. "The death of Eduardo Vianone doesn't fit."

"Did the younger brother get rid of the elder one?" Matthew cocked his head as he played with the coffee mug. "Maybe the elder brother wasn't so fond of Luigi's way of business."

"How do we tie Vianone to the murders? And how do we find out whether Bianchi did what Vianone ordered?"

"It's not Bianchi alone. He's got more men on his payroll than our local police department has officers."

"We don't have the manpower to put surveillance teams on every member of Vianone's army of goons."

"We need someone inside Vianone's business."

Matthew made an angry face, put a cigarette between his lips, and lowered his voice as far as he could. "You mean someone like me? The bruiser from next door? The bully you feared as a kid? The tough guy with the tendency to hit first and ask questions later? I can show you my brass knuckles, if you want me to."

Nicolas needed some time to sober up from his overbearing laughter. "All right, you got me on this one. Nice Chicago accent. No, I don't think they're hiring new strongmen. I mean, we need bugs in Vianone's main office, his HQ."

"How very disappointing." Matthew spat the cigarette onto the desk. His voice was normal again. "You're no fun. Anyway, how do we do this?"

"Vianone has several offices in DC, and from what we know, he lives in the suburbs. We'll follow Bianchi and place surveillance gear."

"I'm with you. As long as *you* tell Sullivan."

Umberto couldn't tell what was harder — to leave his lover behind or meet his new so-called employer face to face in his office again.

"What about Cooper?" Luigi asked, coming around his massive desk like a threat on two legs.

"He's dead," Umberto answered, flat-voiced.

"I know that. What about his widow? Did you press her?"

"She's protected by the police. Nobody gets close to her."

"Try it anyway."

Umberto wanted to ask what part of the information Luigi had not understood but knew he'd waste his breath. "His business executive is running the business now. I would — "

"Why are you still here?" Luigi waved a hand with his cigar. "If you can't get to her, burn down the factory."

"No." Umberto had a hard time keeping his voice down. "I'll find out who got the last shipment of concrete pumps. We'll steal them."

Luigi arched his brows, and his words dripped with condescension. "Too smart by half, huh? Well, I'll let that slip. Go."

Umberto wished he had the guts to punch Luigi's face like he had hit defaulters many times. He wished he had a concise plan of how to kill Luigi and get away with it. But first he had to make sure Luigi's loyal henchmen were either out of the way or could be turned to support him instead of this brazen idiot, in whose wake people died or factories were burned to the ground.

Casting his eyes down so Luigi wouldn't see his flaring rage, Umberto left the office.

Cooper's widow, Diane, sat on a chair in front of the room at the ICU where her son was being treated, sipping coffee from a plastic cup. Looking up, she made a face, and Nicolas hoped it had to do with the bad quality of the black brew and not with Matthew and him showing their badges.

"I'm sorry to disturb you, Mrs. Cooper, but we have questions concerning your husband's company and customers."

"FBI? I thought the homicide division was on it."

"We are taking over," Matthew said with his honey-soft voice.

Mrs. Cooper's blue eyes held enough rage to give her words credibility. "Find the bastard and break his bones, or I'll hire a man who will."

"We're trying to find the murderer to—"

"Ben was threatened, so he did what he thought was right and called the police." She put down the cup on the next chair and got up. She was a tall, sporty woman in her late thirties, wearing white pants, boat shoes, and a knitted sweater in blue and white. Her short haircut added to the aura of a woman being constantly moving, unable to sit back and relax. She crossed her arms in front of her bosom and looked Nicolas straight in the eyes. "Their promise of protection was a joke. Where were they when he needed them? Ben died because that's what this . . . bastard promised would happen if he didn't sell the blackmailer's company the pumps he wanted."

"How is your son doing?" Matthew asked quietly.

Mrs. Cooper kept staring at Nicolas. "My son lost his

father, and I lost my husband because a hardcore criminal thinks that he can dictate who Cooper Industries sells pumps to. If I could, I would close the factory so he can't get any of them. But, of course, there are a hundred and fifty jobs at stake, not to mention our income as well. So the only chance is to find the man who killed Ben and bring him to justice." She narrowed her eyes. "Is that what you're going to do?"

Nicolas wasn't surprised by Mrs. Cooper's harsh reaction. He'd learned that parents of disabled children were tougher and much more sensitive to injustice than others. They learned to fight for their children from day one, and they never gave up faced with setbacks. He believed that Mrs. Cooper would hire a sharpshooter if she thought the FBI didn't do enough to capture the murderer.

"The FBI has taken over because we assume this murder wasn't the first one. A team of agents is working on these cases." Her frown said she wasn't convinced. "The police will keep protecting you and your son while we continue the investigation. What can you tell us about the day the bruiser showed up at your door?"

"You know that I made my statement to Detective Bennett, right? Why are you asking me the same question? I didn't see anything. I stayed upstairs with Lionel to sooth him because he couldn't stand the noise and the stranger cursing and threatening Ben in a row. I told the detective that the bruiser wasn't the smartest man. His language was simple, obscene. He was used to threatening people, I bet." She held tight to her upper arms. "I feared he would club my husband to death. When he left, I hurried downstairs, found him, and we called an ambulance and the police. You know the rest." She huffed. "I contacted a private security company. They will provide security around the clock, here and at home. I never thought I'd ever need a bodyguard."

"It's the right decision."

"It would have been better to give the goon what he wanted." Though she was fighting it, Mrs. Cooper couldn't stop a tear from trickling down her cheek. She wiped it away angrily. "I asked Ben whether it was worth the risk, and he told me he wouldn't bow to any random criminal. If he did, there would be others, and he would be out of business in six months."

"He was a strong-willed character."

Although it was meant as a consolation, Mrs. Cooper glared at Nicolas. "His strong will helped built the company. It helped building a home for our son and make sure we could afford the treatment he needs. But it didn't protect him from a hideous killer."

"Had your husband been threatened before?"

"Not that I know of. You might talk to his proxy, Anton Wicker. My husband trusted him, so he would know of any threats." She shook her head slowly. "But I don't think there were any. We've never been in trouble before." She gathered her strength to meet Nicolas's gaze once more. "If you'll excuse me, I have to look after Lionel."

Nicolas made room, and she went through the door without a second glance. Though she hadn't said a word, he felt too inept to satisfy Mrs. Cooper's demand for justice.

On the way back to the car, Matthew lit a cigarette. "She didn't look at me. Hell, she didn't react to me in any way. That's a first."

"She's as strong-willed as her husband was. That much is clear."

"And that means she can ignore me?"

Nicolas opened the car door and slipped behind the wheel. "We'll have a hard time catching the killer first."

"Because?"

"I bet she didn't just call a security company, but tried to reach out to a contract killer."

"A Sarah Connor in disguise?"

"She's that kind of woman." He started the engine when Matthew sat down beside him, blowing out the rest of smoke while the door was still open. "We'd better hurry, or she'll have found the goon faster than we can."

Matthew smirked. "What would be so bad about that?"

Security was weak at Cooper Industries. Umberto's skills were sufficient to break into the office while the staff joined the assistant manager for lunch at a nearby restaurant. He was astonished to find the computers still running and more astonished that he could use the program without entering a password. Happy about the employees' sloppiness, Umberto called up the latest customer list and their addresses to save them on a USB stick. Without being detected, he left the office and returned to his car. Luigi's incompetence and bottomless urge for vengeance nagged him endlessly as he looked back at the large factory building. Cooper Industries was a solid company, employing more than a hundred men and women. It would have been a shame to ruin the business because of Luigi's tantrum and anger about Benjamin Cooper's rejection. He had learned from Eduardo that there were always other ways to reach the goals you were seeking. You had to be clever and patient.

Flinching as he compared Eduardo's business strategy to Luigi's once again, Umberto started the engine and drove back. It was his duty to hand over his findings to Luigi, but the list burned a hole in his jacket. All he wanted to do was to handle the job alone, take the responsibility, and send his boss to hell.

The day before, Umberto had contacted Steve Arcuri, one of Eduardo's long-time bookkeepers and an upright man in his late fifties. Like others, Arcuri was afraid of Luigi Vianone's methods and the cruel clean-up his goons had begun in Miami. With a giant brush, Luigi had swept away former trusted employees and replaced them with men loyal to himself. Arcuri had so far kept his position, but feared he would end up like two others — drifting to shore after being left out to die in the ocean. Arcuri begged Umberto to stay away and leave him alone. He wouldn't risk his neck to support Umberto on a suicide mission to undermine Luigi's evil schemes. He was too old for that and would retire should Luigi offer him an acceptable sum of money.

Umberto held back that Luigi was capable of granting Arcuri a money-cushioned way out, only to kill him a week later. His supporters dwindled, and acting alone against Luigi was a call for a bullet in the head — if he got off easy. Umberto did not intend to give up so early in his life, not the least because of his new lover.

Eduardo had educated him, taught him the moves of the business — how to learn about your enemy before you chose the best way to get rid of him and how not to be blamed for the strike. Luigi was a weasel, but clever enough to surround himself with bootlickers who would pull the trigger in his name anytime.

It would not be easy to throw Luigi out of the race. He decided to call Farrini and learn whether his second man in Miami possessed more backbone.

Nicolas was happy to deal with the case again, because it kept him from pondering why wearing a chastity device had so intensely spurred his sexual appetite. He couldn't remember ever having been in such a state of frenzied desire. His mind told him that the visit to the club had been an outstanding experience — totally new and exciting. The primitive part of him, the one that provided him with sexual interest, cackled malevolently and told him bluntly that the complete surrender to Jacklyn's superiority had granted him the best sex ever. He loved her, needed her, granted her power and felt great doing so. The memory of the hour after returning home from the club flashed through his mind so overwhelmingly, he had a boner and zoomed out of the real world.

"Nick?" Matthew stared at him, brows raised and with a mischievous smile reserved for occasions when he mocked his partner, but didn't dare say it out loud.

"What?"

"The information just popped up. FBI in Miami arrested Leila Prescott in Orlando while she was visiting a friend. They're interrogating her as we speak. Well, *I* speak, while you're traveling the Twilight Zone."

"I'm right with you." Nicolas took a deep breath and shifted on his seat. "How come?"

"Well . . ." Matthew raised his eyebrows, then lifted the little finger of his right hand. "Tight?"

"The case?" Nicolas asked impatiently.

"The case. The agents report that a friend had seen her in her old neighborhood and called the police. She was arrested by the FBI without resistance."

"Did she admit having killed the mayor?"

"Slow down, pal. She admits—and that's odd—that she was paid to leave Florida." Matthew glanced back at the screen. "Someone approached her after the murder of the mayor and told her she would get a lot of money if she left immediately. He didn't give his name, and her description is vague. She claims she talked to an old man on the phone. How does she know he was old? Because she works as a nurse for the elderly. She can judge a person's age by the way he speaks."

"What's the FBI's course of action?"

"She will be accused of the murders of Lubock, Boman, and Matusky. If they find enough evidence, they will also accuse her of killing the Mayor of Orlando, Stuart Norton. That leaves Eduardo Vianone's death and the subsequent ones in the DC area still open." He shrugged. "If there is no evidence that she traveled north to continue her killing spree, there could be a second killer — especially if you regard the different poisons."

Nicolas bent forward and rested his elbows on the desk. "Do they honestly assume she is able to kill in cold blood?"

"After all, her husband died of an accident at one of Lubock's skyscrapers in western Orlando. If she killed Lubock and found it appealing to take matters into her own hands, why should she stop? All companies neglect worker protection and pay little compensation for injuries. Maybe she went on a crusade."

"That wouldn't explain the murder of Norton. He was known to act against corruption, had made a name for himself by fighting illegal activities, especially in the construction sector. She should have praised and not killed him."

"Mm-hmm — so she went for Lubock only?"

"If she was paid for leaving the state, someone wanted her to become a scapegoat." Nicolas sat back more comfortably while his erection abated. "I'd bet she's not responsible for any murder. She's a nurse for the elderly. This requires compassion and helpfulness."

"Shall I write that as a reply to the agents in Miami?"

"They'll find out that someone used her anger against her. And she needed the money, I assume. After her husband's death, she left everything behind. She was forced to start from scratch." Nicolas shook his head. "When did she get the money?"

Matthew checked the data in the report. "In May."

"Before Eduardo Vianone died."

"Yes." Matthew emptied his coffee cup. "You think he was the old man who paid her?"

"Or someone was clever enough to use a pretender. Prescott fell for it, took the money, and left Florida immediately. Why did she return?"

"She claimed she was homesick." When Nicolas looked at him, brows raised, Matthew snorted and went on, pretending to lament. "Yeah, all right, I get it. A woman who comes home because she's homesick can't be the one who kills four men with poison." His look became as hard as the tone of his voice. "Don't you think you're too soft-hearted to work here? The most cunning criminals are women. Did you know that? When it comes to scheming, to pretending interest, even love, women perform their roles in an outstanding way."

Nicolas knew of Matthew's deceased wife's criminal activities and let the harsh tone slip. "I will believe that she's a hired killer when the agents find the poison and a bank account filled with more than a few bucks."

"Do you wanna bet?"

"I never bet. I asked Addleton to find out where the Rattler got the atropa. He told me that the plant is so common, people are warned not to eat the berries because they look tasty." Nicolas got up and took his jacket. "I'm calling it a day. Go home. We won't receive the court order for the bugs in Vianone's rooms until tomorrow."

"You're granting me a free afternoon? I'm impressed." He pointed a finger at him. "That proves my assumption that you're going soft. By the way—are you going to see Jason, or will you drift into the Twilight Zone you came back from a few minutes ago?"

Nicolas grinned. "Jason first, Twilight Zone later."

He heard Matthew whoop behind him, but left the office without turning back. He didn't want to see any obscene gestures.

CHAPTER NINE

Umberto told Michael on the phone that he wouldn't be home for dinner. To his surprise, Michael didn't press him for reasons or whine about staying home alone. He expressed his disappointment — which Umberto had expected — but decided to stay at the dance club and gym longer than usual. Umberto imagined Michael's muscles straining while working out. He wished he could join him instead of heading for his duty.

Relaxed as only a man in love could be, Umberto gathered four of Luigi's men to brief them about the break-in he had planned for the night. He forced his voice down to business as he explained the plan. He had to appear like the man in charge, a man people trusted. The construction site was guarded, but the security service carried no weapons and could be overwhelmed. The next morning, several valuable pieces of equipment, including the concrete pumps, would be missing, and if they were lucky, the police wouldn't find a clue as to how the theft had been done.

"Does Luigi know?" Drago asked as they stored their burglary equipment in an unmarked van.

Umberto swiveled around to stare the man down. "Luigi wants results, and that's what we're gonna give him. If you want him to grant you permission to piss, go ahead and ask him. In the meantime, I'll find another one to replace you, dimwit."

"Hey, don't cut off my head!" Drago lifted his hands in defense. His bull-nosed face twisted into a grimace. The other men standing around laughed, and Drago grumbled, "I just thought . . ."

"Go someplace else with your thoughts. I need men to work with me, not question my decisions." Umberto turned away to check whether they had their tools loaded. To steal the pumps, he had borrowed three trucks with rope winches to lift the pumps onto the loading area. Since the construction site was way off highways or major streets—these, too, were under construction—their chances of being caught by the police were slim.

Umberto looked at Drago. He didn't trust the forty-something man. He wasn't smart, but was one of Luigi's loyal troopers. Umberto would have chosen differently, but knew that politics—in this case including Drago to please Luigi—were as important as burglary skills. That didn't mean he would tolerate incompetence or truculence. Should Drago become a problem, he would deal with him.

The Rattler was an apt player who planned his moves to the last detail—a valuable skill that enabled him to stay ahead of the police. He was proud of his deeds, of his genius. Where other contract killers faltered, the Rattler thrived on finding a solution. When he had taken over the first job, he had thought about adding a personal touch to the murders—such as a snake tooth on every victim killed by the poison he had administered, but the stealthy mode of his killing prohibited such significant trademark. He liked the nickname the FBI had chosen—he was as much a snake as he was a person who rattled victims and the police alike. The newspapers—always a friend to serial killers and the best medium to stay informed—conjectured there could be more victims to be credited to the Rattler—bodies still concealed or killed so expertly that the medical examiners had not found the poison and credited their deaths to natural causes.

He supposed that this was what had happened when Benjamin Cooper died. The paper wrote that the executive had been killed in a brutal car crash on his way home. If that cause of death was consistent, it wouldn't be added to the list of the Rattler's victims. It was all the same to him. He made decent money with his contracts, and his current client was a vindictive person who craved being recognized. This special client had already issued a long list of possible next targets, expecting the Rattler to prepare for an immediate *displacement* should he call and give the order. The Rattler had never before worked for a client with such a thirst for violence. Usually, he contracted for one murder, expertly executed, to rid the client of an unwanted spouse, husband, competitor, or a person the client hated so much he wanted him dead and buried. The Rattler understood that kind of motivation, though he hadn't used his expertise on foes he had made in his adolescence. The conviction that he could end the life of everyone who had done him wrong made him strong, and yet forgiving. He had found a way to live and enjoy what he was doing even though he wouldn't be credited by the press the way other serial killers were.

Satisfied with the outcome of his last enterprise, the Rattler folded the paper and put it back where he had found it. He had observations to make and preparations to finish, so he inspected his supply of poisons and reached out to his contacts to get some more.

Jacklyn pulled up her legs on the armchair and reclined comfortably while talking to Lesley on the phone. "How did Raiden take the evening at the club?"

"I freed him from every shackle before we sat in the car, and he was okay with that." Lesley laughed. "Only in the parking lot of a club can you open your lover's pants and fumble with the key to the chastity device without being arrested for indecent behavior."

"I bet it was an awesome scene."

"We were getting comments about why we didn't do it inside the club, but, hey, no one gave us trouble."

"Did anything else happen?"

"I already told Nick that the two guys were only making out, and when they had enough, the taller man paid, and they left. The younger one didn't look as pleased as he should be, and I wonder whether their night was as fulfilling as ours. What about you? Did Nick keep his pants on until you were home?"

Jacklyn's voice dropped. "I never expected him to turn into a beast that's so . . . wild, beyond my imagination. He knows that I love to see him struggle, but that . . . was much more than on any night we've spent together. He was a savage. He'd have pushed his rod through my intestines if I hadn't been careful."

"Oh, you lucky girl. He finally let go. Good for you."

"He thinks it was the chastity device."

Lesley clucked. "It was the club, the atmosphere, the other guests making out on the couches. I see it in my dungeon—if you have several guys waiting for their mistresses, they are hyped up much more than when one man is waiting alone. Nevertheless, if it spikes his arousal, keep him chastised."

"He doesn't want that—it's a distraction from work and it could be in the way should he . . . well, you know. He explained to me it was impractical to wear it at work, and I believe him. But . . ." Jacklyn paused.

"But you liked his savagery?"

"What does that say about me?"

"That you like your rides better if there's wildness and danger involved. Will he play along?"

"I think so. He's visiting Jason after work, so I expect him home in an hour. Maybe he's in the mood."

"My fingers are crossed for you. It's a pity you don't have that kind of beam in your home you had at the boat house."

"The pictures were amazing, right?"

"Has he added muscle since I last saw him in the buff? He looks fantastic. He doesn't know about the pictures, huh?"

"Of course not. He'd refuse to play." Jacklyn sighed. "It's not that he's squeamish, but he claims when there are pictures, they could be misused. I wished he would change his mind and I could record our sessions. The last one was . . . well, I've got no words. What's your plan for tonight?"

"Raiden presented a new boat to a customer today and is out partying with his partners. I don't expect him home until late. So there's no playtime for us tonight. Do you want me to come over and help you out?"

"Don't you dare!"

Lesley laughed until Jacklyn disconnected the call.

Matthew stared at the information about the murder victims assembled on the whiteboard, written in both Nicolas's and his own handwriting. Though he wouldn't say it out loud, he missed Jason—at least a little—and decided to ask Nicolas how the father of the newborn baby was doing.

Matthew suppressed the thought about having a family. His wife had cheated on him, had given him up to the Chicago mob, a crime that had cost Matthew his friends, his home, and almost his career at the FBI. He didn't want to think of her betrayal and the family he never had. He remembered their conversations about having a baby, and the pain was still raw after all the years. In the wake of those ill memories, Matthew had not asked Jason about Elaine's pregnancy nor desired to pay the family a visit. He had donated generously to the baby shower, though.

He concentrated on the post-its again. Four builders and an old patriarch were dead in Florida, a builder and a company owner had been killed in Maryland. He studied the details, then went through the files once more and phoned the company managers to find out about the latest business contracts they had acquired or applied for. He added the information to the board. "Municipal buildings," he murmured to no one in particular. "They wanted the contracts for city development projects." Huffing, Matthew turned around and checked the cities' homepages. For an hour, he spoke with staffers of county governments about writing down a list of public works and the companies that had successfully competed for the contracts. He added another row of post-it notes to the board before he dove into the jungle of company connections and sub-contractors to find the main companies behind them.

Frustrated that he couldn't clear the jungle from the lianas, Matthew threw his pen across the desk. When he looked up, Nicolas was entering the office, looking like a Nordic god and in a devilishly good mood — full of energy to tackle the day. Even though he didn't smile openly, the majority of female agents turned their heads to look in his direction as if hit by a wave of testosterone.

Matthew sighed deeply. The man had what he wanted — a good-looking woman and enough sex to keep him satisfied, like a stallion grazing with his mares on a lush meadow. Matthew dumped that image immediately. It was much too depressing.

"Good morning, Nick." Matthew pointed at the whiteboard. "So far, we knew about the projects the companies had and for which they already had investors. But all of them were after the big municipal deals — building a new kindergarten, a high school, a new wing of a university. They were after the deals for train stations or the remodeling of the mayor's office. That's what we didn't know."

Nicolas looked flabbergasted. "All of these murders were committed so that they couldn't pick up contracts for public buildings?"

"Exactly. For me, this explains the murder of the mayor, because we know he would've investigated every fraud. The various companies behind the contracts might lead to Luigi or Eduardo Vianone, but the jungle is thick. I asked for help, and Agent Spring is contacting the department of white-collar crime."

"That's great." Nicolas helped himself to a cup of coffee.

Matthew noticed two thin scratches behind Nicolas's ear, reaching down beyond the shirt collar. He shivered. The idea of a woman scratching him and forcing him into obedience by shackling him—Nicolas's chafed wrists were proof of that—gave him the creeps.

"The evidence points in Luigi Vianone's direction—without hard proof to back it up. We cannot connect him to any of these murders, though they benefit his companies—I think—and increase his influence in the building sector. I checked his income—four-hundred million dollars last year—bottom line. He's a wealthy man."

"And pays his taxes and looks innocent as a lamb. Did the judge send the authorization to tap Vianone's phones and bug his homes?"

"Yes, he did, but he added that this kind of surveillance has already been tried without success." Matthew pushed the piece of paper across the table. "We're not the first ones trying to find him guilty of murder, blackmail, and racketeering. He's the top dog in his business without ever having been dragged before a judge."

"Nevertheless, it's worth a shot. Who's going to do the

work?"

"I already told the technicians to put it on their to-do list."

"Thank you." Nicolas frowned. "Did you sleep at the office?"

"Of course not, but I don't have a lady that keeps me from leaving the house." Matthew got up to fetch another cup of coffee, if only to avoid his partner's smug grin.

Umberto had not expected Luigi to praise him openly, but the man's matter-of-fact attitude when listening to the success story enraged Umberto so much he wanted to smash the concrete pumps with a large hammer and be done with them.

He controlled his temper, as he did most of the time with increasing difficulty, summed up that the pumps and the other equipment they had stolen were deposited in a warehouse close to Fredericksburg and ready to be used wherever Luigi needed them. Smoking a cigar, Luigi pursed his lips, nodded curtly, and dismissed Umberto with a generous wave of his hand, claiming he had business to do and whores to bed.

Umberto wanted to smash the hideous grin off Luigi's face and castrate him on the spot.

After sunrise, Umberto arrived at home—tired, grumpy, and reeking of sweat. He was in no mood to meet with anyone, not even his lover. His plans consisted of a hot shower and ten hours of uninterrupted sleep. He put away his gun in a lockable drawer in his study, then dropped his clothes on the way to the bathroom, sighing with relief when warm water splashed onto his body.

Umberto grunted when Michael joined him in the shower, partly out of surprise, partly because he had cherished his solitude. He didn't say a word when Michael reached for a sponge and rubbed his back. Thankfully, Michael remained silent throughout their mutual shower and uttered no comment when they towel-dried and went out.

"Do you want coffee?" were Michael's first words.

Umberto held him back from walking to the kitchen, embraced and kissed him, his bad mood almost forgotten. "Thank you. Yes, I'd like a really strong cup of coffee and you at my side."

Michael offered him a flash of his wonderful smile, clicked his tongue and said, "You gonna get what you deserve."

Umberto dropped the bitter and biting thoughts about Luigi Vianone, the motherfucker who'd stolen Eduardo's business, and went into the bedroom to get dressed.

Nicolas and Matthew spent most of the forenoon calling county governments and public construction authorities to find out about the latest proposal offers and the companies involved. Then they compared the offers to the companies they assumed belonged to Vianone. Their ears ringing hot and their mouths dry from talking, Matthew and Nicolas compared their results over the two sandwiches they had for lunch at their desks.

Senior Agent Sullivan emerged from his office to hear the latest revelations.

Nicolas swallowed his bite to answer. "Sir, we found three objects that match Vianone's interest. They are large enough to catch his eye and would wash ten to thirty million each into his accounts. The other offers are smaller. We intend to call the competitors and ask them whether they were contacted like Cooper—threats and bullying."

"Fine. Whatever helps getting this bastard behind bars."

Nicolas exhaled when Sullivan turned to speak with another agent two desks away. "He wants him bad. If we make a mistake on this one — "

"He'll want us bad out of the job."

When Nicolas returned to his desk with a fresh cup of coffee, the telephone rang, and Agent Hillbrock from the bureau in Miami told him they had identified the man who met with Bianchi at the *Freaky Like Me Club* on July sixth.

"It's Ennio Marchesi. According to his tax papers and contract, he's a book accountant at the Parkland Building Company, but we know he worked for Eduardo Vianone. If I had to bet, he was close to the old man. Now that I know he made contact with Bianchi, I'll meet him someplace safe and ask him a few questions. Maybe he'll be shocked enough to cooperate." Hillbrock snorted. "Interests are shifting in Miami. It looks like new folk have come to town, taking over vacant positions at the enterprises the old Vianone ran."

"Luigi Vianone is sending his henchmen to replace those loyal to his elder brother. Is that correct?"

"Looks like it. The companies are tight. Everything they do has a legal appearance. It's not like they brag about bullying other company people. They do it behind closed doors, and if the injured parties don't press charges, there's no prosecution. I've seen that happen too often."

Nicolas took his time thinking about it. "All his life, the old Vianone ran an illegal business. What's different now that Luigi took over?"

Hillbrock let out an exasperated sigh. "Dead people in dark alleys. Listen, I talked with older colleagues and called up old files. Eduardo Vianone blackmailed competitors to oblige, but when they complied, he left smaller parts of their businesses to them, stuck to his promises, and left the people alone. Yes, he threw many executives out of the job, pushed those hardest who were in his way, and he had people killed. There's no doubt about that. He wasn't working for the Salvation Army.

By and large, the old Vianone held enough power in the greater Miami and Orlando area to cow competitors without killing or maiming entire families. It's a fact that—if you played along—there was a kind of cooperation. Again, this wasn't fair. It wasn't for fun, but Luigi's the bad kind. If he doesn't get what he wants on the spot, he offs them. He doesn't care about collateral damage, either." After a pause, he said, "You must stop him somehow."

"We're trying, but so far, he's slick. There's no connection between the murders and him. We can't even prove that the company who took over the contracts belongs to him. Well, not yet."

"Luigi must have a handful of people he trusts with errands and with the killings. Anything about them?"

"We're observing several men he ordered from Florida after the elder brother's death. Looks like we have to be patient." Nicolas ended the call and lifted his brows when Matthew looked at him. "And what have you got?"

"Two companies bailed out immediately. They received threats on the phone, telling them their families would end up like Sorenson should they not cooperate. That was enough—considering the major news coverage the case got. They claimed no contract was worth being killed for. But one guy's outraged about the threats and says he'll help us if we can protect him."

"What do we know about him?"

Matthew read from his notepad. "Mr. Warren Burmeister, son of German immigrants two generations ago, founded a building company in Orlando, Florida specializing in the interior design of rooms for the natural sciences in schools and universities. His business expanded to Virginia late last year. He's been successful in many ways and proud of it, or so it appears." Matthew looked up. "The German qualities, you know."

"Right."

"He was threatened on the phone to withdraw his offer, but told them right away that he's not Sorenson." Matthew raised his brows. "Easily said. As far as we know, he's got his parents, who live in Tulsa, Oklahoma, but he doesn't consider them in danger."

"If Vianone is behind that threat, he'll have evaluated his opponent's weaknesses. What did Burmeister tell you about himself?"

Matthew blew out air while his hand reached for the pack of cigarettes and a lighter. "Forty-two years old, second generation in the building sector, renowned executive of his company, pays his rents, his taxes, has a fondness for fast cars." He looked up. "I bet they're well insured. Vianone couldn't pick a fight with him about the cars."

Nicolas reclined, frowning. "If he can't threaten him, what's his angle?"

"Nothing but the man's life. We can offer personal protection until the deal's done."

Nicolas got up and grabbed his jacket. "I'll report to Sullivan, you gather Spring and Addleton for the babysitting job."

"Will do."

Umberto sipped the excellent coffee, and while Michael cooked ham and eggs on the stove, mulled over his position. He had to please Luigi and play by his rules until he found a strategy to knock him from his throne without being stabbed in the back. Luigi's rambling about the latest contract offers and the need for action was the signal to demonstrate his usefulness. Umberto decided to take matters into his own hands and please his boss—hopefully to lull him into false security. Umberto couldn't wait for the day when he would start an open rebellion.

By now, he knew Luigi's henchmen well enough to differentiate between followers, and workers who took orders. The workers could be persuaded by money, the followers must be convinced that Luigi was a bad boss who needed to be replaced. From the beginning of Luigi's unspeakable takeover, Umberto had used small talk gatherings to throw around some anecdotes about insufficient leadership and that Luigi had left men standing in the rain. He masked his bad-mouthing by repeating that he told facts, not fiction. They could check for themselves. Eduardo had told Umberto enough stories about his younger brother to make all narratives sound credible. Umberto waited for the rumors to spread and stir unrest. Rumors had the tendency to grow and leave the source they'd come from in the dark.

Umberto counted on some workers to tell their friends. When the time was right, Umberto could recruit and incite them to act against their boss. Without support from his Miami contacts, this was the only chance he had to oust Luigi and get what he deserved.

The Rattler knew the old saying — what you don't want anyone to see, is best hidden in the open. The executives of the building companies in Florida had not posed a problem. Their daily routines were easy to analyze. The poisons went into their food or drink, and he left the scenes before their deaths occurred.

The Mayor of Orlando had brought forward a different problem. His routines were known only to a few trustworthy assistants, but the Rattler found out about his mother who lived in the city, and she knew everything about her son. Nothing worked better than charming the mother of a local celebrity and cherished politician about his younger years. She loved to brag about her son and told him so much more than he needed to know, it was amazing. One detail was the mayor's love for strawberry pastries — that he had devoured them when he was little and hadn't stopped since. If it hadn't been inappropriate, he would have embraced the old lady and thanked her for the information.

Then there was Eduardo Vianone. He proved to be the hardest target to find and eliminate. The Rattler patted himself on the back for this stroke of genius. He had executed a damn complicated trick, one he had first thought impossible to accomplish and which had pleased his client the most.

He looked at the list his client had written. More research was waiting for him, for he'd better fulfil his obligations or he might end up dead with a bullet between his eyes somewhere in a dumpster. His client was a rich guy, but no one would bet on his sanity.

Umberto's cell phone rang while he was enjoying his third cup of coffee and complimenting Michael on the excellent breakfast. He excused himself to take the call in his study. "Hi, Steve, what's up?" Umberto asked, bewildered that Steve Arcuri, who had told him to stay away, contacted him.

"Just a quick bit of information and you didn't get it from me. Luigi has had a woman kidnapped. For blackmail. You know how it works — to convince her husband to step out of a deal. In this case, Luigi wants the husband's company. I know where she's being kept."

"But that's somewhere in—"

"I'm telling you the address. You call the police. I won't." Arcuri was breathing heavily. "Listen, two of his most trusted men are with the woman right now. You can . . . well, ruin their lives, if you want to."

"Give me the address and county." Arcuri spelled the street name and told him it was outside of Orlando, an industrial complex, deserted by its former owners. "All right. Lose the phone, go about your business, I'll take care of the rest." But the line was already dead.

Umberto collected his wits. He hadn't expected his old friend to come out of hiding to deliver two henchmen on a silver platter. He prepared a few sentences to use, then dialed the number of the police department of Orlando and pretended to be an elderly citizen who had watched two men pushing a woman into an empty building. The police officer took down notes, asked for his name, and Umberto coughed and stuttered, then gave him a false one and said he couldn't breathe anymore and had to end the call. Umberto checked his watch. Even if the police monitored calls, this would've been too short to pinpoint his position.

Pleased with himself, Umberto returned to the kitchen and his cold coffee, but Michael had already cleared the table. "Hey, where's my coffee?"

"You ran off. I thought you didn't want it anymore."

Umberto heard mild reproach and bridged the distance to put his big hands on Michael's shoulders. "I'm sorry. It was important."

Michael turned his head to look up adamantly. "So important that you locked yourself in your study—a room I'm not even allowed to enter?"

"That's the point? Yes, I need some space just for me. You didn't mind that back in Miami."

"But this place—we moved in here together. I don't hide anything from you." Michael moved away from Umberto's hands to continue washing the dishes. "Whenever the phone rings, you act like you work for the CIA—all hushed whispers behind closed doors."

"I can assure you I'm not with the CIA. I couldn't meet their clothing standards." His chuckle died when Michael didn't join in. "My company demands that I keep business talk private, and I stick to that. Sorry, Mikey, these are the rules, and I've pointed them out several times."

"Don't talk to me like a teacher. I'm not your student. I want to spend my life with you, but there you go—no, don't shake your head." Michael dropped the towel on the sink. "You keep secrets. You don't want our relationship to become public. Bert, we're living in the twenty-first century. Why should an insurance company or any of your friends respect you less because you're gay? Don't you think that there's talk among the neighbors about why two men moved in together? I bet there's a lot of gossip around here of how we spend our time. What's the big deal?"

"So this is no longer a discussion about my work, but about me hiding that I'm homosexual?" Umberto huffed. "You're right. I don't want anyone to know. We both can pretend that we're straight, and no one will doubt us. It's better for both of us, believe me. Remember? You were bashed that night on the sidewalk because that goon hated gays."

Michael lowered his gaze. "You're right. I just wanted to go home, and he . . . he must've watched me before." He shook his head, and his voice was low and depressed. "The first hit was the worst. So much hate. Without you . . ."

Umberto's heart opened to Michael's misery, and he regretted having mentioned the dreadful assault. He took Michael in his arms and pulled him close. "Mikey, I want to share so much with you, but I won't go against the rules. I didn't make them, but I can't afford to lose my job. Not now. Not yet. Bear with me that time will change. I promise." He kissed Michael's forehead affectionately. "I'll be there for you."

"Unless you're in your study," Michael replied, looking up.

"Unless I'm in my study."

CHAPTER TEN

Nicolas and Matthew used the back entrance at *Burmeister Commercial Furnishings*. An employee led them to an unused office on street level where the company owner waited for them.

Warren Burmeister was a small man, almost bald, with prominent dark brown eyes, a stark contrast to his fair, clean-shaven skin. It wasn't the contrast that caught Nicolas's eye but the missing left ear. The scar was old, misshaped, leaving a small remnant of the earlobe. A thin line of scar tissue stretched to his neck, giving the impression that the mutilation had been meant to go beyond the ear or that the kidnapper had had an unsteady hand. Burmeister wore an expensive dark blue suit, tie, and despite the hot weather, a vest. The watch at his left wrist was a Rolex, and the signet ring on his right hand carried the emblem of Harvard University. Though not even of average height, Burmeister gave off the impression that he was in charge.

Burmeister reached out for a handshake, his smile waning and quickly disappearing. "Nice to meet you, gentlemen. I apologize for the inconvenient way of meeting, but you said it should be in private." He cleared his throat. "If we fight, we want to reach the finish line, won't we? And not get busted on the first mile."

"May I ask—"

"Yes, I'm missing an ear." He invited them to sit down on comfortable armchairs around a low cocktail table and offered refreshments. "I was kidnapped when I was eight. My father was supposed to pay two million dollars, but before he could deliver the money, I slipped the kidnappers' grasp and called the police." His smile revealed expertly made false teeth. "The papers were full of the small boy courageous enough to escape the evil goons." He shrugged when he sat down with a glass of lemonade. "The men served a lifetime sentence. They were so stupid, it was like a comic book. Yes, I could use an orthopedic ear, but, you see, I don't care about my looks. People stare and then I explain the circumstances. I never want to forget—" He broke off. Then, after a moment, he smiled again. "My mind's racing like a car on a fast track. Since the moment this guy called me and told me to bail out, I'm wondering when the deadly strike will come and hammer me down."

"We'll try and protect you."

"Yes, yes, I'm sure you will. My father had hired a security company—it didn't do any good. The kidnappers caught me on the lawn behind my family's property. I used to play there and always got carried away, thinking of foreign lands, stories, you know? The security guys were kind. They didn't bother me or order me to come back. I think they thought it was a safe neighborhood. But that's when fate strikes, right?" He drank and put down the glass, frowning. "My mother didn't take the kidnapping well. She was proud, yes, that I had escaped, but she tried to keep me inside, guarded, for the next two years." He looked Nicolas in the eyes. "Can you imagine that? I wanted to explore the world, and it suddenly ended at the fence around our home."

"What did the caller say to you, Mr. Burmeister? What do you remember?"

"He asked whether I'm still bidding for the contract, and I said yes. He told me to bail out—not even unfriendly. He said that it would be better for my health. And when I replied that I didn't think so, he added that I'd end up like Sorenson. I had heard of Sorensen's death, right? He had a kind of . . . glee in his voice, like he had won with this threat before and expected me to give in immediately. He gave me a day to consider, and he expected me to withdraw my bid without further explanation." Burmeister shrugged. "That's it. He hung up."

"Describe the voice, please."

Burmeister closed his eyes and exhaled. "Male, cultivated, without accent. He was menacing, but not in a Christopher Lee kind of way. He sounded certain he'd get what he wanted. No drawl in it, no lisp. Even if I tried, I couldn't place him in a state." He opened his eyes. His smile was brief. "Unlike you — I hear that you're from the east coast."

"Quite true. Has anything else happened since the call?"

"No."

"Strange cars in your street, people following you?"

"No. Or more precisely — not that I noticed. I expected someone to observe me and not wait till five o'clock today to see whether I withdrew my bid." Burmeister emptied his glass and clicked his tongue. "On the one hand, I want them to come after me, so that you can arrest them. On the other hand, I'm scared that — don't get me wrong — they're faster than you are."

"I understand that you're scared," Matthew said. "We'll take shifts to accompany you wherever you go and keep an eye on you."

"Chicago," Burmeister said, smiling brightly. "See, if there's an accent, I hear it."

"That's right." Matthew gave a slight nod. "From now on, we'll stay close to you, and you make sure that we know of your daily schedule."

"No problem." Burmeister stood and hitched his belt. His expression told of worry, cloaked by a false smile. "Before we go home, I need something stronger than lemonade, and I know a place to go, agents."

Umberto wanted to make up with Michael, apologize—though rationally there was no reason to be sorry for anything he had done. Michael had accepted Umberto's rooming-in conditions back in Miami, and nothing had changed. And yet, a big deal had changed that his conscious mind didn't acknowledge. Umberto wanted Michael in his house, in his bed. He wanted him close, day after day, and not to quarrel with him about his false job at the insurance company or that he excluded him from his study. It had to be locked. Umberto kept his weapons in a safe, but there was more—files he kept about business operations, and also a bunch of photographs he might use when the time was right. Umberto could not risk Michael glimpsing this part of his life. He was eager to learn of the two kidnappers and certain that if the police caught them, Luigi's fire spitting would shame any dragon worth its legend.

Michael had left the house taciturn, not really angry, but distant in a way Umberto disliked. He had left early, and Umberto took that as a bad sign, too.

He locked out thoughts about Michael the moment he met with his boss in one of the locations Luigi had rented through intermediaries so that his name wouldn't show in the papers. He'd been doing that a lot. Some properties were rented, some bought. It was a clever trick to keep the police out of the loop. Only his trusted men knew the addresses. For reasons Umberto couldn't fathom—and that worried him—Luigi had changed quarters from DC to Lorton, Virginia. It was a small house, compared to the residences Luigi preferred, and that fact unsettled Umberto even more. There were only three bedrooms, two baths, and not even enough space for a snooker table. The guys close to the boss had retreated to playing poker at a small table in the living room. To Umberto, it looked like his boss was hiding. Until now, Umberto had assumed Luigi wasn't afraid of anything.

"You wanted to see me?" Umberto asked politely.

Luigi's face was an unhealthy red, his brow beaded with sweat, and his eyes narrow. The thick artery at his temple looked like a cord, pulsing rhythmically. He chewed on the cigar between his lips, then spat it out across the table. Ash flew like glitter across the wood. "Tell me about all your contacts in Miami. Right now. All of them." Luigi poked the table with his finger, his gaze fixed on Umberto. "Spit it out!"

"What kind of contacts do you mean?" Umberto's heart jump-started to hammer forcefully against his ribs. *Does he know about Arcuri's betrayal?* "I know a lot of people in Miami."

"Don't gimme that shit! I want to know about all the men who were loyal to my brother! All of them! Someone tipped off the police!"

Umberto raised his brows. "Why don't you tell me what happened?"

Luigi stared at him like a bull close to charging. "My men were arrested an hour ago for kidnapping. Red-handed! And how did the police know? Someone called them and told them where to look!"

"Damn!"

Luigi's eyes narrowed further while his nostrils widened. "Don't you even try to look shocked. You don't understand what that means. It's a big deal that's slipping through my fingers. Eighty million worth—at least! The husband was about to sell his company to me!"

"So you had your men kidnap the company owner's . . . spouse . . . wife?"

"That's what I'm saying, right?" He walked two steps to fetch another cigar, then dropped his hand, and looked back at Umberto. His tone was harsh, seething with accusation.

"Did you know about this? The kidnapping?"

"No, I didn't." Umberto was careful not to say a word too many. If he gave away Arcuri, his friend was as good as dead, and it wouldn't be an easy death.

"But you don't seem . . . surprised." Luigi pursed his lips. "You do have friends in Miami. Tell me about them. Give me the names of the men who were close to Eduardo."

Umberto recited a short list of people. Some of them had already been replaced by Luigi's men in the first wave of the take-over, others were too intimidated to act against Luigi. He added Arcuri to the list because leaving him out would have alerted Luigi that something was wrong.

Luigi nodded to every name, reached for a cigar again, and rolled it between his fingers. "I'll try and find the leak, I promise, I'll do that."

"What about your men the police arrested?"

Luigi's expression changed from thoughtful to annoyed. "What about them? Shall I send my lawyer? It's impossible to get them out of jail on bail. They were caught red-handed — if you didn't understand it when I first said it. They'll stand trial." He pounded the table. "Damn! Fuck! Eighty million dollars!"

Umberto felt a cold shiver down his spine. If he was right, Luigi would rather hire someone to kill the men in jail than help them with legal advice. "Anything else?"

"No. Unless you know the traitor."

The sentence gave Umberto pause. He thought Luigi might have ordered him to his abode to confront him with the facts, then see his reaction and know instantly that Arcuri was responsible for the kidnappers' arrest. He resisted looking over his shoulder to see whether one of Luigi's bootlickers was pointing a gun at him. "No, I don't."

"But you contacted the men around Eduardo. Isn't that true?"

"Not recently."

"Broken up all the good connections?"

"And building up new ones in DC, yes." Umberto turned to walk to the door.

"I'll stay here for a while. By the way, take Drago and pay this weasel Birks a visit while you're driving back to DC. He owes me more money than he sent. Rough him up—just for good measure." Luigi looked through the large window. "The next meeting's here, too. Bring me the money tomorrow."

"All right." Umberto left the house and got into his car. His fingers shook when he turned the key in the ignition. If the lie about no recent contacts with old friends of Eduardo hadn't convinced Luigi, he would have been executed on the spot. It was a bad thought that accompanied him all the way back to Washington, DC.

The bar overlooking the Potomac wasn't exclusive, just a modern glass palace to hang out and meet other business people for an after-work drink in a nice atmosphere. There were more lights from above and behind the well-stocked shelves with liquor bottles than in other establishments. The barkeeper—appropriately dressed in a white shirt and a black vest—recognized Burmeister, nodded, and mixed him a black Russian.

While Matthew made a face and remarked about the absurd sweetness of the drink that would pull the fillings out of his teeth, Nicolas swept the room with his gaze, memorizing the interior, the exits, the staff on the move, and the guests sitting at the bar and farther back in the room. The music was a mix of modern jazz, politely distant and so soft it didn't interfere with the conversations.

Nicolas scrutinized the bartender unobtrusively, but the man, trained to observe guests like Nicolas was trained to observe suspects, sensed the scrutiny and asked for their order with hardly cloaked reserve.

Though Matthew and Nicolas were on duty, they tried to look like Burmeister's companions for an afternoon drink. They ordered whiskey on ice without the intention of drinking and asked Burmeister about his recent projects. The executive understood and went into a short summary of how interior design for schools had developed during the last decade. He warmed up while talking, and his sentences, clipped and with pauses in the beginning, became more eloquent and entertaining, spiced with little anecdotes.

Without missing any of the conversation, Nicolas watched the entrance. A man and a woman entered, both looking grim, as if they'd been in an argument on the sidewalk and decided to have a drink, hoping to improve the mood. They chose seats at the end of the bar, the woman ogled by a mid-thirties overweight man who was making love to his gin and tonic. The bartender took their orders. Another man, bent like an old tree and with more wrinkles in his bearded face than a Shar Pei, came next and shuffled toward a table where he slumped on the chair. He lifted his hand briefly, and the bartender nodded in understanding. Having taken the couple's orders, he filled a tumbler with bourbon, delivered the glass to the elderly man with a few kind words, and took his ten-dollar bill on the way back.

Nicolas heard Matthew say, "I read that you aren't married. Do you have a girlfriend, or any good friends an enemy would use to blackmail you?"

Burmeister sipped his drink, then stared at the dark liquid. "I have a lover, an acquaintance rather—I wouldn't call her a girlfriend yet. We met only recently. She's a teller at the local bank where I run my business accounts. We've been on a few dates. They went nicely." He looked up. "I don't think anyone knows of this. I haven't told anyone, that's for sure."

"We assume the killer observes his potential victims," Nicolas said quietly, only for Burmeister to hear. "How long have you been dating her?"

"Three weeks. I don't have much time for fancy dinners and . . . ." He huffed. "I'm not the most social person."

Nicolas would have bet on that. "We need her name and address and will order protection for her."

"Yeah, I guess that'll be the best. I hope that won't push her away. I . . . I hoped to have a relationship once again. It's been some time."

Burmeister drank and spoke in clipped sentences about how his life was going—he spent many hours at work, had little time for dinner and parties, and was afraid of saying the wrong thing or a woman shying away because of his looks.

It dawned upon Nicolas how lucky he was. He worked at a job he loved and had a woman at his side who was dedicated to him and would do everything in her power to sustain their relationship. He had parents who supported his decisions. They were healthy and had their lives in order. There was no evil brother or sister determined to ruin his happiness because of his manic nature. No psychotic neighbor who envied him his beautiful lover. Despite his dangerous job, Nicolas considered himself on the safe side of life. He had what he wished for and prayed that fate would grant him to live in peace. His primal fear was to lose the love of his life. If anything happened to Jacklyn, Nicolas would mourn for a lifetime. He had lost his friend Thomas Zutarski eight months ago to the viciousness of a criminal on a revenge trip. Thomas's young wife, pregnant with his child, had been heartbroken. The couple's son had been born healthy, but despite the happiness about the new life, Charlene was still depressed, and it was uncertain when she would recover. Nicolas wished her all the best, though in his heart he knew that no person would fully recover from such a strike of fate.

Out of the corner of his eye, Nicolas watched a bearded man of indefinable age enter the bar, dressed in loose-fitting, stained pants and an oversized parka that must be much too warm for the summer weather. He stopped beyond the threshold, squinting in the sudden dimness of the room as if deciding whether he was at the right place.

Behind the counter, the bartender mumbled, "Oh, not this guy again."

"What guy?" Matthew asked, turning around as well.

"He's trouble."

"I bet." Nicolas tensed on his seat.

The new arrival spilled out a cluster of curses that would have shamed a marine with twenty years of professional experience, and the bartender ordered him harshly to leave. Unexpectedly, the man pulled a stone as big as his fist out of the depth of his coat pocket and threw it at the bar. It happened so fast, Nicolas gaped at the man for a split second, then pulled Burmeister with him to the ground. They landed with a hard thud, and Burmeister yelped with surprise while behind them glass shattered. A guest shrieked to call the police while diving for cover. Several guests fled the scene toward the rear exit.

Matthew evaded the stone, drew his weapon and pointed it at the intruder. "Hands up! Get on the ground! Now! Down, get down!"

"Down? I'll give you down!" His voice was loud and harsh, tinted by the influence of alcohol.

"On the ground, or I'll shoot!" Matthew yelled, stepping closer.

"Yeah, yeah, whatever." The man made it down to his knees with considerable effort, swayed, then used his hands to steady himself on the floor. "It was but a stone, man, not a missile!"

"Down on the ground!" Matthew approached, looking

toward the entrance, then back to the intruder.

Nicolas was back on his feet, weapon in hand, pointing at the bearded man and nodding his agreement when Matthew signaled he would holster his gun to take out the handcuffs. Nicolas looked at Burmeister, who made it to his feet, slowly. "You okay?"

"Yes, I think so." Burmeister exhaled noisily. He had visibly paled. "He's here for me? Then it was a miss." He turned to look at the shattered glasses and bottles. "And a crude one."

Matthew handcuffed the intruder. "Who are you? What's your name? And why did you throw a stone at the bar?" He pushed him on the nearest chair and pulled out his cellphone to call two more agents from the bureau.

"He gave me the boot!" the man shouted and pointed with his chin at the bartender, who reappeared behind the counter, pale around the nose. "I wasn't drunk the last time, but he doesn't want no normal people here! Just the rich putzes!" He spat on the table.

"Oh, really. Just a disgruntled guest." Burmeister climbed the bar stool and quaffed off his drink. "My god, what a day!"

Nicolas checked the entrance and the sidewalk in front of the bar, but there were no more men waiting with stones or clubs to stir unrest.

"Spring and Addleton are on their way," Matthew said, putting away his phone. He turned back to the handcuffed drunkard. "All right, your name?"

"Brad Pitt."

"I won't play that game with you." Matthew searched the man's pocket, but didn't find an ID or wallet. "Great. I bet you're in the system. It's a matter of time until we get your name."

Nicolas turned back to the bar. The whiskey with the melted ice was tempting, but he resisted. "Are you hurt?"

Burmeister shook his head. His hands were trembling. "No, no, you did the right thing. Could've been something much worse than a stone. I mean, I hadn't expected something like that." He squinted at Nicolas. "Sorenson wasn't clubbed to death, was he?"

The bartender frowned at Nicolas, then abruptly turned away to fetch a hand-broom and dustpan. Along the bar, the few guests who had remained were getting up again and returned to their seats cautiously. The couple who had entered in a bad mood looked shaken. He pressed her hand in assurance, and she replied with a small smile, darkened with worry. He helped her sit down, and she quickly emptied her glass, mumbling words Nicolas didn't understand.

"We'll need the video footage from the time span of the attack," Nicolas told the bartender. "Just to be on the safe side."

"Sure." The bartender finished sweeping up the broken glass, went into the adjacent room and returned, shaking his head. "Sorry, sir, no can do. Something's wrong with the recording. Looks like it didn't start when I opened up."

"It usually starts automatically?"

"Yes, it's on a timer so we can't forget it."

"Great. Did you have any visitors prior to opening today? Maybe a craftsman? Someone you didn't know but who wanted access to the rooms behind the bar?"

"No, not that I know of."

"Is there a locked door in the back where you keep the recordings?"

"No. When I open up, everything's open." He scoffed. "It's not locked like a bank, you know."

Nicolas turned his attention back to Burmeister. "Sir, what's wrong?"

Burmeister opened his mouth and touched his chest. "Can't breathe," he muttered between gasps. "It's . . . it's getting hard to breathe."

"The drink. Fuck!" Nicolas found the counter empty. "Hey, where did you put the glass?"

The bartender looked offended. "In the sink. It was empty, so I—"

"Damn it!" Nicolas pulled out his phone and dialed nine-one-one. "This is FBI Agent Nicolas Hayes, I need an ambulance at the *On the Rocks Bar* on Ninth Street. Possible poisoning." He added the symptoms and told the dispatch that the assassin might have used fentanyl. On the other side of the counter, the bartender's eyes widened while Burmeister held tight to the counter rim. When Nicolas finished the call, Burmeister looked close to collapsing. "The ambulance will be here in a few minutes." He looked at the bartender. "Lock the back door, don't let anyone go. I'll have some questions for the guests."

The bartender nodded and walked off.

"Poison?" Burmeister asked weakly and allowed Nicolas to help him sit more comfortably on a chair. "Yeah, right, Sorenson was—" His breathing was labored, and his eyes were about to close.

"Videotape?" Matthew asked.

"No."

Matthew turned to the intruder once more. "Who told you to throw the stone?"

He spat out again. "I won't give you nothing, you miserable fuckers."

"I will give you what you deserve—a sentence for complicity in an attempted murder."

"Are you fucking crazy? I threw a stone! That's vandalism, if it's anything. I know my rights!"

"Your distraction was used to poison the man's drink. So once again—who paid you?"

"Poison?" The intruder turned his attention toward Burmeister, who sunk down on the chair, breathing laboriously and with increasing difficulty. "I didn't know of no poison!"

Nicolas soothed Burmeister with words, yet when the executive looked up, he saw panic in the man's eyes. "The ambulance — do you hear the siren? It's coming."

"You don't know what poison, do you?" Burmeister wheezed.

"Not precisely, no, but I have a guess."

"Oh, great." Burmeister closed his eyes and went limp in Nicolas's arms.

Nicolas lowered him to the floor, putting his jacket under Burmeister's head. He checked his pulse. "He's going down fast. It must've been a high dosage."

Matthew shook the intruder. "Once more — who hired you?"

"It . . . it was a man. Fuck! I don't even know what *I* look like! So how should I know about him? He was just a man with cash." The intruder stared at Burmeister on the floor, then looked up at Matthew. "He paid me a hundred bucks for following the man with the one ear into the bar and throwing a stone." He shrugged, and his voice got a hysterical note. "I was just here to throw a stone!"

"What did he look like? Remember it, man! Was he here when you came in?"

"No! I don't know . . . anything anymore. Leave me alone, for fuck's sake!"

"White? Young? Old? Tall?"

"White. Beard, sunglasses. Can't say how old. An adult, that's for sure. Quite good clothes. Looked expensive."

"Damn it! That's nothing!"

"I told you!"

"When did he hire you?"

"Two days ago, outside the diner on the other side of the street."

"Directly in front of it?"

"No, in the alley."

Two paramedics rushed into the bar, looked left and right, and quickly knelt beside the unconscious Burmeister. "Gimme the details," the first man ordered Nicolas, who summarized the situation. "Fentanyl, you say?"

"Or any other clear liquid poison that would work in a drink, and quickly."

"All right. We'll take care of him."

Next came Spring and Addleton. Matthew brought them up to speed and asked them to help interview the guests. The paramedics left the bar with Burmeister on a stretcher.

"I'll drive with them," Matthew decided. "You take care of the guests' statements."

"Will do.

Matthew exhaled noisily. "I hadn't thought this would go south so fast." He shook his head. "I need a smoke. Man, I need a smoke."

Nicolas couldn't agree more. He turned toward the shocked guests and started asking questions.

CHAPTER ELEVEN

The couple who had argued on the way into the bar remembered the guest sitting to their left and closest to Nicolas. Both described the stranger as an overweight white male in his thirties, dressed in a dark suit and matching tie. He wore glasses and a beard and had ogled the woman without saying a word. The woman said she had seen his perfect teeth when he smiled. Both guests remembered that he had made a move to the left when the stone flew, and that he dove to the ground next. After that, they hadn't seen him again and assumed he had left like several other guests through the back door while the couple had taken shelter under a table.

Nicolas ran a hand through his hair, took down the names and address of the couple—they were indeed married—and thanked them for their cooperation.

The bartender confirmed the description and added that the man had ordered a drink in clipped words, paid, and then sat quietly until the attack had happened. Miraculously, his lowball glass had vanished with him. The bartender hadn't detected any accent or identified the man as a frequent guest. He didn't remember any unmistakable tattoos or rings on the man's hands, only that they had been clean and well-manicured.

The elderly man at the table, who had ordered the bourbon, explained he had seen the man with the glasses lean across the counter for a moment. He remembered the move because everyone else tried to get away from where the stone hit. He couldn't tell what the man had done, but to Nicolas it was obvious that the intruder's stone attack had been a diversion to gain the second the murderer needed to empty a vial with poison into Burmeister's drink. The elderly man had also noticed how quick the stranger had been—very agile. The stranger had hurried for the back door, much quicker than the elderly guest would have given him credit for, considering his paunch.

At the first table, the intruder whined about the harsh treatment and that he didn't know why the stranger had wanted him to throw a stone. Somehow, the strange benefactor must have known about his grudge and had played on him in the most efficient way.

Addleton looked at Nicolas. "Your guy is clever. If I have it right, he had this planned at least for a week. Any idea?"

"Take down the description, needle him for details. Maybe our guy had something on him that might help identify him."

"Will do. I also checked for cameras near the diner. Nada. Well, there are traffic cams, but not one is directed at the alley. The guy knows exactly what he's doing. Oh, by the way, if you had Umberto Bianchi on your mind as a suspect—forget him. The surveillance team said he was out of town, somewhere in Lorton, Virginia, in a house of . . . well, I'd say it belongs to Luigi Vianone, but no one has seen him. Umberto's not your man, not in this case."

Nicolas stared at the floor, hands on his hips, pondering why Vianone had left DC and whether he knew about the surveillance team. In that case, their efforts to find evidence against Vianone were doomed to fail.

Umberto's fighting skills and his strength impressed the average shop owner. When *Umberto the Bruiser* arrived, they paid their debts to prevent him from demolishing their stores. Umberto wasn't keen on destroying shelves and counters. He aspired to more important tasks. He wanted to become a re-spected man beyond his ability to bully frightened citizens who had the misfortune to run their shops in districts Luigi Vianone controlled. Sighing with regret, he collected Birks's money, stuffed the thick envelope in his bag, and went back to his car where Drago waited, smoking like he always did. Umberto considered his partner a walking dead man—al-ready preserved from the inside. He couldn't believe that a chain smoker like him would turn forty-four in a week. He had already announced a big party, and Umberto regretted he couldn't take Michael with him. However, his private life had to remain private. If anyone watched him kiss Michael, the crew would reject him, and he wouldn't put it beyond Luigi to kill him for such *scandalous behavior.*

Umberto sat behind the wheel, ignoring Drago blowing smoke out of his lungs. He wished Italian men were open to change, but their conservative view of the world prohibited acknowledging the mere existence of homosexuality. If any-one asked, Italian men would deny vehemently that a man could feel love for another man. Catholicism didn't permit thinking outside the box. Even if the members of the clergy knew under the radar that priests and bishops had sex with men inside and outside the church, no one dared to say a word about it. If Umberto wanted to stay with Michael, he would have to do so secretly.

His lover was on his mind during the ride. He dropped off Drago downtown and headed home. If anything, he wanted to drag Michael through the house, tie him up, and do him as hard as his lover permitted. His growing member pressed against the fabric of his pants, aching dully the longer the ride lasted. Umberto wanted to shake off his clothes and indulge in sex for the rest of the day. He missed a stop sign at a cross-roads and gasped when a car coming from his right braked at the last moment. Wild honking followed, shaking Umberto out of his trance of anticipation. His heart beating in his throat, he slowed the SUV and concentrated on the traffic ahead.

Michael's car was in the driveway, and Umberto hastened into the house. "I'm home!" he shouted, as joyous as any cartoon character. Quickly, he stashed his bag and weapon in his study and locked it from the outside when Michael turned the corner, wearing his dazzling smile.

"Now, you're in a fabulous mood."

"I am, indeed." Umberto kissed Michael, taking in the scent of his cologne, and relieving him of his shirt while placing more hungry kisses on his lover's cheek and neck.

"Wo-ho, you've been deprived of attention all day, huh?"

Umberto was breathless. "I would like to —"

"Do it." Michael seemed pleased with the sudden development. He opened his arms wide, smiling broadly. "Do with me what you want, and I promise I'll use the safe word when you push me too far. All right?"

Umberto was genuinely surprised. He looked into Michael's beautiful eyes and found the agreement he had hoped for. His lover would play along. Umberto's voice dropped as he pushed Michael toward the bedroom. "Lose your clothes."

Michael made a show of undressing, looking like the incarnation of a sex god — all temptation in a perfectly sculpted body. He cocked his head. "Like what you see?"

"I want —"Umberto stopped, wiped his mouth, and nodded curtly. "You'll do what I tell you." He dropped his pants and underwear to the floor. Michael understood his wishes without a word and knelt in front of him. Half-erect already, Umberto closed his eyes as he pressed his member against Michael's lips. "Suck me. Suck me hard."

Michael obliged.

Sitting on a plastic chair at the hospital, waiting for the results of Burmeister's examinations, Nicolas's thoughts returned to Jacklyn and her skills. Because Jason couldn't name Elaine's closest friends—he had met only a few of them—and admitted he didn't know how to organize the baby shower, Jacklyn had volunteered to prepare their house for the party, invite guests, and order food and drink. Jason was genuinely happy that Jacklyn instead of his mom contributed to the success. From their long years of partnership, Nicolas knew that Jason, son of rich parents, preferred to ignore the fact that he had been born with a silver spoon in his mouth.

When the Beckhams had arrived at the party, they'd attempted to blend into the guest crowd but failed as miserably as a tiger at a party of antelopes. Mr. Beckham senior made a noisy entrance of hugging and kissing both Elaine and the baby, and Mrs. Beckham looked like she would faint with excitement about being a grandma, finally.

Nicolas wasn't surprised they'd made a show out of their gift—a fifty-thousand dollar donation to a bank account, meant to earn interest over the years to supply their granddaughter with money for her college years and beyond. Jason had looked like he wanted to drop into a hole and vanish— not because of the money, but because of his embarrassment about his parents' show of generosity.

Elaine, the positive, always happy looking and indestructibly charming wife, hugged both her parents-in-law, praised the gift, and had a picture taken with the family and the account check. The Beckhams were very happy, more so when she claimed that their gift was very much appreciated.

Later that day—when the Beckham seniors had left—Jason apologized to the remaining guests about his parents' obtrusive behavior. He blushed when he was praised for behaving so unlike his elder parents. He confessed to Nicolas that such behavior was the reason he didn't invite his friends to a party whenever his parents were involved. They tended to make a show of everything.

Nicolas missed having Jason at his side.

The doctor appeared from the opposite room, and Nicolas and Matthew got up.

"What can you tell us about the poison?" Matthew wanted to know.

"It was fentanyl. Yes, you have every right to be relieved. Your assertion and the fact that the victim was brought here so quickly saved his life. The dosage was high enough to kill a horse, if you don't mind my wording."

"So Mr. Burmeister will recover?" Nicolas asked.

The doctor was in his early fifties, white-haired and severe looking. His nametag said *Dr. Coster*, and he would have fitted in with every daily hospital show on TV. "We administered the antidote, but because of the amount of fentanyl, he'll take a while to recover." He looked at Nicolas across his half glasses. "You can't talk to him right now, if that was implied by your question."

Matthew frowned. "To let him off the hook, Mr. Burmeister must be declared dead. He's become the victim of a clever killer" — he interrupted the doctor's contradiction — "if we can save his life by lying, we will do it."

"As you wish." Dr. Coster huffed and pressed his lips tight. "But I'm not willing to tell his parents that their son has perished. That's either your task, or you inform them about the scheme."

"To make it work, he must be transferred to another wing of the hospital, as quietly as possible."

"I'm aware that secrecy is needed." Dr. Coster bristled. "Be assured that our staff handles patients with great care and discretion."

"All the better," Matthew said. "Do it right now while we call for reinforcements to have Mr. Burmeister protected."

When the doctor left, Matthew turned to Nicolas, smiling. "Congratulations. You saved the first victim of the Rattler without breaking into a sweat."

"We were lucky."

"Oh, come on, take a praise when you get it. You can invite me for a coffee while we're still here."

"Hospital brew? No, thanks. Addleton told me Umberto Bianchi can't be the killer. He was out of town. We're back at square one."

"Not quite. Vianone is behind these killings—I'm sure of that. The White-Collar Division confirmed that a few of the companies we named can be traced back to him. It's obvious the goon wants to push competitors out of the race and bring the building industry around DC to heel. If he can't cow competitors to drop their offers, he has them killed. As we have seen in the greater Miami area, the companies falter, and Vianone can either buy them or destroy them. He's trying the same MO here. If the executives don't grant the contracts to him, he acts—quickly and brutally."

Nicolas rested his hands on his hips. He was exhausted, and it showed in his way of speaking. "These kinds of murders need preparation. The killer was sure that Burmeister would appear at the bar today. He had the old man bribed for the attack and was already there when we came in. Even the fact that Burmeister showed up with company didn't give him pause. He's a very crafty fellow."

"And cocksure that he would get away. He was right beside you. What did you see?"

Nicolas felt like being hit in the gut. *Right beside him* meant he should have been able to arrest the man before he could pour poison into the victim's drink. "The same man the couple saw—a cleverly disguised murderer. I bet nothing on him was the real issue."

"Only his eyes. You can't cloak the eyes."

"He was wearing glasses, and they reflected the light behind the bar."

"Well, damn."

"But his skin was . . . too smooth for a man in his thirties. He had a tan, and the beard was too dark to match the hair." Nicolas frowned, trying to recall the details. "I bet he's younger than thirty and cleanly shaven. Let's assume that the suit was also part of the cover."

"You mean like a fat suit to pretend he was overweight?"

"Yes. A cushion under the shirt looks like pounds of belly fat. And the elderly guest said the man was very fast as he headed for the back exit."

"If I add this up, we're looking for a guy in his twenties, probably of normal weight. He's highly intelligent, knows about special effects and makeup art, and he does a lot of research about his potential victims way ahead of the crime. Which means he must have known about Burmeister bidding for the municipal contract the moment the offer was placed."

"Let's stick with Vianone for a moment."

"Can we take a stroll to the coffee machine? I need caffeine."

They walked down the aisle to a guest area with small tables and ten plastic chairs.

Nicolas used his fingers to specify. "Vianone knows the market in DC and in the larger cities in Maryland and Virginia. He knows who his competitors are. He would be able to provide the killer with the names so the man can prepare for eventualities—like Sorenson. He had ventured into DC territory just recently and already made connections. Sorenson's company was big enough to snatch larger contracts and thus take what Vianone considers his."

They reached the vending machine, and Matthew fished some coins out of his pants pocket. "You say Vianone handed the killer a list and just tells him where to strike? That's rich."

He got a cup of coffee and cautiously tested the hot brew. "It's not that bad — for a hospital."

"Fact is, his goal is to take over the market. If we declare Burmeister dead, Vianone won't find another opponent." He looked down the aisle to Burmeister's room. "I want to draw the killer out. Let's say Burmeister's in bad shape, in the ICU. The killer can't let that slip. Vianone wants results — the deadline was today at sixteen hundred. Burmeister didn't withdraw his offer, and he is still alive." He met eyes with Matthew. "We take Burmeister out of the line of fire and lure the killer in to complete his goal."

"Do we have a one-eared agent we can use as bait?"

His first rush of arousal sated, Umberto leaned back against the headboard of the bed, still breathing raggedly. He patted Michael's muscular leg and when his lover turned on his back, then extended his hand to caress his shaft and scrotum. Michael looked at him through half-closed eyes. He wasn't smiling. Umberto had taken advantage of Michael's obedience and felt bad about it, in spite of his lover's permission to do what he wanted. It wasn't Umberto's intention to misuse the freedom Michael granted him so willingly. The comparison to a toy entered Umberto's mind. Making up for the mistake, he bent forward to kiss Michael's salty lips. "Thank you," he whispered full of emotion. "You were wonderful."

Michael lifted his head an inch. "That sounds like a line from a bad movie — it's the moment before the lover turns into a killer and murders his victim in cold blood."

Umberto huffed. "You take me to be a killer?"

"I just said you sound like an actor in a movie. I don't think you'd kill anyone over bad sex."

"I might. But you're on the safe side," Umberto replied, laughing. "The sex was *a-fucking-mazing*." He kissed Michael again, more sensuously. The attraction was great enough to stir his interest right away. He felt invigorated in Michael's presence, like a man regaining strength after a long period of weakness. He would find a way to get rid of Luigi. Then he would take his lover and move somewhere to start a new life. They would have plenty of money and no one to fear. The name Umberto Bianchi would stand for perseverance, for righteousness. He would do what Eduardo had not been able to do because someone had the old man killed at a time when Eduardo had been pondering his successor. By now, Umberto assumed that Luigi had killed his elder brother and no longer accepted the story that a foreigner had tried to take over Eduardo's business in Florida. Luigi's ruthlessness knew no boundary. "I want more," Umberto whispered in Michael's ear. "Let me tie you up."

"Gladly, but could I get a break and a bite? My stomach's rumbling."

Umberto smacked his lips on Michael's belly and helped him get up. "I wouldn't want you to starve." He winked at him. "Would be less fun for me, huh?"

Michael smiled instead of answering. When he got up from the bed, Umberto remained behind to watch the curves of Michael's back and ass—how the muscles rippled beneath the tanned skin as he moved gracefully. Michael looked back over his shoulder, and Umberto wished he had a photo of that pose.

"Are you coming?"

Umberto slipped off the bed and cupped Michael's smooth butt cheeks. "I'll follow you wherever you go. And right now, I won't let you have more than a bite before I claim you again."

"That's a promise?"

"That's a promise."

The FBI press release contained the information that agents of the FBI bureau in DC had warded off an attack on the company owner Warren Burmeister in the afternoon. Burmeister was alive and in the ICU. His condition was stable, but the doctor claimed he wasn't out of the woods yet. Burmeister's parents arrived in Washington, and the reporters beleaguered them on their way to the hospital entrance. Mr. Burmeister senior informed the assembled journalists that he offered a reward for any clues that would lead to the identification and arrest of the murderer. When pressed by reporters about the murder of Sorenson, FBI Senior Agent Sullivan added, grudgingly, that the killer might be responsible for more murders in the DC area. The news shook loose a cacophony of questions Sullivan answered as briefly as possible before he accompanied the parents into the building.

On his way home, Nicolas heard a clipped version of the press conference on the radio. After security for Burmeister had been established, Sullivan selected an agent who matched Burmeister in size and appearance — excluding the detail of a missing ear — to take over the victim's place in the ICU unit for the night. Matthew and Nicolas expected the killer to strike fast to please his client. The agents at the hospital were dressed like male nurses and clinic staffers and should be present all night. An additional agent waited in the ICU room while the other one rested in the bed.

Matthew had joked that Sullivan would go nuts should the killer not appear in the next few hours, because he had his speech about the successful arrest already in his drawer.

However, there was no way to foresee the *Rattler's* actions. No one knew how clever he truly was or whether he had an accomplice working at the hospital supplying him with information. Superstitiously, Nicolas assumed the killer had friends everywhere, for it seemed unreal how much he knew and how fast he reacted. He prayed that the killer would go for the bait and consequently deliver himself to the FBI authorities.

The search around the bar in alleys and dumpsters had been in vain. The *Rattler* had not left behind incriminating material. A camera caught him jogging toward an alley behind the bar, but the agents could not identify his face. A bulge in the jacket pocket confirmed that he had taken the empty glass from the bar to avoid leaving fingerprints. Nicolas hoped the man was in the system, which would explain his wish to go undetected. So far, this knowledge hadn't led to further action. Nicolas was furious that the FBI had no tangible clues though he had sat right next to him.

As on many occasions, Nicolas hoped to digress from his daily grind at home. Jacklyn didn't react when he called out to her. He took off shoes and jacket, locked the gun in the hallway cabinet, and went searching. He saved the bedroom for last and found a note on the bedspread.

"If you want to play, lose your clothes and chain yourself to the bedpost." Nonplussed, Nicolas looked around, expecting her to show up from behind a curtain. A pair of thick, lockable foot chains rested beside the note. "Jacky, *ma chérie*, that's not what I expected. And, no, I won't risk being locked up when I might get a call and have to go back to work." He looked around again, but Jacklyn remained hidden.

Intrigued, Nicolas searched the house once more, and when he couldn't find Jacklyn, he took a shower and dressed in casual clothes. He heard a sound upon leaving the bathroom. Instinct told him to fetch his gun, but he wouldn't risk a delay should the intruder try to sneak through the bedroom and get away. Heart beating in his throat, he moved as quietly as possible toward the sound, aware that his chance of defeating a burglar lay in surprise.

He burst open the bedroom door, ready to go into combat.

Jacklyn jumped to the right, shrieking with surprise. To the left, Lesley flattened against the closet, torn between shock and laughter.

"You scared the bejesus out of me!" Jacklyn complained, pressing a hand on her heart.

"Me, too." Lesley gave herself up to hilarity. "You should've seen your face."

Nicolas exhaled, lowering his chin to his chest. After Katherine Nelson's assault, his sense of security at his home had diminished, so he needed a moment to digest that he wasn't in imminent danger. "This isn't funny, Jacky, not in the least."

"I thought it was very funny." Lesley snorted, pointing at Jacklyn. "I told you he wouldn't go for it."

Only now did Nicolas notice that both ladies had dressed up in their mistress apparel, consisting of a lot of black leather and a short whip at the hip. He wiped his mouth, trying and failing to detect the fun in the situation.

Jacklyn came to him to gently caress his back. "Too much? Too surprising?"

"You're in luck I didn't fetch my gun first."

"Uh — uh." Lesley made a face of disgust. "You'd shoot the love of your life over a prank? After all, what more could she do than announce her appearance and what she wished you to do?" When Nicolas remained quiet, she passed him by on the way back to the living room. "I said I'd bring Raiden with me, tackle your sub, and tie him up. But you didn't want that."

Nicolas looked Jacklyn in the eyes. "I ruined the prank, huh?"

"I'll live." Jacklyn kissed him chastely and whispered, "You thought we were burglars?"

Nicolas saw the sparkle in her eyes and the blossoming smile. "Yeah. I was prepared to fight."

"Well . . ." She cocked her head. "What about putting up a fight with *me* and then surrendering to my superior . . . fighting skills?"

"Jacky, some days you kill me."

Michael regarded Umberto like a force of nature that could shine bright or glow dark—the latter was ominous. This late afternoon, Umberto's sex drive had taken a turn to the dark side—harsh and demanding. Michael couldn't shake the image that his lover might hit a switch in his mind that would cause him to spin out of control. It was a first for such a reaction, and Michael wondered what else his lover had in store that he didn't know yet.

Michael hoped that Umberto loved him as much as he did, so he pushed the idea away that his lover featured a dangerous streak that would lead to harm. The rational part of him realized that Umberto carried a weight on his shoulders that had nothing to do with his job as an insurance agent.

His bottom hurt. Umberto had reached the limits of what Michael could endure. The sex had been great, as always, and yet Michael enjoyed the hot shower to relax and come back to his senses. He was hungry, too, for he had gone without a decent meal since morning.

"I made us dinner," Umberto said quietly when he handed Michael a towel.

"Thank you."

"Don't be so damn surprised." Umberto's mouth twitched, but the smile didn't last. "I know . . . I know I was . . ." He took a deep breath, then pulled Michael close for a kiss. "I saw your expression. I know I went too far, but I needed . . . never mind." He tousled Michael's hair. "Come on, let's have a bite."

Michael slipped into boxers and shirt and followed

Umberto into the kitchen, where the delicious aroma of peppers and grilled meat watered his mouth. The table was set with large plates heaped with steaks, and a bowl with green salad and tomatoes. The peppers came sautéed in garlic oil with mushrooms and potato slices.

"All right, Mikey, before you bite your tongue — just spill it out."

"My tongue?" Michael sat down, grinning.

Umberto huffed. "Beer?"

"Water."

"Killjoy."

"I didn't know you had it in you," Michael said when Umberto poured water for him.

"Setting the table?" Umberto sat down and helped himself to steak and salad. "Or knowing how to use the stove?"

"Probably both. You leave preparing meals to me, usually."

Umberto opened a bottle of beer. "Next you'll claim that I didn't know where to find the kitchen in the house."

"You knew." Michael chose a small steak and filled the plate with mushrooms and peppers. "You found the table where to sit down and eat."

"Thank you so much."

"Yes, thank you for this great meal." Michael lowered his gaze but still observed his lover. He hadn't figured Umberto would feel regret. Maybe he was overreacting, and Umberto had the evening planned exactly like this. It was one more reason to love the Italian, in spite of the previous hour.

Michael's bottom would hurt for another day.

Nicolas was in a bad mood and not willing to play the women's submissive. Instead, he sat down with Lesley and Jacklyn for a beer and red wine and listened to their conversation. In the back of his mind, he pondered what he could have done to keep the *Rattler* from escaping. Senior Agent Sullivan had stressed his disappointment vociferously and demanded that the agents should work overtime until the killer was caught—along with Luigi Vianone as the mastermind. Matthew had apologized that he hadn't taken the killer's presence into consideration, but Nicolas saw through the charade. It had not been Matthew's task to watch the guests at the counter. It nagged him that the *Rattler* had him outmaneuvered on his own turf.

Nicolas looked up and found Lesley ready to depart. She kissed his cheek and left. Moments later, he heard her van leave the driveway.

Nicolas wiped his face with both hands. "I'm sorry I spoiled the mood," he said when Jacklyn returned to drain her glass of wine.

"Let's say, it could have gone differently, but that's the risk we take. If you come home tired and grumpy —"

"I wasn't grumpy."

"If you come home tired and grumpy, you don't have to play. We would've loved to take you away from those grievous thoughts that occupy you, but, hey, if that's not on your list for today, it's okay."

Upon his invitation, she sat on his lap. He kissed her shoulder and her bosom, breathing in her scent, enjoying the moment of closeness. "I looked forward to coming home and . . . it wasn't the right time for Lesley to be here." He glanced at her face, slightly flushed from the alcohol. "Maybe we should talk about your plans in advance?"

"No way, my Beast. That would ruin the fun." Jacklyn kissed his nose. "I won't tell you, and you don't want to know. Unless it's a special weekend."

Nicolas buried his face at her bosom and mumbled, "Yeah, special weekends. Looking forward to another one." He exhaled, looking up into her beautiful face. "But it has to wait."

Jacklyn lowered her chin and raised her brows. "Your job comes with a heavy weight on your shoulders. You need time to relax or you'll burn out."

"I know, but this case —"

She put a finger on his lips. "It's this case or another. I told you I want you to stop working and enjoy your life. My parents would provide us with money, no questions asked. My mother stressed that when we met."

"Could we, please, get past the point that I'd be the one who gives up my profession? I help putting bad guys behind bars, and when we were visiting your parents, you stated that you support me with what I do."

"Of course, I do support you. But that doesn't mean you're gonna do that for the rest of your working life."

"Maybe I'll fall up the ladder and have a job at the desk when I turn fifty."

He meant it as a joke, but Jacklyn didn't buy it. Concern showed in a steep wrinkle on her brow. "Until then, you'll risk your life and brood over cases and killers and methods of how men could be murdered. Any average guy could turn into a murderer." She lifted her hands and dropped them. "Isn't this the case? The average neighbor can become a murderer — sometimes out of revenge, sometimes out of necessity."

"I'm dealing with a contract killer. He makes money from the hits."

"He's a professional, then. It means he's making a living out of killing people. Nice company, huh?" She slipped off his lap to clear the table. "If this was my job, I'd do everything to look like the typical John Doe. I'd be nice to my neighbors and mow the lawn every Saturday. Hell, I would even learn to cook a meat loaf! I'd do everything to go under the radar."

Nicolas smiled while Jacklyn warmed up to the subject.

"First thing is — I need a credible façade, a real job, an income that I can show the IRS. Then I need enough spare time to fulfill my contracts." She closed the dishwasher with her butt and switched on the program. "If I work sixty hours a week, I won't go shooting victims, that's it." She came back to wipe down the table. "I need a secret place to stow my weapons and such, so that any official visitor to my home won't stumble over my equipment."

Nicolas frowned. "Have you ever thought about changing professions?"

She smiled mischievously and pushed a strand of hair behind her ear. "I could do a lot of professions if I had the time. But I'm too busy treating patients, which means I wouldn't keep up the assassination business and satisfy clients. That's what counts. You can't become a wanted hit man without time to do your job." She wiped vigorously at some stains. "Other than that, the idea is to kill people without being caught, right? The façade is the most important instrument."

"And being a physiotherapist wouldn't do?"

Jacklyn pursed her lips as she swirled the cloth in her hand. "I could arrange it, I guess. Now that I've got two full-time assistants, I might find enough time for stakeouts and killing the targets."

He reclined, cocking his head and replying to her smile with an appreciative nod. "As I see it, you've thought that through."

"Of course, I did." She took the cloth back to the sink in the kitchen. "As I heard on the news, the man's very clever. If you want to catch him, you must know his potential victims and protect them."

"We're doing that. We checked all relevant projects, county or state, and informed the possible contractors to be extra careful. Those executives who bid for large municipal constructions received protection by local police and are advised to eat at home and check every package to see whether it's still sealed."

"Food poisoning is his preferred method?"

"His range is much wider, but, yes, he did this four times." Once more, the image of Burmeister breaking down at the bar assaulted his mind, accompanied by a wave of guilt that made his breathing difficult.

Jacklyn returned with a glass of water in her hand, thinking. "He needs space for his equipment. A supplier. Time on a stakeout."

"Believe me, we know all of this, but the man is like a ghost." Nicolas wiped the bridge of his nose. Tiredness washed over him. "He's very careful. Cleverly disguised."

"Yes, one could meet him on the street and not know he's able to kill a person when the money is right."

Nicolas stood, unable to continue the discussion without feeling depressed. He plucked the glass out of her hand, set it onto the table, and embraced and kissed her sensuously. "You are wonderful, my love. But let's go to bed, okay?"

"Oh, an invitation to brainstorm with you? How could I resist?" She linked arms with him and led him straight toward the bedroom.

CHAPTER TWELVE

Luigi fumed. First it was a mindless trail of words, spat out at high speed, but then he suddenly turned to Umberto. "I should've sent you! I know we have our differences, but I know you're tough. You can do your job. You're reliable. That hit man . . . not so much."

"So you've hired a professional contract killer?" Umberto asked as nonchalantly as he could. His heart raced. Until now, he had assumed that Luigi had handed the task to one of his henchmen he had known for years, a man known for his skills and discretion. Such an intimate could be found and eliminated, but a contract killer—an outsider hired for nothing else but pulling the trigger—was like a shadow. Suddenly, the murder of Eduardo Vianone appeared in a different light—the contract killer had somehow gotten to the old man even though very few people knew of the location of his abode. Until now, none of Eduardo's former intimates had a clue how the poison had been added to the old man's protein shake. "For how long?"

"That doesn't concern you." Luigi drained his whiskey glass and slammed it onto the desk. "Fact is that Burmeister is still breathing, and that the killer—the man I pay a fucking lot of money—has done nothing to change that. He vanished somehow and doesn't answer my calls. No news this morning that the bastard is dead. If that asshole recovers, he'll grab the deal, and I can't do anything about it."

"You could still kill him," Drago said quietly, hesitantly.

Luigi swiveled around like a snake that found a new prey

178

to attack. "Still kill him? Yeah, right, maybe throw him under a bus when he leaves the hospital—all alone and on his own, which is very likely! Would you, please, take over the job and take his hand? I bet you're very qualified for that."

Drago frowned, and Umberto looked at the floor to hide his smile. Drago was unable to fathom the degree of irony Luigi was lashing out at him. When Drago opened his mouth, Umberto signaled him to shut it again. Drago obeyed, grumbling something unintelligible.

Luigi held out his glass for his secretary to pour more whiskey. "I want the hit man found. I want to ask him face to face why he failed so miserably. His . . . fucking stupidity cost me ten million dollars!"

The secretary had a hard time pouring whiskey while Luigi ranted on. If the matter hadn't been serious, Umberto and the rest of the men would have laughed out loud. They stood rooted, waiting for more slander and for tasks that would allow them to leave the room. Umberto couldn't remember anything being as stressful as meetings with his new boss.

"You, Umberto, take care of Burmeister. No matter the cost, I want this bastard dead and his company burned. You, Guido, take two men and try to find the hit man. I'll give you what I have on him."

Umberto was close to asking to switch tasks, but then didn't dare to appear too eager to look for the professional killer. He clenched his fists and kept his poker face, though it cost him.

"You can leave," Luigi told him, waving his hand. "Put a bullet in the man's head and be done with him."

Umberto left for his car, astonished and at the same time wary. For the first time, Luigi had given him an important task—in the eyes of the boss—but Umberto was reluctant to fulfill it, mainly because Luigi wanted Burmeister dead despite the dangerous circumstances. *Is this his strategy to get rid of me?* Umberto pondered his options of acting against his boss. If there had been a possibility of handing Luigi to the FBI and salvaging the enterprise, Umberto would have done it. However, involving the federal agency implied the entire empire would be dismantled and his inheritance ruined. Umberto wanted to retire with style on a small island, not work at some packing company for a few bucks. If he wanted to get to the top, he had to move carefully and keep the boss pleased until the time was right to kill him.

Unfortunately, that included killing Warren Burmeister.

"Nothing during the night?" Senior Agent Sullivan asked pointedly as he stood at Nicolas's desk.

"No, sir. The night was uneventful. I had the entire food and beverage stock at Burmeister's home examined." He made a face. "The killer had the filtered water in the refrigerator poisoned. He must have been at Burmeister's home prior to visiting the bar."

"Video surveillance?"

"No, sir."

"So I assume you have no new leads on the killer, right?"

"Not at this time, no." Nicolas faced his superior, bracing for more accusations about why he hadn't arrested the Rattler when he was close to him. "The agents on the ground changed shifts. Burmeister is recovering, but couldn't add any useful information."

"And the man who threw the stone?"

"He's still in custody. Montagna and I will talk to him again in an hour."

Sullivan cleared his throat. "Summing up, we have more chances to find the killer using the reward the Burmeister family promised than with the entire equipment of the bureau." He left with a distinctive stare.

Nicolas assumed his boss held him responsible for the failure. Grumpy and searching his mind for a solution, he picked up the phone at the first ring. "Agent Hayes."

"This is Burmeister. I'm calling you because your fellow agent told me that you're still searching for clues to the man who poisoned me."

"Do you remember something?"

"His shoes." He laughed when Nicolas remained quiet. "Yes, I have the knack of accents but also of shoes. Maybe I'm a woman and don't know it. Anyway, the shoes were expensive—I'd say handmade in Italy. Finest leather. They were like glued to his feet."

"Thank you, that's a good piece of information."

"It's my hope that if that runs true, you might find the dealer in town. Since they are exclusive and expensive, there can't be so many people buying them, right?"

"That's true. How are you feeling?"

"Much better. The doc said something about washing the poison out of my system, and it works. I hope to be home by tomorrow."

"Maybe not home, but out of the hospital. Until we'll have found the man, I advise you not to return home. The FBI has a safe house."

Burmeister was silent for five seconds. "Not a chance that I can return to my work, either, huh? I should've bailed out and done with it. But I'm not willing to give a crook what he wants."

"We'll keep you protected." Even when he said it and Burmeister remained quiet, he felt foolish. "At least, we'll try," he added.

"That's what we all do, isn't it?"

The Rattler knew what he was worth—a man for hire, a

contract killer with success guarantee. The failure at the bar was a stain on his reputation. It bothered him in many ways — future clients wouldn't trust him, and — worse — the current client would threaten him with retaliation even though he didn't know him. They had never met in person.

He played out every possible scenario — how could he kill Burmeister without alarming the FBI right away? It was obvious that the FBI had set a trap. The announcement of Burmeister being in critical condition was meant for the killer to come and try to fulfill his mission. The Rattler considered the possibility that Burmeister was dead — given the amount of fentanyl he had poured into the drink. Only if the agent had reacted on the spot and judged the poison correctly would the victim stand a chance.

From what he had learned watching the streets surrounding the hospital, the police and FBI forces were present like spiders waiting for the fly to show up. He dismissed the chance that he might get into the hospital unnoticed. Maybe he could get to him later, at a safe place, at an unknown place, when the FBI was less vigilant. Even that option had only a ten percent chance of success. Used to killing stealthily, the Rattler avoided clashing with police forces. He wasn't equipped for a war-like combat situation.

He assessed the amount of poison he had left. If his client continued to have him murder people at this insane rate, he must buy more fentanyl from his dealer and hope that the man would keep his mouth shut. He expected every dealer to become a whistle-blower eventually. If threatened hard enough, they would give the police or the FBI what they wanted. Cautiously, the Rattler put out feelers to two dealers in a different district. The enterprise was time-consuming and risky, but he had no choice.

In the afternoon, he had what he needed and looked at three missed calls from his client, most probably demanding results — Burmeister dead. He couldn't help his client in this case. The FBI protected Burmeister to a degree that made it impossible to get close — not as a nurse, not as a false doctor. The Rattler was a professional, not a magician. When he replied to the insistent calls, his client told him he would find another assassin to get rid of Burmeister and terminated the call, shouting obscenities.

The Rattler didn't know whether he should feel insulted or relieved. He took the decision lying down and hoped that the chosen assassin would get an overview on the ground before drawing his weapon. Should that man be successful, the Rattler would bow and buy him a drink.

Though he had hoped to detect a weakness, Umberto had to admit that he could not get into the hospital to kill Burmeister as Luigi demanded. The hospital swarmed with FBI agents — he could smell their presence on the streets and on the corridors. Umberto dropped the idea of entering the hospital pretending he needed help with a head wound when the first guy he met wore a small, wired headset. Quickly, before any one of the staff noticed him, Umberto left again, heart pounding against his ribs, barely maintaining a normal gait instead of breaking into a run. The hospital looked like an outpost of the FBI headquarters — too dangerous for the average criminal.

Outside in an alley, where he had parked his car, Umberto leaned against the wall and drank whiskey from a flask he carried in the car door. His breathing returning to normal, he went back to his observation point. He knew that Burmeister's parents were in town, so he tried to place a call as the victim's father. It was a shot in the dark — he didn't know whether Burmeister senior was with his son right now. When the nurse answered the call and he asked after the victim's well-being, the nurse — a young woman if he judged the voice correctly — told him with honest regret he had missed him by five minutes and that he was leaving the hospital.

Umberto thanked her and hung up. Still standing at the car with the flask in his hand, he wondered whether this was just another clever trap or an inexperienced nurse wanting to help people.

Though he was a trained marksman, he lacked the qualification of a military sharpshooter. "Indecision doesn't help," he murmured, stoppered the flask, and dialed another number on his phone.

Nicolas was at Burmeister's side on his way to the elevator. At their first meeting, the victim had been ready to spit into the gangster's face. Now, Burmeister looked tired and worn out, all vibrancy gone from his walk and his voice. He wouldn't make the same decision again — he'd rather hand his business over to Vianone and restore his peace. The miracle of life was a gift, not something you risked two days in a row. Burmeister wiped his face, took a deep breath, and asked for the fifth time whether the elevator and the garage had been checked. For the fifth time, Nicolas assured him that all kinds of precautions had been taken, and that he should consider it a positive sign that no intruder had tried to enter the hospital to get close to him.

Burmeister's silence was the same as a denial.

The elevator took them to the basement. Flanked by Nicolas and Agent Spring, Burmeister made it to the waiting black FBI van.

"This might not look like much, but the windows and doors are bullet-proof. Should an assassin try —"

"Don't tell me the odds, Agent Hayes, just get me out of here and someplace safe."

Nicolas helped him sit down and buckle up. A third agent

was driving the van out of the garage. When they came to street level, Nicolas expected an interruption—a bullet into the windshield, a car braking right in front of them, a group of heavily armed gangsters about to deliver a hail of bullets at the van. When nothing happened and the van filtered into traffic, he let go of the breath he had been holding unknowingly.

"How long do I have to hide?" Burmeister asked quietly.

"I can't tell you the exact date, sir, but we're trying to catch the killer and the man behind the assaults."

Burmeister huffed. "Cryptic FBI statement? I have a company to lead, and I can't do everything from afar. My employees need to see me in person. I have to oversee their work. They can't make decisions on their own, and some of my managers will sprout heads of greed knowing that I'm too far away to stop them." When he went on, he sounded weak and exhausted. "I didn't found this company to see it ripped apart by some kind of mob, but I won't let it go down because of bad management, either."

"I can't—" Nicolas stopped, noticing that Burmeister wasn't waiting for an answer.

The van took them out of Washington, DC, and into Virginia until they reached a quiet estate, set back from the street, in Manassas. Four agents were waiting on the premises, and Nicolas explained to Burmeister that he would be protected twenty-four-seven for as long as it was necessary.

"Don' tell anyone where you are. If you need files taken to your office, one of the agents will do it for you. Use the phone, email, video conferences—you've got the necessary equipment in an office upstairs."

Nicolas got out of the car warily. It was possible they had been followed. It was possible that the assassin had waited for Burmeister to leave the hospital because he had found out that he stood no chance against the FBI agents inside the building. Nicolas looked around, but the neighborhood was quiet, the inhabitants gone to work. He signaled Burmeister to leave the van.

"All right, get out and into the house quickly." Nicolas made eye contact with the agent to his left, then gestured Burmeister to leave the van. "Don't show yourself at the windows, and don't leave the house if it's not necessary."

"I'll lay low, if you mean that." Burmeister had obviously lost his combative stance. His smile was a vain attempt to show good spirits. He walked toward the entrance as fast as he could but was still too weak to trot. "After the ordeal, I'd be pleased to take a nap, but I can't. I have to tell Dean, who runs—"

A burst of rapid gunshots erupted from a thick shrubbery beyond the small street.

Two bullets hit Nicolas's back and propelled him forward, knocking the air from his lungs. He pulled Burmeister down with him across the patio, into the house, onto the floor.

The second agent closed the door and knelt at his side. "Are you all right?"

Nicolas wheezed as he turned away from Burmeister. His back was on fire, his lungs too tight to allow breathing. He nodded curtly, grimacing with pain.

Burmeister lifted his head wearily. "Now I understand why you insisted on a bullet proof vest. Hey, are you all right?"

"Yeah . . ." Nicolas hurt from his shoulder blades to his waist. With help from his fellow agent he made it into a sitting position while the agents outside returned fire. "What about you? Can you get up?" he asked, reaching out.

Burmeister knelt on the floor, gasping and retching. "I'm . . ."

Nicolas made it to his feet, pain coruscating across his back. He wanted nothing more than to take off the vest and breathe normally again. "I'll take you to the living room so you can lie down." Nicolas tried to help him get on his feet, but Burmeister shook his head wearily.

"I'm fucked up."

"No, you're not." Nicolas ignored the increasing pain in his back and concentrated on the bright side — neither Burmeister nor he were severely wounded. He pulled himself together even though he wanted to turn away and call it a day. "Look, sir, we're doing what we can to get you through this."

Burmeister turned his head slightly to meet Nicolas's gaze. "Don't sugarcoat that this was the second time in three days that someone tried to kill me. I want to vanish somewhere. I want to hide in a hole and not come out until you bring me the heads of those monsters on a platter." He sounded on the verge of a hysterical fit, only repressed by sheer will. Then he wheezed and with the help of the second agent made it to the couch in the living room. Burmeister looked small and vulnerable, not like a man in charge of a large company. "I survived an abduction in my youth and hoped that nothing would ever happen to me again. Hell, I thought that the fucking abduction was the worst thing that could ever happen to a man! I was wrong." He accepted the glass of water the second agent provided. His hands shook. "Thanks. Will you catch the goon with the gun?"

"The agents are here to do just that."

Burmeister scoffed again, sipped water and reclined, exhaling shakily. "And if they fail — is it another safe house then? Even more remote than this?"

"Yes, probably." Nicolas took off his jacket and the vest, slowly and carefully. He tried to put it out of sight, but Burmeister had already seen the bullets sticking in the back.

"Those were meant for me."

"And they didn't do any harm." Nicolas managed to sound positive. "I told you —"

"No, don't say it again. I know what you're trying, and I thank you for the effort." He set down the glass and rested his head against the soft couch, closing his eyes. His hands still trembled, and his voice was depressed. "This is a fucking nightmare. He'll find me sooner than later." Upon a sudden sound, he opened his eyes again and looked at Nicolas. "The time for the offers is over. Either I won or not. What's the reason for sending a killer after me now? It doesn't make sense."

Nicolas knew enough about Luigi Vianone to judge his vindictive nature but wouldn't reveal to the victim that the Italian syndicate boss had killed for far less than a ten million dollar contract. "I don't know. Maybe the killer can't be called off, and we must stop him."

"Great." Burmeister closed his eyes again. "Losing an ear hurt, but this here — this hurts worse."

Wincing, Nicolas agreed.

Michael came home, parked the car, and unloaded the groceries in the kitchen. He filled the refrigerator and cut a cucumber for the dinner salad. When Umberto didn't show up, he tried the door to his study and found it locked, as always. Unable to control his curiosity to learn more about Umberto than his lover wanted to reveal, Michael decided to take matters into his own hands. If Umberto didn't want him to know about the contents of his precious study, he would check for himself. The previous night, Umberto had locked himself up in the room on the second floor and had not come out for half an hour. Eavesdropping hadn't delivered results. Either Umberto had spoken too low or had done something else that didn't make any noise. Michael loathed secrets in general, but he certainly did not tolerate them with his lover. He considered himself worthy of knowing all secrets his lover had. How should he trust Umberto if he kept so much from him?

Vincent had never kept anything from him. From day one, Vincent had told him about his private life, his business, and how he had managed to become successful. Theirs had been a relationship on eye level. This memory was the benchmark for every other relationship Michael started.

He put on sneakers, walked into the garden, and pretended to take care of the rose bushes until he was convinced there was no neighbor working or relaxing in the adjacent gardens. In a fluid move, Michael picked up a stone the size of his fist and threw it against the window on the upper floor. The glass shattered. Michael dropped to the ground, then rushed to the back door in the shadow of the thick, outgrown hedge that needed trimming but was perfect for Michael's stealthy disappearance.

Inside, he kicked off the shoes and hurried upstairs, a set of tension tools in his hand. He needed thirty seconds for the simple lock, but hesitated to open the door, fearing his lover had a burglar alarm installed. After a moment he shook off his indecision and entered.

Michael had not expected an outstanding design with golden knobs and *Tiffany* lamps, but he was nevertheless astonished at the room's tasteful furniture and decoration. The walls were covered by large landscape paintings, the floor carpeted in a soft yellow, complemented by an old and probably expensive rug in front of the broad wooden desk. On the left side of the room, matching the hazelnut desk, stood two wooden cabinets with ten drawers each, made for storing small items or papers. Michael opened the first drawer and found some stationery. The next one held old photographs, some letters, even postcards from friends. Michael smiled. He hadn't considered Umberto to be the sentimental type who would hold on to postcards as keepsakes. He stretched his hand to finger the depth of the drawer. The lower board moved upon touch. Intrigued, Michael pulled out the drawer, emptied it and lifted the bottom. He found neatly stacked pictures, snapshots of people he didn't know, taken on streets, in restaurants, and in bars, even at a bowling alley. Some pictures carried names, some only dates. Michael flipped through the stacks without recognizing any face. Carefully, he returned the stacks to their places and pushed the drawer back in its place. Two more drawers contained plastic envelopes filled with a handkerchief, a handwritten letter, a ripped off button — all of the items hidden under the main contents of the drawer. He couldn't stop wondering what these things meant to Umberto.

Michael turned to the large paintings and detected a wall safe behind one of them. The desk drawers were locked, too, and he assumed he would have too little time to search the entire room until Umberto showed up. The computer and two screens — large enough to serve as TV sets — were switched off. Michael had no illusions that he would get access to Umberto's files without a password. He wondered, though, when Umberto had brought the equipment into the house. He couldn't remember any of the furniture or the computer being part of the move from Miami.

Walking back to the door, Michael couldn't shake the notion that his lover had secrets he couldn't even start to reveal.

Downstairs, Umberto's large SUV roared onto the driveway.

"Any luck?" Nicolas asked when Agent Addleton entered the living room.

"Traffic hampered our pursuit." Addleton sleeked back his hair and checked his appearance in the reflection of the cabinet's glass door. He adjusted his tie. "The killer got away, but narrowly."

"Do you have anything on him — license plate? Car make

and model? What he looked like?"

"Plate, yes. Make and model, of course. The BOLO is out, but I don't think we'll find anything. The killer will abandon the car in a few minutes. Where's Burmeister?"

"In bed. I urged him to take a nap. He was worn out."

"Small wonder. You look like death warmed over, too." Addleton went to the kitchen, and Nicolas followed, suppressing a whimper.

"The killer must be desperate to get to the victim." He winked at Nicolas while he poured a glass of orange juice from the refrigerator. "Do you think Vianone is leaning on him? After all, it's the first mistake the hit man has made so far."

"At least hard enough to force him to change his MO. He risked his freedom to try and shoot the victim."

"Obviously he isn't a good shot. Hence his usual, more secretive method." He pointed with the glass at Nicolas. "One more note for your whiteboard, huh? I wonder where such a young man learned how to poison people. Do you consider him a sociopath?"

"I consider him a contract killer." Nicolas's back hurt as if he had taken a severe beating. With every breath, he felt his lungs expand painfully. "He's determined, a good observer, very clever. The man who threw the stone at the bar told us that the killer had approached him a day after he had been thrown out of the bar. This means he observed not just Burmeister but also the old man. He must have a lot of time on his hands. I asked for surveillance tapes of traffic cameras, but they only keep them twenty-four hours."

Addleton leaned against the counter, frowning. "I called the HQ and asked about another safe house. They're sending an unmarked car as we speak."

"Burmeister is right—it doesn't make sense to kill him now that the deadline is over. He didn't even check whether he won the bid."

Addleton made a face. "We have nothing against Vianone without catching the shooter."

"Even if we nailed him—why do you think he'd give away his boss? Vianone survived in this business for so long because his men are loyal." Nicolas was unable to stand still, in spite of the pain in his back. The situation got to him. He wanted the killer caught and Vianone with him, if it was only to clean the stain on Nicolas's reputation. He had almost failed Burmeister twice, and he didn't trust in another location. If the killer had been able to follow them once, why shouldn't he do it a second time? The irrational thought that the killer had accomplices everywhere, even in this residential neighborhood, hit him again. He despised the notion that he was superstitious.

"There's always a trail behind a killer, something we can work on," Addleton said. "First, I would like to know the man's identity. He took the glass from the bar. That tells me that he's in the system, maybe a convicted felon. If we obtain his fingerprints and identify him, we're much closer to catching him, don't you think?"

"What about the shells? Did you find them?"

"Yes. We know the ammo he used, but as far as I can tell, we won't find fingerprints. He isn't dopey. That's not the way to catch him."

"I'll go check the perimeter," Nicolas decided and ignored Addleton's reply that there were already two men outside. He had to move or he'd go mad.

Chapter Thirteen

Michael closed the door but couldn't lock it again. He hastened downstairs and into the kitchen where he had left tomatoes, a cucumber, and lettuce. After washing his hands, he reached for a knife and a chopping board to prepare the side dish for dinner. His heart raced as he went over the words he had prepared.

Umberto embraced him from behind and sighed deeply when he rested his chin on Michael's shoulder. "You smell great, you look great, and I bet you're preparing a great dinner."

Michael grinned as he turned his head. "You're chipper tonight, huh? Hungry, too?"

Umberto pretended to bite Michael's shoulder. "Ravenous. Would you believe me when I said that this hunger won't be sated by salad?"

Michael opened his eyes wide and exclaimed, "No! Don't tell me you're turning into a naughty boy now."

"Naughty, yeah . . ." Umberto kissed Michael's shoulder and neck, exhaling with what Michael interpreted as growing desire. "Let me change clothes and freshen up, okay?"

"By then, I'll have dinner ready." Michael detected alcohol on Umberto's breath but didn't ask whether he had stopped for a drink.

"Whatever you say as long as you are ready."

Michael watched Umberto walk upstairs. He couldn't have wished for a better start to the evening. Grinning, he continued cutting vegetables, seasoned the salad with vinegar and oil and then turned to the small pork filets he had marinated.

Umberto's whistling suddenly stopped. He cursed loudly and came running down the stairs again, taking two steps at a time.

"Did you enter my study?" he hollered as he grabbed Michael at the shoulders. His face was contorted with anger.

Michael gasped and dropped the spatula he had taken from the drawer. "I know that I shouldn't so —"

"Did you?" He shook him.

"No! Why do you ask?"

"The door was unlocked, and someone threw a stone through the window." Umberto shook Michael again, harder. "Be honest! Did you walk in there?"

"You keep the door locked, don't you?" Michael freed himself from the hard grip, intimidated and yet annoyed. He retrieved the spatula and put it in the sink to fetch a new one. "I came home only minutes before you, changed clothes, and went into the kitchen. I didn't hear anyone throw a stone. I was happy that I managed to get here soon enough to start making dinner." In a tearful tone he added, "I know that you like pork, and there was this special offer —"

Umberto stepped closer. "You didn't go in there? Didn't see who threw the stone?"

"No! Damn it, Bert, don't treat me like a goon. I'm your lover, and when I tell you I wasn't in there, I wasn't, okay?" He stepped back, irritated by Umberto's rage. "You must believe me."

Umberto ran a hand across his head and breathing heavily nodded. "All right. Looks like a kid's prank. I'll call a glazier tomorrow and have the window replaced." He turned toward the stairs. "Sorry, but . . . I don't want anyone to go in there, not even you."

"Family secrets?" Michael smiled tentatively.

"Yeah, something like that."

Michael turned back to the stove and poured oil into the pan.

Though the dinner was delicious — light and tasty — Michael couldn't calm down and relax. Umberto had believed his lie — maybe he thought that he hadn't locked the door in the morning. Remnants of fear remained. Michael knew that Umberto was cunning. There was a restlessness, an energy about the man that was both intriguing and frightening. Michael didn't want to be in the center of the man's fury, and the scene in the kitchen was the closest he ever wished to get to his lover's dark side.

They cleared the table together, still in awkward silence. When Umberto proposed watching a movie, Michael obliged and started searching the online services. Umberto's cell phone rang. Rolling his eyes, Umberto took the call and retreated upstairs, as he usually did. Michael remained in the living room, straining in vain to catch part of the conversation.

When Umberto came downstairs, he was completely dressed and had his car keys in his hand. "I'm sorry, but something came up. I have to go."

"Company business? Again?"

"Don't be glum." Umberto kissed Michael's forehead. There was regret in his eyes. "I'll be back as soon as I can."

"What kind of boss calls you late in the evening and expects you to show up in person? Can't you —"

"I have to go." Umberto put on his shoes. "I'll make up for this."

Michael forced a laugh. "Ah, really, now you sound like a husband talking to his wife of twenty years. And she knows that nothing ever changes, and that you can't make up for anything."

Umberto frowned, but left without another word. Michael

sat on the couch, pondering whether Umberto would have locked the room. He had no interest in a movie anymore.

If there was anything Umberto loathed more than someone trying to betray him, it was Luigi Vianone's constant complaining and bickering. This evening was no exception. When Umberto took his place in front of the small desk at the hideout's main room, Luigi was smoking a cigar, drinking whiskey, and rambling about competitors and how hard it was to find qualified people, who know how to do their jobs.

Umberto braced for a two-hour monologue of how bad Luigi's day had been while his thoughts were with Michael. His lover had looked annoyed upon his departure, far less understanding of Umberto's *work situation* than before. The idea that Michael had indeed entered his study crossed his mind, though he wanted to believe his young lover with all his heart. Doubts remained because he was certain he had locked the door.

"Oh, you," Luigi exclaimed, pointing with the cigar. "You've left me a fine mess! Great! A trained ape could've done better!"

"What are you talking about?" Umberto asked with the coolness of a man who had nothing to hide. "I did what you asked for and trailed Burmeister."

"But the fucking man isn't dead! Still. Not. Dead!" He emptied the glass and crashed it on the desk. "Drago! Why the fuck did you task Drago with this, for fucks sake? Aren't you man enough to pull the trigger yourself?"

"You told me time and again what an excellent shooter Drago is. That's why I called him. I told him to follow me to where the FBI was heading with Burmeister, and he did the rest." Umberto shrugged, pretending to be shocked by the failure. "I didn't know he couldn't pull it off." He looked around deliberately. "Where is he? Did the FBI arrest him?"

"He's not that stupid, you moron!" Luigi walked toward the large open doors leading toward the patio and back again. "He's in hiding. He got rid of the car and the weapon. The only clever thing he did today." Luigi shook his head. The thick vein at his neck was pulsing rhythmically. "Damn it! How hard can it be to off one single man?"

Hard enough to fail twice. Umberto kept his mouth shut. By granting Drago the honor of killing Burmeister, he had shown his obedience to Luigi's preferred soldier, and—now that Drago had missed—he celebrated his adversary's deep fall from grace. Drago knew he shouldn't show up, not only because he might lead the FBI to the safe house but for fear he might end with a bullet in his heart and a grave at sea.

Luigi took up pacing again. "It's not over yet, but that's not my main concern." He turned his focus on Guido. "Where's the fucking contract killer? I gave you the leads, so where is he?"

"It wasn't much," Guido said with a touch of defiance, but he avoided direct eye contact. "We tried to find him through the money, but it was a dead end. It appears he changes accounts frequently. The one you gave me—it was already dead. That's not the way to find him. He could be anywhere."

"No, for fuck's sake! He's still in town. I'm sure of that. I sent him the name of another target, and I bet he'll go for it." He crashed the stub of the cigar in the ashtray. Ash flew in every direction. "He won't forego the money."

Umberto wondered whether this was wishful thinking—a killer with this reputation would find work everywhere—when a shot crashed through the patio door, knocking Luigi off his feet. Umberto thought—hoped—that the contract killer might have turned his allegiance and fired at his boss. He pulled his gun and took position at the left door. He didn't see the shooter through the trees and shrubbery as long as the man stood still. His accomplices stood to his right while another one pulled Luigi out of harm's way.

"What the hell's happening?" Luigi screamed. The Italian millionaire and top dog when it came to illegal businesses suddenly went pale in the face. His voice was high. "Shoot that damn bastard, whoever he is!" Cursing viciously, he held his right arm where blood seeped through the shirt. "Shoot him! Go! Go!"

Weapons drawn and ready, Umberto and Guido entered the patio. Quickly, they made out a silhouette running for the back fence.

From the left, another of Luigi's goons joined the hunt. "He's heading south!" he shouted into his headset.

Umberto was the fastest of the three men and took his stance when the intruder reached the back gate to slip through. He fired two shots in quick succession, and the enemy went down, screaming.

Guido ran past him and knelt beside the unmoving stranger. "Two hits and he's still breathing."

"The boss wants him for an interrogation, I'm sure of that," Umberto replied in the deepest voice he could manage. He had aimed to kill, but obviously it wasn't the day for a killing. Holstering his gun, he asked, "Does he have anything on him?"

"No. Probably left his stuff in the car." He handed Umberto the keys.

Umberto turned to the third man. "Alonso, check the surrounding streets, find his car, and come back with anything you find about him—papers, receipts, anything that tells us who he is and who sent him. Be thorough!"

"Eagle's eyes, you know." Alonso took the keys and jogged down the street.

Umberto and Guido put the man back on his feet and dragged him toward Luigi's office. The boss was sitting on a broad armchair, and his secretary buzzed about him, cooing like a mother hen. If this had not been a serious, even life-threatening situation minutes ago, it could have been a scene from a comedy. The secretary wore a short skirt and high heels, a blouse with too many open buttons, and so much makeup, it was like she was auditioning for a movie role. She had cut away the sleeve and was staunching the bleeding with gauze while Luigi rambled how he would take revenge on anyone trying to snuff him. As far as Umberto could see, Luigi had suffered a superficial wound to his right arm, mainly because he had turned to the left the moment the shot had been fired. Umberto kept a poker face to hide his disappointment. It would have been a wonderful evening with Luigi dead and the shooter caught. In order to establish a grand standing, Umberto would have tortured the assassin and then shot him like an executioner. Luigi's men would have applauded him for his brutality and then pledged him their allegiance. *Wishful thinking*.

"That's the fucking assassin?" Luigi hollered. "I'll have him castrated first and killed last!"

Umberto pressed the stranger into the second armchair. The man's head lolled to the side. He was still unconscious from the impact of two bullets in his right shoulder blade. The stranger wore black jeans, black shoes with rubber soles, and a canvas jacket with ten pockets in which he had stacked ammunition, a small spyglass, a pack of cigarettes, and a lighter. A larger one contained a water bottle. Judging by the crew cut, the black leather gloves, and the fact that he came prepared for a long observation, Umberto's first assumption was relevant again. Had the contract killer turned against Luigi? It was logical in a way — he couldn't kill Burmeister, knew that his client would come after him, and therefore decided to get rid of him. If he was as clever as they assumed, he would know of the investigation into his former accounts.

What a pity that he missed. Umberto spread the pocket contents on the small table while Guido slapped the assassin's face to wake him up. Smelling salts finally did the trick. The stranger's eyes flickered open. As he assessed the situation, his expression was bleak — he didn't expect to survive.

"Who hired you?" Luigi shouted, dismissing the secretary's attempts at bandaging the wound. He was obviously fighting to get a grip on his emotions, but his voice betrayed him. "Who told you to kill me? How did you find me?"

The secretary tried to continue delivering first aid while Luigi waved his arm. Umberto turned away to hide his grin.

The stranger tried to lift his head. Grimacing with pain, he looked from Umberto to Luigi. He curled his lips into a pain-filled smile, and he whispered, "Sorry that I missed."

Umberto couldn't agree more. He wished so vehemently that the assassin had been a better shot. He clenched his teeth as he watched his boss rise from the armchair the moment the secretary secured the small bandage with a strip of tape.

"I'll shoot you in the fucking face if you don't talk!" Luigi spat spittle with his words. "Who hired you? Who paid you money to kill me?" He held out his hand, and Guido gave him his gun, safety off. "Talk, fucker, or I'll blow your brains out!"

"Excellent idea." The stranger coughed and grimaced when the pain hit him with full force. He looked like he would drop unconscious any minute. "Shoot me right away."

Umberto considered it possible that the man was the contract killer — only the method of killing was different. Wouldn't the professional killer, whose first choice was poison, prefer to spice Luigi's drink? Or deliver food with rat poison as a special ingredient?

Luigi pressed the muzzle against the man's forehead. "Last chance! Who hired you to kill me?"

"It's a long list, you bastard," the stranger replied. "I don't have all night to tell you, so just be done with the shooting."

Luigi pulled down the corners of his mouth, inclining his head. Then, slowly, he lowered the gun toward the man's midsection, waited, and shot him in the thigh. The assassin howled at the top of his lungs. Umberto forced himself to remain quiet and expressionless, teeth still clenched firmly to keep words from spilling out. On the one hand, Umberto wanted to learn the name, on the other hand, he didn't give a damn. The man had failed to clear Umberto's way to the top. The problem was still the same — the small arm wound would anger Luigi but not keep him from doing business.

Luigi appeared equally frustrated, albeit for a different reason. His voice was shrill, on the edge of hysteria, not becoming to a man who pretended to be the toughest criminal this planet had ever brought forth. "The name, fucker! Tell me who hired you or I'll shoot the other leg, too!"

Umberto wished the shooter would stay quiet and die decently with a bullet between his eyes, but the pain was unbearable. It was a matter of moments until his defiance crumbled. When Luigi aimed at the left leg, the man hissed. "All right, I'll tell ya!"

Luigi's hand didn't waver. "Talk!"

"A guy I know told me that someone wants you out of the way."

"Gimme his name!"

"No names. We talk via . . . dead drops, fake emails, that sort of thing."

"If you don't gimme a name, I'll shoot your foot next!"

"I don't know his name!" the assassin shouted. He looked up, baring his teeth. He sounded exhausted, accepting his inevitable fate. "It doesn't matter. He leaves the money, I do what he wants, and that's it."

"Is this a personal hit?"

"It's never personal." He lowered his chin to his chest, breathing raggedly. "Just . . . that . . . it's for a woman."

"A *woman*?" Luigi couldn't sound more flabbergasted if he'd been told that the Russian president had ordered his execution. "What woman?"

The assassin closed his eyes, giving in to the pain. He licked his lips. "He said something about . . . right something wrong. She wanted . . . justice . . . for her husband. He was killed . . . by you." His chin dropped to his chest.

"What kind of woman?" Luigi hollered as he shook the assassin hard. "Why?"

The man was unconscious, and no shouting woke him up again.

Umberto stood with his back against the desk, pondering whether there was actually someone who would take over killing Luigi for him.

Nicolas met with Matthew at the office to go through the information they had gathered so far. Burmeister was with yet another team of agents in an even more secluded safe house in Virginia, waiting for the FBI to do their job. Nicolas felt the pressure of Burmeister's words on him. *How long should I wait until it was safe to go back home, go back to work, or meet with my girlfriend? Is the FBI able to arrest Vianone, and find him guilty of the many crimes they assumed he had committed? Will I live in fear of Vianone's wrath for a long time to come?* Nicolas had been unable to answer the questions. He felt like he was losing his touch for his profession.

"The man who threw the stone — Clifford Harris. He's a DC resident, currently unemployed but not broke. The killer's money, though, was well appreciated. He's got an inclination for shady operations. He says he's testing the bars."

"Be that as it may, he couldn't add anything useful to our investigation other than claiming he didn't know about the assassination attempt. He didn't know the man, hadn't seen him before." He looked up. "I conclude, the contract killer observed Burmeister first, found out about his preferred afternoon whereabouts and then was in luck that Harris was thrown out of that bar. Harris was the perfect distraction. I wonder what he would've done without him. Start a fire?

"He's clever and also convincing. You need a thorough knowledge of human nature to convince a snubbed customer to throw a stone as retaliation. Harris could have said no and just walked off to another bar. When I asked him how the stranger convinced him, Harris paused and then said that at the end of the conversation he *wanted* to throw a stone because the bartender had treated him so unfairly." Matthew frowned. "Add *cunning* and *persuasive* to the list of attributes of the killer."

"I should never have allowed Burmeister to take us to his favorite bar. Damn it!" Feeling defeated, Nicolas consulted his notes. "There are three shoemakers with a good reputation in DC and vicinity. We sent them the information we have about the killer, and one of them replied that he has young customers, too, because he supplies the high society of DC—men who were either born rich or became famous in various professions. They wear fine shoes, but they have to be *fashionable* to go with their wardrobe." He looked up. "Yeah, smile like the Cheshire cat. I felt the heat of his voice creep through the telephone line."

"He sounds proud of his work. Could he identify the customer by the meager information we provided?"

"No. There were several on his list. I would like to drop by and have a chat with him."

"And you want me to accompany you," Matthew concluded, using a high and very female touch in his voice before cracking down with laughter.

"Yeah, that would be great."

Matthew put the fingertips of his right hand on Nicolas's shoulder as he batted his eyelashes. "Believe me, honey bunny, I'll be right by your side."

The stranger didn't regain consciousness, but it was unclear whether he had died of a heart attack or blood loss. Luigi didn't care about the cause apart from the fact that he had died without revealing his client and the name of the woman behind him. He rambled on as usual, causing Umberto and the other men present to take deep breaths and suffer quietly until their boss was done. Umberto couldn't tell whether Luigi needed the monologue to calm himself or to convince his goons that he was still in charge. As far as Umberto could see, Luigi had lost credibility by screaming like a ten-year old girl throwing a tantrum.

Other than Luigi, Umberto considered the wife of the dead Mr. Cooper, who had refused to sell his concrete pumps to his boss, a possible client of the assassin. He wouldn't say a word about his assumption. He left it to Luigi to come to that conclusion himself. Umberto would not lift a finger to kill Mrs. Cooper. To him this would look like shooting himself in the foot, and he wouldn't do that, either.

Alonso returned to the office out of breath and bathed in sweat but with a grin. "Did I miss the party?" he commented on the body lying on the carpet. No one laughed. "Oh, okay, no party at all. I get it." He put the car keys and the contents of the stranger's car on the desk. "That's all I could find. Looks like he rented the compact two days ago and drove around a bit."

"Any clue how he knew of this place?" Luigi demanded to know, already nourishing on another drink.

"He had pictures of you and of several of our buddies." He pointed at an envelope Luigi hastily emptied.

Umberto was shocked to find pictures of Guido and Alonso. He met gazes with Luigi, whose eyes narrowed immediately.

"No papers, no ID, nothing." Alonso clapped his hands. "Looks like he dined at a fine restaurant in Arlington. I could ask around if anyone remembers him, maybe knows with whom he was there." He cackled. "Doing police work, you know?"

While Alonso monologued about possible means to find the client, Umberto's heart hammered painfully against his ribs. If it was possible the assassin had followed Guido and Alonso, Umberto might have been on the observation list, too, even though his picture was not in the stack.

"We have to pack and leave," Luigi ordered in a tone that said down to business and yet was full of suppressed anger. "If there's one attacker, there might be more lurking at the next corner. Hurry!" he barked when the men stood rooted, disbelieving his words.

Umberto felt like his thoughts had reverberated through Luigi's mind. He pulled himself together. There was no time to call Michael. He had to hope that the assassin was the only one and that neither Michael nor he were targets. Umberto regretted that he had allowed his lover to move in. Though he cherished their living together, he was taking a big risk.

"Let's see if that was my contract killer," Luigi mumbled as he stuffed papers into a box. "Let's see what happens next."

For once, Umberto agreed wholeheartedly with his boss.

The Rattler had survived in this business for years because he was even more careful than a rat on the streets constantly threatened by enemies. He had learned that caution paved the road to success, not the money. He would forego money anytime to save his hide. He had done so before. If circumstances told him the job wasn't kosher, he withdrew his offer and told the client to go to hell.

The recent information that someone had tried to find out his whereabouts via his offshore accounts troubled him. Moreover, he'd learned that one of Vianone's henchmen had inquired about him. The search had not revealed anything, of course. The Rattler changed accounts for his money frequently, avoiding police investigations. The actions were time-consuming but worth every minute. His charming personality had established good connections to tellers and online brokers so that he received information without begging. He wondered whether the tellers knew they were dealing with a criminal.

Sometimes, the Rattler thought about giving up the job and retiring somewhere, but the thrill of dominance over the lives of others pushed him. He needed the excitement and the adrenalin in his body, even if the stakes grew higher with every job. His clash with the FBI agents at the bar had pumped so much blood through his body, he'd been about to burst, even more so when he had escaped the establishment with his empty glass and the knowledge that Burmeister would almost inevitably drain his drink as a stress relief. This had been much better than learning of the target's death in the newspapers.

The Rattler had fought his initial urge to dance down the alley to blatantly demonstrate his genius. He refrained from showing the FBI the middle finger on tape because of passersby who might find his behavior strange and would remember him. He didn't want to be remembered. He tried to look like an ordinary guy, a person people looked at and forgot immediately. He chose disguises so carefully, even professionals tended to overlook him in a crowd. He was proud of his demonstration of genius at the bar and his easy escape.

The FBI agents had looked like fools, and the Rattler bet they had suffered their superior's browbeating. He laughed out loud, and the stillness around him swallowed the sound.

Nicolas sighed exaggeratedly when he slipped behind the wheel of his company car after visiting Andrew Lloyd—no *Webber* behind it, as the owner had stated, chuckling—in his upscale shoe design shop. The shoemaker, a slim man in his sixties, was the politest person Nicolas had ever met. He apologized about fifty times for being such a forgetful businessman that he couldn't identify a single customer. He showed the FBI agents his handmade shoes, praised their quality and heritage, and elaborated on the dying art of shoemaking.

He admitted regretfully that there were customers who paid cash and also those men—even fewer—who didn't return for another pair of his outstanding, Italian-inspired exquisite shoes, though no man of high standards should go without. With that sentence, the businessman had looked pointedly at Matthew's and Nicolas's off-the-rack shoes that didn't fit the artist's requirements. After a brief pause, Mr. Lloyd continued his lecture about the need for excellent shoes, especially in the businesses of circus artists, dancers, and—not least of all—political representatives. They all needed fine shoes to do their work and, of course, impress people.

"Another three hours wasted," Nicolas said on their way back to the bureau.

"Our killer's behavior pattern is consistent. He avoids places where he can be identified, uses cash whenever possible. Probably he has offshore accounts, but we can't get to them if we don't know the sums he's moving." Matthew sighed. "He must have made millions of dollars in just a few years to go shopping like this."

"The shoes were expensive, but not *that* expensive."

"Not the shoes alone. His lifestyle. The shoes are just one small part of his style. He knows how to hide in a crowd. He knows about disguises. Remember, he approached every victim in his own area without being spotted. He got close enough to each of them without the victims' colleagues and relatives noticing him. No one could describe a stranger. In cases with descriptions, they were worthless because every witness described another kind of person." Matthew huffed and added contemptuously, "I bet he could walk right up to us, and we wouldn't recognize him. He's a bold motherfucker."

"A very familiar FBI term."

"Up yours."

"Are you a tad sensitive about the matter?"

"Sullivan chose my ass to gnaw on the last time he met with me at the office. He doesn't like me anyway, and such a slow investigation is just what he needs to bite my hide."

"Do we have other potential candidates Vianone would want to kick out of business?"

"Trying to distract me? Fine. Whatever. Yeah, we do have two more company owners on the list, but it'll take a lot of diplomatic shit-talk to persuade them to work with us."

"That's right up your alley."

"Up—"

"Don't you dare say it again!"

CHAPTER FOURTEEN

Umberto wished he was a smoker and could calm his nerves by drawing on a cigarette like Drago did all the time. While he oversaw the move, it was Luigi who ordered the assassin's client found. Umberto had diligently nodded, without the intention of lifting a finger to do his boss's bidding. From what Alonso had found out while talking to his contacts on the street, the dead stranger wasn't the contract killer but some hired gun with a debatable reputation, and no high-class professional. Umberto wanted, needed to find that damn hit man and shoot a clip of ammo into his face to revenge Eduardo's murder. After that, he would turn on Luigi by revealing to his gang that the younger brother had ordered his older brother murdered. For what? Money. What else should there be for the offspring who had never learned to cherish what he got, but always hungered for more riches?

Umberto had no doubt about his own criminal behavior. From his teenage years on, he had never aspired to a job in a company—no matter the branch—to earn money legally. His father had worked for the Vianone syndicate, constantly bragging about the money lying on the street but without mentioning the bodies he left behind. Umberto followed his father's example under the impression that the Vianones praised and rewarded loyalty. Eduardo had handled family matters in the best interest of his staff. He would never have left a family member at the hands of the police. He paid highly talented lawyers enough money to fight for their clients regardless of the kind of crime.

Therefore, Umberto despised Luigi's ruinous dealings with loyal henchmen. He would do everything differently, more like Eduardo. He would become a respected leader, not a laughing stock. "First things first," he mumbled as he left Luigi's latest hideout. "Find the killer."

At the office, Nicolas called back Agent Hillbrock from the FBI bureau in Miami. The agent reported his secret conversation with Ennio Marchesi, who was more than simply nervous about Luigi Vianone getting wind of him talking to a federal agent.

"What I found out," Hillbrock said, "is that Eduardo Vianone was about to retire. He wanted his empire, as he called it, in safe hands. He'd been a competitor all his life, and Marchesi told me that the old man had decided to split his enterprise between his younger brother and a member of his long-term team." Hillbrock made a sound in his throat as he consulted his notes. "Here. There were several aspirants he considered worthy of leading a part of his enterprise, among them Umberto Bianchi."

"Did Marchesi consider it possible that Bianchi killed Vianone to take over the enterprise?"

"Not likely. Marchesi stressed the good relationship between Eduardo and Umberto—that it was much better than between the two brothers. To avoid a clash and murder, Eduardo had decided to not let his brother go without any inheritance." Hillbrock slurped and then belched. "Sorry. I was just out to grab a bite, and the sandwiches were spiced like dragon fodder. Anyway, I would rule out Umberto as the killer. He moved to Alexandria to serve the younger brother. Luigi is the one who's leaving behind dead bodies wherever he walks."

"He's never present at any crime site."

"No, he's not a gawker, because he never pulls the trigger. He's got his men to fulfill his orders. And a contract killer, that is."

"Would Marchesi repeat his statement in court?"

Hillbrock laughed briefly, which led to a snort. "No way. He's so afraid he pees his pants the moment he leaves his secure home. If anything, he'll vanish like mist when the sun rises. I was lucky I found him and that he was willing to give me some clues. If Luigi learns about this, Marchesi is history."

"Anything else worth knowing?"

"One thing, actually. Marchesi said that Luigi probably — most probably — doesn't know about Eduardo favoring Bianchi and that he considered granting him a part of the business. If Luigi knew, I bet he would've killed Bianchi on the spot instead of ordering him to come to Virginia and work for him."

"But then Bianchi has every reason to hate Luigi. Why not kill him?"

"You don't kill a man with so many goons backing him. Vianone is protected. Many men follow him, adore him, do his bidding without thinking. He's generous to those loyal to him. That's all that matters — loyalty. It's on you to decide whether this loyalty is real — according to Marchesi, it was with Eduardo's men — or based on money alone."

"So Bianchi takes up working for the younger brother, and though he might know by now that this man is responsible for the older brother's death, he can't act against him. Unless he finds a way to let it look like an accident."

Again, Hillbrock snorted. "Yeah, try to fool a bunch of goons. Good luck. I wouldn't put my money on Bianchi in this case."

Eduardo had maintained solid and well-bribed connections

to the treasury department. Umberto didn't know how the old Vianone had established it, but he was willing to try his luck to see whether he could bribe or blackmail the man into obedience. Neither was necessary. Mr. Walter Lombardi was a distant relative of the Vianones and asked amiably how he could help. Umberto's request to check an account yielded a company name that led to purchasing contracts for three small warehouses in Hialeah, Florida, St. Louis, Illinois, and Annandale, Virginia. Walter promised to dig deeper, maybe to find a name that would yield the account holder. Umberto told him he would call again.

Umberto chose to pay the nearest warehouse a visit. After observing the three-story, unadorned concrete building for an afternoon and learning about the various tenants—none of them had ever met the owner—he explored the second level. Half of it was vacant, according to the old janitor, who was as loquacious as any housewife with nothing more to do than watching people and collecting gossip all day.

Umberto broke into the rooms without causing damage to the lock. Once inside, he checked the corridor, but no one had followed him. He closed the door quietly. The unknown owner ran a shop for clothes and accessories, for makeup, false beards, and wigs. Most of the clothes fit a man of average height and weight, some were made for men with a paunch and fat bottom. All of the clothes had a used look but were made of fine quality, especially the suits. There were also uniforms from various professions—jumpsuits from a delivery firm, gray jackets and pants with the logo of an electricity company, various lab coats with different nametags. It was a mélange of disguises every theater owner would envy.

If he had been a forensic expert, he might have found fingerprints on the dresser and the three-fold mirror, but without the expertise, he relied on his observations. Umberto had found the killer's lair. It was a tremendous, a magnificent breakthrough that increased his chances of finding the killer. His search for poison and other weapons was in vain, which meant that the murderer had more than one hideout or kept his supplies close to him, not trusting any warehouse or safe. When further search revealed no clues to the owner's identity other than his assumed height and build, he stood rooted for minutes before he decided to return to his stakeout.

Walking back to the car, Umberto hoped that Luigi's claim about the killer's need to accept the next contract ran true. During all his bragging, Luigi had not dropped a word about the next victim's identity or when the hit should take place. Umberto slipped behind the wheel, pushed back the seat, and tried to get comfortable. However, after two hours of uneventful waiting, his thoughts returned to Michael and how much he wanted to smooth the crinkles in their relationship. He wanted to return home. They had to talk about the locked room, about the upcoming months, and about his intention to leave the country. Umberto started the engine and drove down the street.

Approaching the driveway after a gruesome tour of three hours in heavy traffic, Umberto wished that Michael was faithful, that he could trust him. He needed someone to trust in this world full of deceit. However, Umberto knew he had locked the door to his study because it was his habit—moreover, a compulsion, like putting his gun in its holster before leaving the house. His heart wished that Michael had not inspected the forbidden room and found out about his picture collection of known criminals of the Vianone enterprise and the collection of weapons and pieces of evidence that would shatter enemies like an earthquake. It was risky to keep all of it in his house, even though it was hidden. If the police entered his office, they would have a field day exploring how many goons had worked or were still working for Vianone.

Eduardo had taught Umberto to be cautious, to be prepared, to have an eye for details — names, numbers, connections. In the week prior to his murder, Eduardo had hinted at a competition between two equal combatants. Without revealing names, Eduardo had smiled his father-like smile, and Umberto interpreted the rest — that he would be the one combatant and Luigi most probably the other. A hideous murder had finished that competition before it had begun, and left Umberto empty-handed and with a heart filled with sorrow, as well as a rage that could not be quelled.

Even more he wished for Michael to be his true companion — his lover, his trusted friend.

Leaving the car, Umberto pondered whether he could forgive Michael his curiosity, if his interest was indeed harmless and not meant to sell Umberto's secret to the highest bidder.

Michael wished Vincent could see how far he had come, could watch his growth. So much had changed in his life, so much that he wanted to share with his mentor, but all he could do was think of him, talk to him as if he were sitting on a chair in the kitchen while Michael was cutting peppers for dinner. Michael missed Vincent in a way he couldn't describe. Even if he had words — who should he tell about the most wonderful teacher and lover? Not Umberto. Any mentioning of former lovers would trigger an outburst of mindless jealousy. Michael was alone in his mourning, his sorrow, and his desire to return to the place he belonged. Vincent was gone after a too short time they had together, and the hole in Michael's heart would never close. In spite of Umberto Bianchi's kindness and caring — he would never replace Vincent.

For a short time, Michael had believed — had wished it to be true — that Umberto could be the one man he needed in his life. But the blunt truth was that the Italian kept too much to himself, lived in a space he wouldn't share, so that Michael doubted a change of mind. He doubted Umberto's announcements, too, that he would change jobs in a year and that they would live on an island somewhere in the Caribbean. Maybe Umberto spoke the truth. Maybe Umberto had his heart in the right place. Michael couldn't shake the notion that Umberto might drop him should the need arise. His claim that Italian men were not permitted to show their homosexuality in public appeared shallow and ostensible. He had never elaborated why and how he had parted with his previous lover, and Michael assumed that Umberto's employer had been involved, maybe threatened to chuck him out. Or worse.

Michael heard Umberto enter the house, close the door, and drop the keys. A heavy sigh followed.

The last few days had been stressful, but Michael wanted his lover to feel at home. He washed his hands to meet Umberto in the hallway. Used to secrecy, he checked whether Umberto had come alone.

"It's just me," Umberto said, smiling.

"Enough for me." Michael lifted his chin for a kiss, then helped Umberto out of his jacket which he put on a hanger, knowing that his lover would simply drop the garment on a chair. "Hungry?"

"Not so much, but it smells delicious." Umberto tousled Michael's hair and ran his hands along the sides of Michael's head. "Later, okay?"

"Whatever you want." Michael was surprised that he meant what he said. Every doubt about Umberto's personality, his truthfulness or his intentions vanished in the shower of affection that Umberto delivered so easily. Michael sighed with bliss upon another sensuous kiss. "Go freshen up. A beer?"

"I won't say no," Umberto replied, already on his way

upstairs.

Michael adjusted the jacket on the hanger, took out the leather gloves, smoothed them, and put them in the drawer right beside the rack. On the way back to the kitchen, he pondered whether he should tell Umberto about Vincent Decker — not referring to him as the most wonderful lover but as a mentor, a man who had shown Michael the world and how to make money.

Cutting peppers again, however, he doubted that Umberto would understand.

Matthew stopped at the door to the cafeteria, out of breath. "Hey, Nick, I just got a call from the surveillance team. They found something. You coming?"

Nicolas stuffed the last bite of his sandwich into his mouth, wiped breadcrumbs off his jacket, and followed Matthew downstairs.

"The team followed Bianchi and checked an address where he was snooping around," Matthew explained on the way to the garage. "They found a storage room." He winked at Nicolas. "Guess what's in it."

Nicolas licked the rest of the garlic dressing off his fingers. "The detailed plans of how to murder effectively without being caught, signed by the killer?"

"Funny, but close. It's the killer's dressing room. They're looking for fingerprints as we speak. You've got some dressing on your lips."

"Thanks." Wiping off his lips, Nicolas slipped behind the wheel and drove the car onto the street. "How come Bianchi knew of this? And why is he interested in the killer's whereabouts anyway? Rivalry? Is he searching for something he can use against Vianone?"

"That's my idea, yes. He wants to get rid of Luigi. If it's

true that Bianchi was in the older man's favor, he can't stomach that he's been degraded to an errand boy."

Nicolas felt the surge of hope rise. He didn't really care why Bianchi had searched the killer's lair and what he would do with this knowledge as long as the FBI got the upper hand and identified the killer. The slow progress was wearing him down. He wanted a success, not to please Sullivan—that would be a vain attempt—but to close the case and make amends. He didn't take it lightly that the killer had slipped his attention at the bar. It would be his fault if the killer succeeded in killing someone else before the FBI could catch him.

Matthew gave him directions, and they reached the warehouse complex in the waning daylight. Three FBI vans parked at the curb, and the agent in charge introduced them to the large room stacked with clothes and other items the killer used.

"Looks like he also posed as a woman," Agent Spring said instead of a greeting. He smiled as he lifted a wig from its rack. "See? He's very innovative which means—"

"He must have a face that fits." Matthew grinned at Nicolas. "Well, your face might be clean shaven like a baby's butt, but with that chiseled chin, you couldn't wear a wig and pass as a woman. Not in this lifetime."

Spring laughed, but Nicolas's interest was with the makeup table. He looked over the shoulder of the forensics' expert who dusted the entire surface and the mirrors for fingerprints. "Anything useful?"

"I think so." The technician looked up. "He was careful, even here, but I found a print of an index finger and the thumb of his right hand. That should be enough to identify him . . . if he's in the system."

"I bet he is." Nicolas turned back.

Matthew was rummaging through the clothes meant for various professions. The killer had used overalls, coats, hats, and also dresses and long skirts. Nicolas tried to imagine the person that could show up as an overweight man in his thirties and the next time as a woman in a summer dress, paired with ballerinas. For no special reason the word *androgynous* appeared in his mind — the description of a person who was neither explicitly female nor male. The killer was able to slip into every role he wished to portray, able to deceive onlookers perfectly. He could meet with a person twice, and that person wouldn't recognize him.

Nicolas unclenched his teeth. He wanted to catch the killer so badly, he lacked the usual patience that was needed to solve a case. "How long until you get the results?" he asked the technician.

"You should have them by morning."

"Thank you."

Matthew shook his head. "I don't know what he's planned, but he could change from TV technician to delivery boy to the lady in red within an hour. I wonder how many murders he's responsible for that we don't even know about."

Nicolas wanted to reply, but again, his teeth were locked in a state of rage.

Umberto came downstairs on bare feet, adjusting his shorts. Michael loved the sight of the man's muscular body. He did not like his lover's cranky expression. Cautiously, he asked, "What's wrong?"

"I thought about my study and that I lock it every day. I always do."

Michael evaded Umberto's gaze, afraid his facial expression might give him away. "That day, you obviously forgot."

"No, I didn't. It's like . . . brushing my teeth in the morning. I just wouldn't forget it."

"What are you trying to tell me?"

"I think you went into the room when you heard the stone smashing the glass. Did you unlock the door, Mikey?"

Michael felt Umberto's presence beside him like a weight that pressed on his shoulders. He couldn't breathe. "No, I didn't."

"And I think you did."

Michael turned to the stove to push the cut peppers, mushrooms, and onions off the chopping board into the pan. He adjusted the heat. "Why don't you believe me?" he asked with an exasperated sigh.

Umberto scoffed as he put his right hand on the counter. "I came home and the door was open. Did you rummage through my things or not?"

"No!" Michael huffed, then turned his head to finally meet Umberto's stare. "How often must I repeat it?"

"I don't believe you." Umberto's eyes narrowed. "I think you opened the door to look for the damage, then decided to look more closely. You are curious by nature. I bet I could've installed a state-of-the-art lock, and you would've tried to pick it sooner or later."

Michael widened his eyes, parted his lips, and yet needed a moment to bring out the question. "You accuse me of breaking into your secret room? How dare you?"

"I just know, all right? I wanted to give you the chance to be honest, but . . . you are not."

Michael's heartbeat skyrocketed. He took a wooden spoon to stir the mix in the pan. His hand shook. "Why are you keeping secrets from me?"

"Oh, not that question again! Let me be clear—I don't rummage through *your* things! So why do you think you can do this with mine?"

"I don't keep my stuff locked away. You're always so secretive." Michael dropped the spoon beside the pan. "Don't you think that I deserve to know what you do? What kind of company do you work for that wants you to show up at night and keeps you busy all through the night, huh? Why do you carry a gun? And when you come back — well, I can live with you smelling of stale cigar smoke or whiskey, but there's another stench that I can't bear. What is it? What did you do several nights ago? You smelled of . . . grease, of something chemical. What did you do?"

Umberto's nostrils flared, and he pressed the words through clenched teeth. "I cannot tell you everything I do, okay? It's—"

"Oh, yes, the oath of secrecy again? Company politics? Gimme a break! I do love you, Bert, I want to spend my life with you, but you're like a clam. You keep so much from me that I don't know who you really are or whether I can trust you. But the more important question right now is — don't you trust *me*?"

Umberto's mouth worked, but he remained quiet. Shaking his head, he went to the fridge, took out a beer bottle and unscrewed it. Michael remained at the stove, suddenly insecure about how this conversation would develop. He lowered the oven heat when the onions began to glaze.

"I want to trust you, I really do." Umberto let out an exasperated sigh. "There are things I can't tell you. It's necessary to keep secrets, and that won't change. Not for a long time."

Michael huffed. Inclining his head, he said quietly, "Because you're doing illegal stuff? Is that it?"

Umberto's face twisted to an expression of anguish. He opened his hand, palm up. "As I said —"

"Are you involved in crimes? Is that the truth? Are you some conman jumping at someone's orders and . . . doing what? Break-ins? Robbery? *What do you do*, Bert?"

"I said, I won't tell you."

"But I—"

"Stop pestering me, Mikey!" Umberto drank from the

bottle and put it down forcefully. Foam spilled across the bottleneck. "That's the last word, all right? We're through with this!"

"Is that so?" This time Michael withstood Umberto's glare. "Do you think I have to shut my mouth and just watch what you do without ever questioning your doings? No, Bert, that's not me. Sharing a life means there are no secrets — not of that dimension, anyway. You either tell me or — "

"Or *what*?" Umberto snapped.

"Or I leave." Michael let the words sink in, anxiously watching Umberto's expression. He remembered that Umberto had parted with his former lover, and not on good terms. Heart beating in his throat, Michael switched off the oven. The sweet aroma of peppers and onions was delicious, but he felt nauseous.

Umberto took another long swallow of beer, and when he lowered the bottle said, "Then you'd better leave."

A hit in the gut could not have been more painful than those four words. Michael parted his lips for a reply, but the words stuck between his lungs and his vocal cords. When Umberto didn't indicate this was meant as a joke or added a sentence about trying to salvage their relationship, Michael turned away. He went upstairs to pack his belongings into a small suitcase, yearning to hear Umberto's footsteps. Desperately hoping his lover would apologize and hold him back. He fought tears as he closed the locks. If he left now, he couldn't come back. He wouldn't come back, because his ego didn't allow it. He bet that Umberto thought the same way.

The image of moving into a hotel room for the night or searching for a small apartment to live alone was devastating. He loved being with Umberto, loved his presence, his way of speaking, his love making. Michael enjoyed company and caring for someone.

When he passed through the hall, Umberto was

rummaging through the kitchen, but Michael didn't bother to check what he was doing. He wouldn't enter the kitchen and say farewell only to realize that Umberto didn't care whether he stayed or left.

Quietly, devastated by the sudden development, he left the house.

CHAPTER FIFTEEN

The Rattler knew that his private rooms had been breached. It was abundantly clear that he couldn't return to his dressing room for a quick change of appearance. The setback came at the most inconvenient time. If he was to eliminate his client's latest enemy, he had to be cunning, clever — a master of disguise. The FBI was looking into the murder cases with a new focus. They had drawn the right conclusions. Their protection of Burmeister proved that they had identified Vianone as the client behind the latest contract — the FBI would be on his heels.

Additionally, Vianone would cry for the killer's elimination should the Rattler fail him again. If the syndicate boss identified and caught him, the Rattler faced a slow and brutal death. The threat — though still vague, but looming — caused him shivers unlike the prickling sensation he felt prior to a hit. For the first time in his career, the Rattler considered his death possible.

Being in the focus of the FBI was just as bad. The shivers turned violent as he imagined the FBI agents who had sat next to him at the bar pointing their guns at him. He feared ending up in prison — it was a terrible thought. He had spent a month in a detention center at the age of fifteen. The time had been stressful, but was nothing compared to what awaited him in a high-security prison. He would be bait for every inmate and not live long enough to apply for a transfer to another penitentiary.

Shivering, he chose a route out of town to head west. He

had options for how to avoid enemies and the FBI, but he needed to act fast.

Exuberant after the findings at the warehouse, Nicolas's mood spiraled skyward when he learned that a police patrol had detected the car with which the assassin had fled the safe house. The FBI agents on the ground reported the car was located on a private parking space in Arlington, and that the vigilance of two police officers on patrol had led to the surprisingly quick success. Another team of forensic agents was on their way to examine the interior hoping to find clues leading to the driver's identity.

Nicolas dropped Matthew off at his downtown apartment, then drove home.

Jacklyn awaited him with dinner and a seductive smile that increased his hope he could expect more than a culinary treat. He freshened up and joined her at the table.

"Oh, you look much more cheerful than the last few days. You are making progress, finally?"

"Yes." Nicolas poured wine for her and water for himself. "I think we're closing in—on all suspects." He raised his glass. "Let's hope we can close the case before the end of the month."

"That would be wonderful, my Beast." An impish smile followed. "A little sooner would be nice."

"Why?"

"My father called. He said that you had such an *intense and revealing* conversation—his words, not mine—that he wants to invite us to stay at their home while he and mom take a trip to Switzerland. What do you say? Between the lines he's inviting us to use the house for a session. He even offered to give the staff some days off."

"If you can wait until after the case is closed—"

"Make sure you'll get some days off. I remember you saying that you had several cases on your desk. I can't wait until all of them will be *off* your desk, because that's not gonna happen."

Nicolas sighed as he set down the glass. "Don't make this a conversation about me dealing with a lot of cases and having no time to spend with you, okay? I'm hopeful I'll get a few days off after the suspects are arrested." He sensed her impatience and that indeed she had hoped he would be able to leave work at once. Since she had hired two full-time physiotherapists to work at her office, her leeway had increased. Consequently, she wanted to spend more time with him than before. It was nice to know that he was wanted, but bad to be unable to fulfill her wishes. "Listen, Jacky, I understand what you want, but we were on the same page when we talked about me working odd hours. There's no doubt about it—I won't have regular working hours, ever. Some days I'm home early, and on other days, I won't come home until late. Remember that because of my unpredictable schedule you started working as a mistress again."

"Part time." Jacklyn made a sound in her throat he interpreted as a concession. Her smile reappeared. "Then we make a cut here and enjoy the night, all right?"

"That's fine with me." He toasted her with his glass.

"It'll be even better once you learn what I've on my mind."

"Oh, yes, ma Belle, I see the sparkle in your eyes."

"You'll see much more than that . . .or maybe nothing at all."

Umberto stood in the kitchen. He loathed the silence. He loathed the aroma of freshly fried vegetables, mostly because Michael had prepared dinner and was not with him to enjoy the meal. His appetite was gone, his mood sank to the bottom.

He pushed the pan to the side, emptied the beer bottle, and fetched another one. Still, it was not enough alcohol to douse his misery. Restless, he cruised the house, looked longingly at the St. Andrew's cross installation in the bedroom, and moved on until he could no longer bear the emptiness of the rooms and the lack of Michael's voice while his scent lingered everywhere. Umberto was amazed how little Michael had packed — all of his toiletries were still in the bathroom. The memory of screwing Michael in the shower stall hurt immeasurably. He whimpered and loathed that his emotions got the best of him.

Umberto slammed the door, changed back into his street clothes, grabbed his gun, and left the house. Sitting behind the wheel, he intended to search for Michael at the dancing studio, but dismissed the idea. The way Michael had fled the house, he wouldn't be in the mood to have a chat about their mutual future, not even if Umberto tried to apologize first. He didn't know how to apologize, anyway. He could not reveal that he was the bruiser for Luigi Vianone and bashed people for money.

Without consciously making the decision, he drove back to the warehouse and found it besieged by FBI vans. Swiftly, he drove by and stopped his car a block away. He sat in the dark, heart beating against his ribcage, trying to make sense of what he had witnessed. The FBI had located the killer's lair — just like he had done hours ago.

He checked the rearview mirror. Had he been followed? Had he been followed by FBI agents *all of the time*? It was bad enough that the wannabe assassin had spotted and observed two of Luigi's men. It was even worse to think that the FBI was on his trail. Mouth dry, Umberto cruised around the blocks, watching the ensuing traffic and trying to spot the one sedan that was on his heels. He spent an hour crisscrossing through Washington, DC, and the neighboring suburbs using every trick he knew to make sure he lost possible pursuers.

Soaked with sweat, Umberto parked his car at the large parking lot of a mall, wiped off his fingerprints, and left the SUV unlocked. He dropped the keys two cars ahead and hoped for a lazy criminal to find them.

He bought a few items for a short trip — starting with a hat to partially cover his face — then searched for a suitable vehicle he could hotwire. A small black compact car was the easiest to steal. Grim yet determined, Umberto set out.

Nicolas was content when he found the results of the fingerprints' examination on his desk by morning and at the same time disappointed that the forensics' expert hadn't put a name to the prints. "The file is sealed?" he asked Matthew, who returned from the coffee maker with a fresh mug. Grumbling, he slumped on his chair. "We need a judge to get a permission to open it?"

"Yep." Matthew blew over his coffee as he sat down. "Already done. I expect the judge to answer any minute." He smacked his lips after the first sip. "Ah, I'm addicted to this stuff." Upon Nicolas's inquisitive glare, he said, "My statement that we're dealing with a possible hit man should speed things up."

"Thank you. Any coffee left for me?" Nicolas got up.

Matthew looked contrite. "Half a cup, maybe."

"You've been here for hours? Couldn't sleep?"

"Ah, Bingo's got the squits, so I was up all night."

Nicolas grimaced with sympathy. "Bad?"

"I won't go into detail. The coffee is too delicious."

"And who's taking care of him now?"

"Now that Bert is back in his cozy home in Chicago, the dog lady does. I told her I can't take a day off, and she understands my working situation. Though, yes, she wasn't amused." Matthew sipped coffee, then swung in his chair to face the monitor. "It's coming." He set down the mug to open the email. "The judge gave permission, and I'll forward this to the police department so they send us the file." He looked up. "If they're fast, we can go after the killer at noon."

"Great." Nicolas returned to his desk when the phone range. "Agent Hayes."

"This is Agent Green. Sorry to report that we lost track of Umberto Bianchi. He dumped his SUV and must've stolen a car. We don't know which one, so we're off his trail. I'm currently checking the stolen car list in the vicinity, hoping that the owner will report his car to the police, but until then, I can't do anything else."

"Surveillance cameras?"

"A few, but they don't show which car Bianchi chose."

"Thank you. Call me if you get any information." Nicolas put the phone back on the table. While he stared at it, he said, "The surveillance lost Bianchi. Which means he knew of our surveillance and lost it the moment he wanted to be alone. Damn it! This isn't getting any better."

The Rattler sat behind the wheel, disappointed to such a degree that he was pondering whether to leave the country. He had enough money to start over anywhere in the world. Given his reputation, he would find work at any location, and yet he hesitated to take that step. He didn't want to leave everything behind. His mentor had taught him everything he knew, and one lesson contained that a criminal worked best on the turf he knew inside and out. Learning about a country's rules, both cultural and historical, would cost him years. He would live on his savings and try to lie low.

This wasn't fulfillment. It would be fun in thirty years, but wasn't the right decision now. He was too young to spend years with reconnaissance and establishing new connections. In the United States, his clients found him, contacted him, and provided him with jobs that he loved to do. He couldn't do the same in Europe or Asia, not without thorough preparation.

Depressed, he drove down the ramp toward interstate sixty-four west. In several hours he'd passed Louisville and was heading for St. Louis. He would clear out that warehouse and get back on the road as fast as he could.

Umberto stopped at a gas station, put on his new hat, and pushed the nozzle into the gas tank. Though the chance was negligible that the car he was driving had already been reported stolen, he didn't want to take a risk. He filled the tank, paid, left a tip for homeless children at the cashier's desk, and headed back to the car in less than ten minutes. If there was a chance at the next stop, he would change wheels again to remain undetected.

The compact car had an inbuilt navigation system that directed him to interstate sixty-four and told him he would arrive in St. Louis in eight hours. He couldn't wait to explore the hit man's hideout.

Ennio Marchesi didn't want any involvement and argued verbosely that Luigi checked on Eduardo's old intimates on a regular basis. But then, after honeyed compliments and—not so honeyed—reminders of their excellent relationship and that Ennio owed him much, the Italian reluctantly agreed to checking the warehouse the killer possessed in Hialeah, Florida. Umberto set the cell phone to the loudest ring tone so that he would hear when Ennio called even if traffic was heavy. He couldn't wait to learn where the hit man had turned to. Either way, Umberto would find and kill him. He nourished his rage while on the road. Nourished it so that he wouldn't hesitate to pull the trigger. Nourished it so he would feel relief, even satisfaction about the man's death. He would take photographs and show them to Luigi's followers. He would explain how Luigi had plotted against Eduardo to gain even more than what he would have inherited anyway. Umberto bet that most of Luigi's men — loyal only because they didn't know his agenda — would turn against their current boss. Maybe one of them would take over killing Luigi to show his dedication to Umberto. He would appreciate that.

Luigi's death would mean the end of Umberto's rage and the beginning of his leadership. He was ready to honor Eduardo's way of leading a business as large as this. If he could accomplish that task, he would make peace with Michael and move on to a better future.

The prospect of regaining his lover's trust took the edge off Umberto's rage. Though reaching the top of the Vianone enterprise was first on his list, reuniting with Michael was a close second.

"I can't believe it," Matthew whispered, staring at the screen, his lips parted, his eyes wide and his brows raised as far as they would go. "Really, it's . . ." He reclined, shaking his head.

Nicolas rounded the desk. "What? What's so unbelievable?" He looked at the same lines Matthew had read, and his jaw dropped. "Oh, shit."

"That's what I'm saying." Matthew inhaled and let out his breath noisily. "Let's find the guy and arrest him."

"Do you think Bianchi has the same information?"

"He might."

"Then we'd better hurry to get to him first, or our hit man will be hit."

CHAPTER SIXTEEN

Nicolas and Matthew retraced the account used to pay for the warehouse. With that information, the White-Collar division helped identifying other items that had been bought or rented via the same account, including two more warehouses — one in Florida, the other one in St. Louis, Illinois. After alerting the bureau in Miami, they arranged for a flight to St. Louis.

Matthew deployed agents to Umberto Bianchi's house to arrest both inhabitants should they be at home and search the property while they were there.

On the flight, Nicolas reclined and closed his eyes, worn out from the time-consuming work on details to stay inside the lines of the law and yet solve this case as fast as they could. Agent Sullivan's high expectations were only the icing on the cake. He wished to bring the hit man to justice far more than his superior did.

"Did you call Jacky?" Matthew asked, coming off a call with the dog lady.

"Yes."

"Oh, that sounds like it wasn't easy."

"It's never easy." Nicolas glanced at his partner. "It'll get worse if I don't get some days off after the case is closed."

Matthew smiled lopsidedly. "You're up for some nocturnal entertainment . . . if you get time off from work? Lovely." He blinked rapidly. "I think it's fascinating what you're doing . . . suffering, living through pain to please your lady."

Nicolas closed his eyes again, smiling. "You can't taunt me, wiseass. I won't tell you details."

"You're carrying the details on your skin, lover boy. No further explanation needed."

Nicolas stretched his legs, getting comfortable, when the cell phone rang. "Agent Hayes."

"This is Agent Hillbrock. We found the warehouse in Hialeah. It's another dressing room. Lots of clothes, makeup, and accessories of many varieties. We've taken position on a stakeout should your man get here."

"Thank you. Keep me posted."

"Will do."

Nicolas shook his head. "No sign of him in Florida. Maybe we're in luck, and he headed west."

"Luck is something that's with the killer, but not with us," Matthew replied gloomily. "And maybe he's got more hideouts throughout the country he paid for with different accounts. I'm not betting on quick success."

"You are taunting me," Nicolas replied as he settled to take a nap. "But I'm not buying."

"We'll see that."

In the industrial district of St. Louis, Umberto slowed the car down to pass by the one-story building at the address he had fed the navigation system. Having parked half a block away, he got out and hoped no one would find it while he was away. Throughout the ride, he had fed his rage, mulling over the wrongs he had suffered which had culminated in Eduardo's death. Eduardo—the great leader, businessman, wise substitute for the father who had hardly been there for him. The old Vianone had quickly acknowledged Umberto's talents and promoted his protégée from errand boy to bruiser to assistant, whom he trusted with negotiating small contracts. Eduardo's death was much more than the loss of an employer—it was the loss of a dear friend and mentor.

Umberto clenched his teeth as he checked the magazine of his 9mm *Beretta* handgun. He wouldn't meet his adversary unarmed. Maybe the hit man was keen on poisoning his victims. He wouldn't put it beyond him, though, to carry a firearm. Umberto decided not to give his enemy the chance to defend himself. He would be in charge of the situation from the beginning to the bitter end.

Ennio had reported on the phone that the killer hadn't shown up at his hideout in Hialeah so far. He was on stakeout and would stay until either the one sought-after arrived or Umberto told him that his presence was no longer needed.

The warehouse was built as simply as the one in Virginia. Behind the white concrete walls lay eight units, locked with blue doors. Umberto saw light through one of the windows. Though he didn't know whether he was about to meet the killer, his heartbeat and breathing accelerated. He swallowed and gripped the gun tightly, safety off.

A light breeze rustled leaves and paper trash in the parking area in front of the building, partly masking any sounds from within. A medium-sized sedan was parked close to the entrance, its tailgate open. Umberto slowed his steps. He didn't want to startle a stranger by pointing a gun at him. At the main door, Umberto stopped when he heard a voice that was faintly familiar, yet so filled with fury that the words erupted in quick succession, more thrown out than spoken. He moved one step closer, and the words became understandable. Umberto felt as if his lungs constricted so hard he couldn't expand them for breathing anymore. Gasping, he rounded the corner and entered the brightly lit room.

"You!"

Agent Addleton reported to Nicolas that Bianchi's house had

been turned upside down. The findings left the seasoned agents speechless. There were several stacks of photographs from known criminals and suspects, but the FBI had also found pictures of politicians and judges accompanied by members of the syndicate or their associates. The astonishing evidence included plastic bags with items that might belong to crimes the FBI had still on the table. A technician was still trying to open the safe in Bianchi's study. Addleton assumed Bianchi had gathered information about several members to use against the boss when the time was right.

Nicolas pointed out that Bianchi was playing with high stakes—trying to undermine Vianone's position as the new boss and getting adversaries under his heel. If a judge could be blackmailed, Bianchi would know how to use him to his advantage.

Agent Spring summed up the information they had gathered for the DA, and they finished the call just as the plane touched ground in St. Louis close to midnight.

Agents from the field office in St. Louis met them at the airport lounge, and they set out to the industrial complex outside of town.

Umberto steadied his suddenly quivering hand. He was sweating profusely, and yet he was cold, startled by the sight of Michael Grayden standing in front of him. He parted his lips, but words failed him. Instead he scoffed, trying to gain his composure, trying to overcome the numbness, the block in his head. He couldn't believe what he was seeing, and yet it was true.

"You didn't expect me," Michael said. He put on a dark brown wig and adjusted it, glancing into the mirror to his right. "Well, I didn't expect you, either." He tried to sound nonchalant, but his voice betrayed his emotions.

"Mikey . . . this can't be. Not you." Umberto swallowed, blinked, but the same person stood in front of him, fifteen yards away, wearing black slacks and matching shoes. His muscular upper body was bare, displaying his shaven chest, triggering memories and feelings in Umberto that he didn't need right now.

Michael made a step toward the dresser to fetch a brown moustache that he attached to his upper lip, further altering his appearance.

Umberto understood now how Michael had gotten close enough to his victims without being spotted, let alone identified. Wearing a suit and tie with the altered facial appearance, he would pass as a businessman, and no one would give him a second or even suspicious look. The realization that nothing about this man was what it seemed to be took Umberto's breath away for a second time.

Though he had a gun in his hand, Umberto felt inferior, unable to deal adequately with the situation. His plans were in shambles, his hopes for a common future smashed by the lover he had trusted. "What are you doing?" It was a stupid question, the answer obvious, and yet his battered mind couldn't come up with anything clever to say.

"I'm leaving. You found out about my hideout in Annandale. That was most unfortunate."

"How . . ."

"How did I know? I had prepared the doorknob, and the residue of the powder was on the gloves you had in your jacket." His glance was condescending. "I'm never sloppy."

"The FBI is on it, too." Umberto couldn't think beyond the devastating fact that his lover was the hit man he had yearned to find. The discrepancy between knowing what he had to do and doing it tightened his chest. "They must've observed me. Or both of us."

"Then you understand why I'm in a hurry." Michael put

on a white dress shirt, buttoned it, and tucked the hem into his black pants. He looked up, flashing his dazzling smile. "We could leave together."

Umberto lowered the gun. His hand was trembling too much for a clear shot. The memory of their first night—how he had found Michael bleeding on the sidewalk, the two hours at the hospital, the ride home, the night that evolved much better than he had hoped for. "So everything was just pretense? From the beginning?" His voice was breathless.

Michael bowed curtly and made a sweeping gesture with his hand. "I hired a man to gimme a short trashing outside the bar. I knew you'd come to save me." He rolled his eyes. "I assure you, the pain was real."

Umberto couldn't believe the words that came out of Michael's mouth. "How? How did you know I'd follow you?"

"You had given me the eye the moment I entered the bar." Michael's voice was unemotional. "You had watched me drink at the counter, followed every move I made. Remember—you even followed me to the john. I knew you'd come, if only to offer me a ride home."

"Bastard."

"I admit, I hadn't taken you to be so caring. I wanted your acquaintance, your trust." Michael laughed, but briefly and without humor. "I never expected you'd fall for me head over heels. Man, you surprised me." He reached for the jacket on the chair.

Umberto steadied his grip on the gun. "All of this . . . for what?"

"As if you didn't know." Michael adjusted the fit of the jacket, glancing at Umberto and sighing exaggeratedly when he remained quiet. "Eduardo's address. I was astonished that not even Luigi could provide the address of his brother. He gave me the names of a few of his associates and told me to squeeze one of them for information." He shrugged. "I considered it less . . . obvious to befriend you."

Umberto swallowed. His voice was strangled, the question an exclamation of anguish. "Why me?"

"It was worth a try. And you were the only one close to my age. The other intimates were by far older, and any approach would have been more difficult."

"You betrayed me." He hated his incredulous tone.

"No, I didn't. I used you to get the information I needed to dress up and deliver a box of fruits to the old man's home. It was a simple sleight of hand to pour the poison into the shake." Michael lifted and dropped both hands. "From Luigi's ranting, I knew that his older brother was a health nut. It was a good guess the shake was meant for him."

"And I thought . . . I thought you fell in love with me."

From one moment to the next, Michael's expression hardened. "Vincent Decker. Remember the name—Vincent Decker. He loved me dearly—like you never could, because you kept secrets from me. You even kept *me* as a secret and didn't stand by my side. You accused me of breaking into your precious study. Vincent—he was really my lover, my mentor, my friend. His love was unconditional, given at any time. He introduced me to the wonderful world of deceit, of great illusion, and of stealthy killing. Vincent recognized my talent." Michael cocked his head and squinted. His gaze was directed at something in the distance. "He knew instantly what I could do and helped me develop my potential. He was a great teacher—in every way. I learned how to administer poison—any poison—so expertly that the victim hardly knew what was happening to him. During his time, Vincent made millions in the business, and he left his heritage to me." His focus returned to Umberto. "I honor his legacy."

"So you killed Eduardo on Luigi's orders," Umberto said flatly.

"Of course I did. It was a masterpiece, considering that I

had to go to great lengths to get his address."

The mockery stung. Umberto's mouth was dry, his voice thin. He knew he should kill the bastard and get away, but he was unable to lift his hand and aim. "You did all of this to gain my trust."

Michael nodded, lifting and dropping his left hand. "Yes, I did. I had to be patient. I had to become a part of your life so that you would never suspect me."

"You knew all the time that I was working for Luigi."

"But I couldn't tell you that, could I?"

"You aren't a dancing instructor."

"Yes, I am. You watched me dance. I have talents far beyond your meager imagination. If you weren't pointing a gun at me, I could show you how well I can defend myself."

Umberto swallowed dryly. He needed to keep the upper hand, but it was obvious that Michael didn't consider him a threat. "It was all a lie? Our . . . relationship?" The word seemed too thick to speak it out.

Michael simpered as he put his wallet in his pants pocket. "The sex was great. And before you ask—I'm gay. That's no lie. You wanted this relationship, Bert, don't deny that. You asked me to roam. You asked me to move with you to Virginia. I just played along."

"Just played along," Umberto echoed. "You played me."

"Because you are so gullible when it comes to relationships. You try so desperately to separate business from love life that you never believed for a moment that I had other motives than fucking you."

Umberto felt the gun in his sweaty hand as if he was holding a kettle ball. He recalled the rage he had sustained during the ride. He felt like he was falling, left in a void from which he couldn't escape. Even though Michael stood in front of him, a part of Umberto's mind prohibited the idea that Michael had betrayed him from the first moment. There was no relationship. There was no love between them. There was no scenario in which they would walk away hand in hand to start over in a beautiful cabin on a Caribbean island. Umberto digested the facts that numbed his senses and denied him any joy. His voice was low, yet lacked threat. "You won't walk away from here, Mikey."

Michael reached for a suitcase and lifted it off the table. "Because you're gonna shoot me? I don't think so."

Umberto was annoyed by Michael's arrogant tone. "Maybe a jury would convict you. Maybe they would be blinded by your smile and couldn't imagine that you're capable of such horrible crimes." Umberto raised the weapon, and this time his hand was steady. "That's why I have to be judge and jury. I decide that the trial is over. And here's my verdict."

Michael's simpering was replaced by an expression of horrified disbelief. "You don't want to shoot me, right? You can't pull the trigger. Remember what we both had together? How you screwed me in the bathroom? How you tied me to the cross and had your way with me? I gave you a lot, Bert, much more than any other lover ever did. You can't possibly end this with a bullet. Yes, I had to kill the old Vianone, but let's face it—you want to get to the top, don't you? You want to get rid of Luigi, and I can help you do it."

"Eduardo was much more than my boss, you bastard. I looked up to him."

"Fine. Honor him and take over his business from this arrogant, stupid pretender. We can take him down together."

"If I agree, you'll kill Luigi and vanish." Umberto shook his head. "That's not gonna happen, Mikey. Luigi will die, one way or the other. I don't need your help."

Michael looked left and right, but even though he was nimble, the room didn't offer cover he could reach faster than Umberto could pull the trigger. "All right, then." He put down the suitcase, rested his hands at his side, and looked

Umberto straight in the eyes. There was fear and yet confidence. "Shoot. Shoot me in the heart, in the head. Aim carefully. Don't let me suffer."

Umberto scoffed. He remembered the report of Eduardo's butler about how the old man had died. He had read enough about the poison found in his blood to know that Eduardo had suffered immeasurably until he finally drowned. He lowered the muzzle an inch, grimly delighted that Michael paled and held his breath. The shot boomed through the room, and Michael went down, pressing both hands on his belly, screaming in anguish.

Nicolas laughed, startling the agents riding with him in the company car. He put the cell phone back in his breast pocket. "It's nothing," he said with a dismissive gesture, curbing his joy to a chortle. "Agent Spring told me that the evidence found at Bianchi's home will solve two FBI cases, *at least*. Maybe even more. He's also optimistic that there's material among the pictures and other items that will help convict Luigi Vianone."

Matthew clapped his hands. "Yes! I told you we'd nail this bastard!"

Nicolas shook his head but was in too good a mood to contradict him. "Let's catch Grayden and close the case with a bang."

"If you don't mind me asking," Agent Thornton, a stocky, almost bald man in his forties, said, "but why didn't you focus on Michael Grayden sooner? He fit the killer's description."

Nicolas shrugged and when he wanted to answer, Matthew was faster.

"The hit man's description varied from one case to the next. We searched simultaneously for a slim young man, an overweight man in his mid-thirties, and an inconspicuous youth with a crew cut. At what point should we have immediately suspected Michael Grayden?" Matthew's brows knitted, and his voice was low but intense. "Never mind, now that you've read the summary of the case, this might seem like the logical explanation, but when we took over the case, Grayden was the friend — probably lover — of an Italian bruiser. He was just a dancing instructor. We had him under surveillance, but he didn't do anything out of the ordinary, so the surveillance team was withdrawn." Agent Thornton's eyes were small slits and he pressed his lips together. When he started to speak, Matthew cut him short. "I met with him. I talked to him. He convincingly portrayed the innocent young man who was happy serving his friend. We assumed he was Bianchi's toy. I admit, he had us fooled."

Thornton huffed. "He must've been at every crime scene."

"You forget that he killed with poison. Even though he had been at the scenes, he was long gone when the victims died."

"But—"

"Take the murder of Cooper." Matthew turned farther on his seat so he could focus on Thornton. "Grayden knew he would take his son to the diner. He knew what father and son would order, so he replaced the cherries with atropa. When Cooper crashed his car on the highway, Grayden was long gone, remembered by the staff of the diner as a young, gum-chewing delivery guy. No one could describe him, only that he had made bubbles with his gum. That's what I mean, Agent Thornton. He wasn't the number one suspect because he was smarter than the usual psychopath."

Thornton raised his brows and pursed his lips, but Matthew's warning glare was enough to end the conversation.

Michael's face contorted with pain so great he had no breath left to speak. He writhed on the floor, trying and failing to cope with the agony that crippled him. Umberto watched his enemy's fight with death, relieved he had pulled the trigger. At the same time, he wanted to take back the decision and forget that Michael was a killer without remorse. The mix of emotions hurt as much as the bullet that had ripped through Michael's intestines and would kill him in less than five minutes. Umberto holstered the gun.

Umberto crouched, put his arms on his thighs, and watched Michael's sweat-covered face. "You call me gullible, but I still believe that love is possible. If two people are honest with each other, they can share much more than their bodies."

"You . . . are in the wrong business . . . for that." Michael groaned and tried to curl up but was already too weak.

"You were wrong accepting Luigi's money. You should've known the guy is bad for business. He leaves dead bodies wherever he walks. He's next on my list. If I show his men that he hired a hit man to kill his own brother, none of them will follow Luigi ever again. The family is everything we have. We trust each other. Beware of the one who doesn't follow the rule."

"You . . . you don't." Michael swallowed, then summoned strength to go on speaking. "You want . . . to be top dog."

"Because I've earned it. Eduardo had prepared me for taking over the business. I just take what is rightfully mine."

Michael coughed, then groaned when another wave of pain hit him. "You're a bastard . . . crippling me like this."

"Your suffering is shorter than that the one Eduardo faced. A bullet in the head . . . no, not for you." The sound of his voice should be revengeful, but utter sadness smoothed it. Umberto felt torn—satisfied to have avenged his old friend's death and yet sorry that he had trusted the wrong person. "I wanted you to be my lover, Mikey, the one I could share everything with. You misled me, betrayed me in the worst way." Umberto pressed his lips tightly together when emotion surfaced. "You misused me to follow your own goals. How could you be so . . . cold, so calculating?"

"It's a game . . . with high stakes." Michael grimaced as more blood welled up from the wound. "I liked being with you," he whispered. "That was no lie."

Umberto parted his lips for a scathing remark when he saw Michael's face slacken. Carefully and with his hand trembling, he closed Michael's eyes. A tear fell on his lover's cheek, betraying the hate, the thirst for revenge, and the inevitable outcome. Umberto knelt for a long time, unwilling to leave Michael behind like this.

He looked into Michael's peaceful face. He would not see him dance again, or smile, or pose. More tears welled up, borne out of regret and the realization of how lonely his life would be.

"There's a car park right in front of the entrance," Nicolas said as the FBI car rounded the corner toward the warehouse. The driver stopped out of sight, and Nicolas turned to the other men. "Let's assume Grayden and Bianchi are here. Both are armed. It's a fair guess they're willing to shoot their way out."

"No need to tell me the odds," Thornton mumbled as he checked the magazine of his service weapon. His expression was grimly determined. He looked like a man ready to go into combat pushing the cross of righteousness in front of him. "Ready? You and Montagna go up front, Alders and I cover the rear entrance."

They got out of the car and approached the warehouse quietly, vigilantly. In the late afternoon it had rained, and the light from the entrance was mirrored in the puddles. Nicolas walked first, his *Glock22* drawn. It was his case, and he wanted to be the one to nail the hit man, to point the muzzle at Grayden and tell him he was under arrest. The disgrace of having neglected the man's appearance at the bar and the near failure of saving Burmeister still nagged at him. If he didn't get him tonight, he would go mad.

He entered the building's main corridor and focused on the open door to the left where light was shining brightly. Both hands around the butt of the gun, finger on the trigger, Nicolas stepped forward, ready to shoot should the enemy await him.

It was quiet in the room, no rummaging, no footsteps, no mumbled monologue. It was still possible that a nocturnal visitor was sorting out his belongings, so Nicolas was careful as he swiveled into the room.

In front of him, a man was lying on the floor, and another one was kneeling beside him, facing the opposite wall.

"This is the FBI. Get up and turn around, slowly," Nicolas said.

"So you found out, too, huh?" The man inclined his head to look over his shoulder. "He framed you as he framed me."

Nicolas recognized Umberto Bianchi. "Get away from him."

"He's dead. I shot him." Bianchi sighed so that his shoulders dropped. "He wouldn't stand trial. You know that. He would blindside everyone and walk out of the courtroom while judge and jury wonder what happened." He shook his head. "I couldn't let that happen."

Nicolas strained to see the man's hands. They appeared curled in his lap. "I said, get up and turn around."

Bianchi's gaze rested on Grayden's relaxed face. "You get to know someone, you believe that you know him inside and out, and yet — there is no way of knowing for sure." He looked back at Nicolas. "Isn't that so?"

Nicolas had the premonition that Bianchi wouldn't get up and surrender. His breath caught in his throat. He pointed the gun at the man's shoulder, ready to act should Bianchi pull a gun. "For the last time, get up and turn around!"

"The worst is that I hungered for revenge. I might have known of Michael's double-crossing if I had *wanted* to know. However . . ." Bianchi's gaze went past Nicolas, and he sighed again.

Nicolas assumed he'd reached inside his jacket. "Don't!"

"You want me to rat on my boss, don't you? That would suit you fine."

"We've already got all we need," Matthew said, "to get you and your boss behind bars."

Nicolas remained quiet but cursed his partner's bluntness. He saw Bianchi tense and the sudden move of his head. Thornton and Alders had opened the back door and approached through the rear corridor. Bianchi made eye contact with Nicolas again. His brows twitched. "Bianchi, no!"

His words had not yet faded when Bianchi pulled a gun out of his holster. It didn't matter where he wanted to point— if he was to shoot Nicolas or the two agents coming in from the other side.

Thornton watched the move, the sudden threat, and he acted as if in training. "Drop the gun!"

Bianchi's expression remained calm, regretful as he completed the move. The muzzle pointed in Thornton's direction as if the gangster knew the new agent would pull the trigger faster. Before Bianchi could steady the weapon, Thornton shot him twice. The echo was loud in the small room, numbing Nicolas as he made another step. He watched Bianchi drop the gun and fall on his back. Two red dots on his shirt right above the heart indicated that Thornton was a good shot and that he had not tried to spare the man's life.

Quickly, Nicolas holstered his weapon and checked Bianchi's pulse. It was a formality. He knew the criminal had been dead the moment he hit the floor. "He wanted this," he said flatly. He avoided looking at the older agent, he did not want him to see the anger that flashed through him and would show in his eyes.

"Doesn't matter," Thornton replied as he confirmed that Grayden was dead, too. "He was about to shoot me."

"He might—"

"Don't tell me how to do my job," Thornton snapped, baring his teeth. "We all saw him draw a gun. That's it. It doesn't matter if his act was provocative. He didn't want to go to jail. So what?"

Nicolas swallowed the answer that wanted out. He was convinced that a non-lethal shot would have done the job and prevented Bianchi from pulling the trigger. Regretfully, he looked at the dead criminals, then sighed and got up. Matthew was already on the phone, calling the coroner and the forensics lab. With Alders's help, he secured the crime scene. Nicolas met Matthew's gaze, but when he looked for sympathy, he found cool professionalism.

Hands on his hips and his chin lowered to his chest, Nicolas exhaled. The hunt was over. He should feel great.

He didn't.

Epilogue

"My parents will be in Switzerland for another week," Jacklyn said, grinning mischievously. She twirled a pair of leather-padded handcuffs around her index finger. "Are you sure you wanna do this as planned? There's still time to bail out."

"You would put away the cuffs, unpack your *heavy-as-a-car* suitcase, and take a ride with me to Disneyland?" Nicolas cocked his head. "Seriously?"

"Maybe not Disneyland." She crinkled her nose and pulled down the corners of her mouth. "Maybe a Dungeon Park."

Nicolas laughed. "Torture in every chamber. Enter at your own risk." He held out his hands.

"Sounds like a new entertainment Lesley would choose to create."

"I bet."

Jacklyn locked the handcuffs around Nicolas's wrists. "Spiffy."

"I'm so glad you didn't insist on me going in the buff just because it's summer."

"Now that you mention it . . ."

"Too late." He showed her his hands. "Can't change that now. I'm dressed and I stay dressed."

She looked to him, dead serious. "I've got a knife."

"I know."

"Hop into the car — on the back seat. You're not done yet."

Nicolas smiled about her enthusiasm and the girlish attitude she showed while playing with him. He could have done the ride to the Hamptons without being shackled in the car, but he was happy to oblige his mistress's wishes. Seeing Jacklyn in such a vivacious mood was the greatest reward he could wish for.

The agents had closed the case, and Senior Agent Sullivan was content to tell their success to the waiting press corps. In his benign reign he had granted both Matthew — with a stern look — and Nicolas five days off. The decision equaled a month of vacation regarding the number of still open cases. Both Matthew and Nicolas had dutifully thanked their superior for his generosity and hurried out of the office before Sullivan could change his mind.

The rental car Jacklyn had chosen was a big SUV so that Nicolas had more room on the back seat. Jacklyn chained his ankles and spread a cover over him.

"I'm the kidnap victim, huh?" Nicolas asked when she sat on the driver's seat.

"You will be everything I want for the next three days."

Nicolas chuckled. "Somewhere in that there's a compliment hidden."

"You have all the time in the world to figure it out." She put the SUV in gear and drove down the street, out of the residential area.

When she giggled with delight, Nicolas said, "You'll have a lot of explaining to do should the police stop you."

"That's why I'm laughing. We could both end up in jail tonight."

"In the Hamptons. That'll be fun."

"Or I land in jail, and you have to explain why I kidnapped you and why you wanted to be kidnapped." She clapped her hands. "That's hilarious." She accelerated, still laughing, and the big motor roared to life as the SUV entered the highway.

"Ma chérie, would you mind . . ."

"I can't hear you!" she shouted in triumph.

"Jacklyn!"

Behind them, the siren of a police patrol grew louder.

It was Nicolas's turn to laugh. "Oh, my wonderful Belle, this is going to be an interesting day!"

The End

ABOUT THE AUTHOR

Ann Raina lives and works in Germany with cats and a horse. Riding and writing are her favorite hobbies. So far she has written thirteen novels for eXtasy Books with more to come. Her latest series, starting with Twisted Mind, turns around a couple determined to live their love life even if they get into dangerous situations here and there.

In all of her books she combines romance, suspense, and humorous elements, for no thrilling story can stand without a comic relief.

For contact turn to annraina@yahoo.com

On Facebook https://www.facebook.com/ann.raina.7

On Instagram #ann_raina_author

www.ingramcontent.com/pod-product-compliance
Lightning Source LLC
Chambersburg PA
CBHW061611170626
46811CB00001B/390